D0556437

The Seductress

She unbuttoned her shabby gown midway to her waist and pulled it off her shoulders. Positioning her hands low on her hips like she had seen the serving maid at The Cock and Crown do, she propelled herself into the library by means of a sway-backed, shoulder-rolling, hip-grinding walk. Needless to mention, all conversation stopped.

She held out her hands as if to ward the older man off. Jerking her thumb toward Rawlings, she whispered loudly, ''It's him I'm fancyin' this day. He's a swell cove, ain't he?'' She leisurely walked all around Kevin, eyeing him up and down as she went. ''Nope,'' she informed him sadly . . . ''changed me mind, I did. I likes me men with more meat on their bones. Gives me somethin' to hold onta, iffen you know what I mean,'' she said, jabbing him a playful elbow in the ribs.

Without a backward glance, she wriggled and bounced back across the room, turning only at the door to wink and blow them both a kiss, before collapsing against the side of the corridor. She hadn't known being a fallen woman was such hard work . . . But it had been such fun!

Other Avon Books by
Kasey Michaels

THE BELLIGERENT MISS BOYNTON
THE RAMBUNCTIOUS LADY ROYSTON
THE TENACIOUS MISS TAMERLANE

Avon Books are available at special quantity discounts for bulk purchases for sales promotions, premiums, fund raising or educational use. Special books, or book excerpts, can also be created to fit specific needs.

For details write or telephone the office of the Director of Special Markets, Avon Books, Dept. FP, 1790 Broadway, New York, New York 10019, 212-399-1357.

THE LURID LADY LOCKPORT

KASEY MICHAELS

AVON
PUBLISHERS OF BARD, CAMELOT, DISCUS AND FLARE BOOKS

THE LURID LADY LOCKPORT is an original publication of Avon Books. This work has never before appeared in book form.

AVON BOOKS
A division of
The Hearst Corporation
1790 Broadway
New York, New York 10019

Copyright © 1984 by Kathie Seidick
Published by arrangement with the author
Library of Congress Catalog Card Number: 83-91188
ISBN: 0-380-86231-x

All rights reserved, which includes the right to reproduce this book or portions thereof in any form whatsoever except as provided by the U. S. Copyright Law. For information address Cantrell-Colas, Inc., 229 East 79 Street, New York, New York 10021

First Avon Printing, February 1984

AVON TRADEMARK REG. U. S. PAT OFF. AND IN OTHER COUNTRIES, MARCA REGISTRADA, HECHO EN U. S. A.

Printed in the U. S. A.

WFH 10 9 8 7 6 5 4 3 2 1

To my husband, Mike, and our children, Anne, Michael, Edward, and Megan, who—thank God—do not believe domestic bliss begins with a clean house!

Prologue

KEVIN RAWLINGS had been the Eighth Earl of Lockport for some six months, but to date he was singularly unmoved by the increased wealth and social status that were part and parcel of his new title.

Perhaps this elevation to the peerage had come too late. After years of waiting for his cantankerous, ancient Great-Uncle Sylvester to finally stick his spoon in the wall and have done with it, years spent alternately borrowing on his expectations or running from his creditors, Kevin's sudden solvency had not brought the instant happiness he had long believed it would.

As for his new title, all that it seemed to bring with it was the responsibility of finding a Countess and setting up his nursery posthaste to insure his line. The mere thought of entering the marriage stakes, that social frenzy that included visits to Almack's, a myriad of senseless to-ing and fro-ing—inane balls, rout parties, Venetian breakfasts, and other nonsense—was enough to make a grown man run for cover. But there was nothing for it—he was duty-bound to find himself a wife.

All the natural speculation as to whom Rawlings would choose as his lucky bride (his name was linked with no less than a dozen young misses in the betting book at Boodles), and the unending stream of insipid infants clamoring for him to throw his handkerchief their way did nothing to pique a spark of interest in him for any of Society's latest crop of *débutantes*. To make matters even worse, it seemed his barely hidden disinterest and almost Byronic moodiness only served to *attract* rather than repel the ladies, and the whole thing was becoming, quite frankly, more than a bit of a bore.

At long last the Season wound down with the annual birthday celebration of George III on June fourth, and London rapidly became rather thin of company, leaving Kevin no nearer to finding a bride than he had been at the onset of the Season.

The Earl was left feeling fatigued, at loose ends, and on the lookout for something different to occupy his time.

For months Kevin had been blissfully ignoring the many impassioned pleas from his new man of business to present himself at his new country holding in Sussex, known for generations simply as The Hall.

Perhaps a change of scene would help to rouse the new Earl from his strange melancholy. Much as he dreaded inhabiting a chamber in the drafty old pile, for even the two or three nights he thought to be the most he would be able to endure, a trip to The Hall might just be in order.

And so, his mind made up, Kevin prepared to tool his new curricle down to Sussex to present himself to his staff and tenants.

As it turned out, it was fortunate his valet had a tendency to overpack.

Chapter One

"THERE HER BE GOIN' AGIN, loppin' off ta the hills ta lay in the long grass—lookin' fer all the world like some dreamin' looney." Hattie Kemp shook her mop of coal black hair (of which she was secretly proud, as it was unmarked by even a single streak of grey, although everyone knew the cook was sixty if she was a day). She turned away from the kitchen door to threaten the maid, Olive Zook, who had taken leave to sneak a peek at the retreating back of the barefoot girl now running swiftly away from The Hall.

"Back ta work ya lazy, shiftless thing," Hattie Kemp warned, shaking her ladle at the now cowering maid who had already begun stumbling from the room.

"Yes'm, yes'm," Olive stammered, curtsying jerkily as she tried to make good her escape—her capacious apron pockets disgorging a myriad of bobbins, pins, wadded papers, and other private treasures that left a trail as she bounced and bowed her way out of the room.

"Daft, silly woman," Hattie Kemp muttered under her breath before taking one last peek at the hills and the departing girl's swirling skirts. "Ach, child, yer smart ta take yerself off whilst yer can. When the new lordship comes, iffen he ever do, tis not likely ta be many more days like this 'un fer the likes of yer." Hattie Kemp wiped away a single tear with the corner of her apron before resuming her work.

Meanwhile, the subject of Hattie Kemp's concern was happily skipping along the ridge of the hill that ran down to the cliffs bordering the Channel, her faded and worn gown billowing indecently high and her long hair whipping in the wind. She sang as she skipped, then whirled round and round in an innocently abandoned dance before finally dropping to her knees to gaze pensively out over the whitecapped waves.

The fresh breeze coming in over the water swirled past the girl who shook her head to encourage her hair to fly back and away from her cheeks and forehead as she lifted her face to the warm summer sun.

The facial features thus revealed were not of a beauty that inspired poetry. There was a short, straight nose, quite an ordinary, everyday sort of nose; an average mouth—if not for the bottom lip being a bit too full; a nicely rounded chin with only a slight cleft; two clear but unremarkable large, round blue eyes; and, clearly her best feature, two tiny shell-shaped ears.

Her coloring, however, was not in the least ordinary. She had finely shaped dark brows and long, equally dark curly lashes that thankfully bore no resemblance to the color of her hair. That mane of hair, for it was indeed a considerable amount, was neither red nor blonde but an almost orangey mixture of the two, and while possessed of a healthy sheen, it must be mentioned that it was stick-straight into the bargain.

She had the typical complexion of the red-haired—milky white and smoothly textured—including the tiresome inclination to redden painfully upon exposure to the sun, in addition to harboring a lamentable tendency to freckle quite noticeably wherever that same sun touched—as it was doing, with the full cooperation of the girl, at that very moment.

Sinking back on her heels with a deep sigh, the girl stretched her arms behind her to the ground, arching her back and allowing her long hair to tangle in the deep grass. This movement revealed in detail her trim, almost boyish figure and long graceful neck. If it were possible to judge her height, taking into consideration her long-waisted body and the size of her slender, tapering hands and bare feet, she could be said to be of average height, neither gangling nor a pocket Venus.

Her gown tended to be less than nondescript; in fact, it was downright dowdy, not to mention ragged, patched and—like the rest of the girl—none too clean.

The girl sighed again, another deep, shuddering sigh, and rolled over onto her stomach to rest her head on her crossed arms. Clearly she was a servant girl stealing a few moments away from her duties. And just as clearly, she was upset about some unhappy thought or other that had intruded on her peaceful idyll.

The sun rose higher in the sky as a few honeybees lazily patrolled the area, their progress undisturbed by the now sleeping girl. She slept on through the afternoon, her even breathing broken only by a few more heartfelt sighs, until a noise too loud to be ignored intruded on her unhappy dreams.

She woke reluctantly, wiping the sleep from her eyes and pushing her matted, grass-filled hair carelessly behind her ears before rising slowly to pierce the misty distance with her gaze, for it was nearly dusk and the mist from the Channel had begun to roll in. It was impossible to see anything clearly but she could hear the jangle of carriage harness and the blowing and stamping of at least four horses.

"Could it be him?" she asked aloud of the grass and the sea, for no one was about. "Could his high and mighty lordship have finally shown fit to arrive and take his rightful place as master? No one ever comes to The Hall anymore so it must be him."

Straining her ears she could hear the gardeners, Lyle and Fitch, babbling excitedly to each other as they, she guessed, took charge of the horses.

She hoisted her skirts up around her knees and began to run surefootedly toward the kitchens at the rear of The Hall. Skidding to a halt at the crest of the hill overlooking the front drive, she could see a smart-looking curricle and four, Lyle and Fitch holding the leaders as they walked the equipage slowly toward the stables. "Well, lop off me legs and call me shorty—*it is him!*"

She sank to her haunches to catch her breath and give some thought as to what the arrival of the new Earl would mean to her. Plucking a length of sweet grass, she chewed one end reflectively as she sat and thought, and thought and sat. She sighed once or twice, scratched at an itch on her nose and finally stood up to slowly walk back toward the sea.

Time and enough for answers come morning, she thought with a shrug of her slim shoulders. She'd share a meal with one of the tenants if she felt hungry later on, which she doubted, and it wouldn't be the first time she'd slept under the stars.

She'd waited six long months for the new Earl to show his face. Now it was his turn to await *her* pleasure.

The first thing Kevin did upon entering his inherited country domicile was to cast his eyes around the Great Hall. The second thing he did was to curl his lip into an aristocratic sneer and grumble under his breath, "The Hall—no imagination, my esteemed ancestors. This place would have been better served to be named The Vault. A person could hide a hundred bodies in this curst place without a bit of trouble. And," he added jokingly, "they would be well-preserved corpses, what with the complimentary cold storage."

After he had stood unattended for some minutes, he took it upon himself to walk to his left and ascend the shallow split staircase from that side of the room, heading for the wide upper gallery and the drawing room behind it.

He entered the damp, shabby drawing room with no one appearing to gainsay him, stripped off his cape, curly-brimmed beaver, and driving gloves and placed them gingerly on a dusky rose satin chair—at least he hoped it was dusky rose and not dusty red!

Using his malacca cane to prod and poke at the furnishings, he strolled aimlessly about the large chamber while his mind reached back in time to his last visit to The Hall some three years previously. He had come only because the Earl's doctor swore vehemently that the old man's time had come, but as had been the case on numerous prior occasions, the doctor was nowhere near correct in his prognosis.

Kevin had arrived with a house party of ten young bucks to bear him company during his deathbed vigil, and they had all proceeded to create such an uproar that the Earl roused himself from his rack of pain to drive the lot of them out of the house at the point of his old campaign sword. "An apoplexy should have taken him off then for certain," Kevin mused aloud, smiling at the memory of his angry great-uncle, red of face and dressed in flowing white gown and nightcap, charging down the stairs waving his tarnished and bent weapon and bellowing obscenities at the top of his lungs.

But enough of fond reminiscences he told himself wryly, before I get utterly maudlin reliving the moments I've spent under this leaky roof. He crossed the room to give the bell cord several mighty pulls, the last proving too much for the aged cloth, bringing its brocaded length down around his shoulders.

With half a hope someone somewhere in the house had heard his call, he proceeded to a window, drew back the shabby velvet drapery with the tip of his cane, and stood looking out over the wreck of the West Park behind The Hall.

As he stood in the light of the dusty sunbeams he looked, even after a long, wearying journey, to be his tailor's best advertisement and his valet's fondest dreams come true. Rawling's tall frame was a rare example of perfection in symmetry. By nature a sporting man, he was well muscled, but not so much so that his manly bulges spoiled the neat lines of his jacket, and his broad-shouldered, slim-hipped torso was wondrously complemented by as fine a set of legs as ever graced a pair of silk stockings.

This beauty of form extended to include the fine bone structure of the true aristocrat, including an aquiline nose; well-defined high cheekbones; a firm square chinline; and a broad smooth brow. Arranged inside this exemplary frame were a full mouth, which when smiling allowed long slashing creases to appear in both cheeks, and two arrestingly penetrating blue eyes that deepened almost to navy or withdrew into an icy paleness, depending on his mood. Finely shaped, mobile eyebrows, which etched along the jutting bones of his brow, could register his humor, anger, surprise, ennui, or disdain with equal facility. Indeed, any actor then treading the boards would have gladly given up his best rouge pot for such eyebrows.

Crowning this magnificent example of manhood in flower were locks of the finest guinea gold coin color, locks that had an infuriating proclivity to escape their modish style to curl about his face, giving him an undeserved appearance of boyish innocence.

Such a fine specimen could only be doing his duty to rig

himself out in none but the epitome of fashion. Kevin did not shirk this responsibility, and this, combined with a natural fastidiousness inborn in the man, made him a person to be envied and aped by all the young dandies as well as sighed over by half (figuring conservatively) the ladies in London.

And so, such was the awe of the housemaid, Olive Zook, that when she at last entered the room in answer to the bell summons and first gazed upon this golden god, for the moment basking in sunlight as if a halo surrounded his entire body, she could only stand silently and gawk, her mouth agape and her eyes bulging in astonishment.

She must have made some slight movement eventually, for Kevin suddenly withdrew the tip of his cane from the draperies and turned leisurely to face the room's newest occupant.

"Ah, my good woman," he drawled affably. "Allow me to present myself. I am, for my sins, your employer, the Earl of Lockport."

"Oh, my Gawd!" Olive Zook gasped, completely forgetting the breakfast tray she had tardily been carrying back to the kitchens, as her hands flew to her cheeks in dismay. The silver tray and its burden of crockery and utensils dropped to the floor with a resoundingly loud *crash.*

"Oh, my! Oh, dear! Oh, wot has I done?" the maid wailed, simultaneously trying to straighten the cap lying all askew atop her stringy, faded blonde curls, gather together the broken crockery, and curtsy at least a half-dozen times in deference to her new master.

The Earl's left eyebrow rose in feigned dismay as he tried in vain to still the maid's nervous flutterings. At last, realizing it was the only course left open to him if he were ever to get some sort of coherent speech from the woman, he put his hands on her shoulders and gently but forcibly pushed her into a nearby chair.

"Now," he said, once peace was restored. "You have me at a disadvantage. I have introduced myself to you, but you have not told me your name."

"Me-me name's Olive, yer worship. Olive Zook," she returned slowly before adding hastily, "Pleased ta meet ya."

She was only kept from indulging in another flurry of curtsies by means of the Earl's firm hand on her shoulder.

Once assured she had settled herself, he inquired urbanely, "Tell me if you can then—Olive, is it? Yes, of course, Olive—is it possible that anyone harboring even a whit of sense is in residence? Excluding yourself, of course, my dear."

Olive, blushing to the roots of her hair and her fumbling hands twisting her apron into an ever-tightening corkscrew, replied disjointedly that Willie, the groom, and Lyle and Fitch, the gardeners, were about somewhere, and Hattie Kemp, the cook, was busy in the kitchen yard wringing a chicken's neck for today's dinner, but Gilly—sly thing that she was—had disappeared, only the good Lord knew where, directly after luncheon, and hadn't been seen since. And the Lady Sylvia *never saw anybody,* Olive supplied almost as an afterthought, so she imagined his lordship didn't want her to go all the way upstairs to ask the Lady Sylvia if she wished to meet the new master, just to be sent back down with a flea in her ear for her troubles.

While Olive's rambling recital was winding slowly down, Kevin had to fight down the urge to quit this madhouse even if it meant he had to spend the remainder of the day in his curricle hunting for a suitable inn at which to spend the night. "Is there no housekeeper then?" he asked without much hope.

"Oh, my stars, sure'n there is. Mrs. Whitebread. Now how did I go and fergit dear, sweet Mrs. Whitebread?" Olive looked up at the Earl hopefully. "Does yer wants me to fetch her to yer, yer worship?"

"I believe that might be a step in the right direction, Olive," he concurred wearily and then added, "And it's 'your lordship'—not 'your worship.' I do believe you have confused me with one of the clergy, a profound error in judgment might I add."

Turning again to the window so as to blot out Olive's painful-to-watch series of bobbing curtsies, all done while retreating step by step to the door, stepping on crockery and eventually crashing her posterior into the doorjamb, Kevin set himself to wait for Mrs. Whitebread.

She was in his presence in less than five minutes, bearing a tray of refreshments before her. Mrs. Whitebread was at least seventy, and that was being charitable, but her tiny, wizened body moved with the speed of a much younger woman. But, alas, her physical preservation did not extend to her hearing. Again and again the Earl presented his questions and again and again he was misunderstood.

"I wish to contact Mutter," he informed the housekeeper, referring to his man of business, seemingly part of his inheritance from his great-uncle.

"Butter, you say? To be sure there's butter. And jam too. Never let it be said Mrs. Whitebread scrimps on one of her snack trays."

Kevin tried another tack. Raising his voice a bit he informed the housekeeper that his valet, Willstone, would be arriving soon, and he required rooms made ready for them both.

"Aye," she answered, nodding her head. "The millstone's been broke these five years and more. We shop in the village now, not that the quality's the same, you know. You'll be fixing the millstone then, your lordship?"

Giving it one last try he fairly shouted, "I need chambers prepared for my valet and myself!"

Mrs. Whitebread sniffed disdainfully. "Of course you do, your lordship. As if Mrs. Whitebread needs to be told such a thing. Olive and I will see to it directly. There's no need to shout, you know, Mrs. Whitebread's been doin' this here job since before the likes of you was breeched, begging your pardon, sir. Now don't you think I should send Willie for Mr. Mutter? He'll be that pleased you finally got here."
Kevin sighed and nodded silently. "Of course you do. I can't imagine why you didn't think of it yourself, you being an Earl and all."

Dumping the tray of tepid tea and stale cakes on his lap, Mrs. Whitebread then departed the room with alacrity, calling loudly for Olive as she went.

"I've got the perfect name for this place at last—New Bedlam. It fits it to a cow's thumb," he told the room aloud. "Wait 'till Willstone sees this—he'll give in his notice immediately!"

But Kevin was wrong in his estimate of Willstone's strength of character. He could no more desert his master to the horrors of The Hall than leave a babe lost in the woods. Why his lordship's wardrobe would be in a shambles by the end of a week, a criminal waste of good tailoring. Besides, the Earl was all his valet could desire in a master, a living monument to his servants' expertise and never one to spill ink on his nankeens or wine on his neckcloth. Why the man didn't even take snuff and only rarely affected those disgusting cigars that caused a man's clothing to reek of repulsive tobacco smoke. And of course there was another reason for Willstone's forebearance—he was convinced the Earl would have his fill of this place in no more than two days and they would soon be posting off to nearby Brighton and Civilization.

Willie the groom came back with the message that Mr. Mutter would be happy to wait on his lordship at ten the following morning as he already had a pressing engagement for that evening (being a fourth at whist with the greengrocer, the vicar, and the local innkeeper—not that he disclosed this to the Earl's messenger), and Kevin had no choice but to resign himself to the delay.

Overruling his servant's reluctance, the Earl had Willstone join him for dinner in the dusty morning room behind the Long Library. The servings were small, which turned out to be a blessing as very nearly none of it was edible anyway. Stabbing a particularly suspicious piece of meat, he was goaded into telling his valet, "This cannot be other than some very gamey meat from a tough, strong-tasting, and stringy rabbit. They can't hunt or trap animals around here; I really believe the cook waits for them to die of old age and then gathers them in like berries."

His only solace was some unexpectedly fine port Mrs. Whitebread miraculously unearthed from the cellars. After imbibing rather freely of two or more bottles, the new Earl was able to retire to his dank, dark chamber with only a small show of dismay and was actually able to fall asleep in his huge, hard, damp bed.

"Mutter, you'd better have a plausible explanation for hauling me down here," he warned the darkness around him before nodding off.

By nine of the clock the next morning, Kevin was sure of two things. He would starve to death if forced to endure much more of Hattie Kemp's cooking, and he would deal with any of Mutter's questions and be on the road to Brighton before noon or know the reason why not.

Normally at least a fashionable half-hour late for any appointment or engagement, the Earl was uncharacteristically early for his meeting with his man of business, and even now he was blazing an impatient path in the dusty rug in the Long Library with his frustrated pacing.

At long last Mr. Mutter appeared, and being a perceptive man, he quickly got down to business. Seating himself behind the late Earl's cluttered desk, he leaned back in his chair and touched his spread fingers against each other like a child making a house with his hands.

"Please be seated, my lord," the lawyer intoned solemnly while Kevin looked about fruitlessly for a single spot in the entire large room that was not littered with books, charts, or other assorted clutter. At last he resorted to tipping a straight-backed chair forward, ridding it of its burden of rolled-up yellowed scrolls, and positioned himself and the chair across the desk from the lawyer.

Silence reigned for a few minutes while the man consulted his large pocket watch. The only sound in the room was the ticking of two or more dozen clocks situated about the room until, as Mr. Mutter raised his head and closed his eyes, the hour struck ten; with each of the dozens of clocks beating out its ten gongs, the echo reverberating throughout the room like the coming of Doomsday.

"Hell and Damnation!" Kevin exploded when at last the din subsided. "I'll give the sack to the next person who dares wind these ridiculous clocks! Of all my late great uncle's eccentricities, this clock collection has got to be the worst."

Mr. Mutter did not comment one way or the other, but merely snapped his watch closed, sucked in his ample belly, replaced the watch in his brocade waistcoat, and began to speak in his high-pitched sing-song voice. He told Kevin that the estate in its entirety was, as per the entail, completely his as he was the nearest surviving male heir. He then quoted the yearly income from rentals and the combined revenue of the farms, herds, forests, and quarry.

It was a considerable sum, but that was to be expected.

Even though the late Earl had allowed The Hall and adjacent grounds to decay for nearly two decades, he had always taken great pride in his business acumen. Considering he hadn't spent an unnecessary groat in twenty years, his fortune must be at least twenty times his annual income.

Kevin's quick mental figuring fell far short of the actual amount of the legacy Mutter quoted. "If I might interrupt for just a moment, my good man, may I ask why, if I am such a wealthy man, you have settled none of the bills I have been sending you these many months?"

Mr. Mutter cleared his throat. He was just now getting to that if his lordship would refrain from any more questions for the moment. It seemed, the lawyer went on, that the late Earl bore his grand-nephew no great love. Mr. Mutter looked to Kevin for agreement and Kevin nodded. That being the case, the late Earl had concocted a confoundedly complicated but perfectly legal Will that, while being unable to keep The Hall or the yearly income out of his nephew's hands, did succeed in tying up the rest of the estate in what could only be deemed a crowning achievement of malice aforethought.

Did the new Earl know, by the way, of the existence of a young female named Eugenia Fortune? The new Earl did not.

Mr. Mutter cleared his throat again and pushed on. Miss Eugenia Fortune, he told Kevin, was the product of a union between the late Earl and a Miss Alicia Falkner, a near neighbor.

"*Miss* Falkner?" Kevin interjected.

"Er—yes—*Miss* Falkner," the lawyer agreed, "though it was thought at the time that there had been a marriage between them. But after young Eugenia was born, a twin you know, but her brother stillborn, and Miss Falkner a bedridden invalid from that day on, the Earl declared there had never been a marriage. With Miss Falkner never seen by any but the servants, and the old Earl already a strict recluse, nothing was ever really done concerning the status of the child. Miss Falkner passed away some eight years ago, never telling her side of the story—I must say that to be honest about all concerned with this delicate situation—and her daughter continued on here as before, as a servant of the house."

"Why have I never heard of any of this?" Kevin asked, a frown marring his smooth forehead.

"How could you? You and the Earl were never close, I dare to say, and you would have overlooked Eugenia on your rare visits here unless she were particularly pointed out to you."

"How old is this Eugenia person?"

Eugenia was about eighteen, the lawyer said dismissingly, and then he got back to the business at hand. "The bulk of the Earl's immense estate was his to dispose of as he saw fit. According to the conditions of the Will, it will be placed in trust for the Society For The Preservation Of The Unfortunate Barn Owl, a Society of his own making, unless you marry this Eugenia child before the year is out. You were running out of time, my lord, and as you refused to answer my requests to come to Sussex, I withheld payments on your accounts hoping it would be the spur you needed to bring you to The Hall. I felt the matter too delicate to discuss in a letter."

Odd, thought Kevin to himself, I doubt there is any subject in this world capable of ruffling this old bird's feathers. "A society to preserve the barn owl? What the devil could the old boy have been drinking when he made that one up?" Kevin drawled, still outwardly calm. "And you're sure the Will is unbreakable?"

"Positive," was the lawyer's cool answer. "There's more, my lord. Even if you do marry the child you must wait a year from the day of the marriage to take control of the money—unless you solve a puzzle the late Earl has sent you. If you solve the puzzle the money is yours immediately."

"I hope I won't be shocking you, Mutter, if I ring for some brandy. You've dealt me a bit of a facer here this morning," Kevin put in as he crossed to the bellpull and rang for Olive.

After downing a neat three fingers of the fiery liquid, Kevin was ready to hear the rest of the details. There really weren't many. Mr. Mutter told him of his guess that the Rawlings family's jewels were part and parcel of this "puzzle," as none of the jewels had been found in the house after the Earl's death. "Solving the puzzle would be a double blessing then, unlocking the funds and recovering the considerable Rawlings's jewels—there are large emerald, ruby, and diamond sets, I recall; exquisite pieces, plus a good deal more."

"And if at the end of a year I have failed to solve the puzzle?" Kevin prompted.

"You still gain control of the funds, but the jewels, if that indeed is what this whole business is about, remain hidden. The late Earl did not take me into his confidence concerning the solution to the puzzle."

Kevin began pacing the small open area of the floor, his planned departure to Brighton forgotten. "I could refuse to marry the chit and still receive the income from the estate. Surely I can manage on that?"

"Have you inspected your holdings, my lord? Since the late Earl's next-to-last illness three years ago, there's been precious little in the way of repairs or upkeep on any of the farms. And the forestry section is in need of—well, you get my point, sir. In order to continue *making* money, you will first have to put quite a large sum of money *into* the estate. This year will be the last one to show a profit if something is not done and done soon."

"Has anyone seen my Elsie?" interrupted a babyish voice. Both men turned to see a plump, grey-haired old woman, her hair done in childish ringlets and her gown twenty years out of date, hovering just inside the room.

"Great Aunt Sylvia," Kevin muttered, his mind recalling the existence of the late Earl's sister. "Good God, I forgot all about her."

The old lady, not being gifted with an answer to her question as neither of the men knew just who this Elsie was, entered the room on slipper-clad feet, casting her eyes about her while crooning in high-pitched baby-talk, "Elsie, where are you my little darling? Come to Mummy, lovey-cakes. It's time for your lunchie-poo and a little nappy-wappy. Ah!" she exclaimed at last, excitedly clapping her hands. "There's Mummy's baby. Come here you naughty little puss. Mummy was *so* worried about her little darling sweetums."

Kevin and Mr. Mutter stared, expecting to see a cat or a pug dog emerge from the clutter, but instead Lady Sylvia leaned down, scooped up, and hugged to her bosom a child-sized china-faced doll, whose head was covered with long blonde ringlets of human hair, its body dressed in a high-waisted white dimity dress and shiny patent slippers. Without acknowledging either of the men, Lady Sylvia retreated from the room, alternately scolding and kissing her precious Elsie as she went.

There was a long silence before Kevin said to no one in particular, "There are times I do believe I envy my great-uncle his happy release."

Chapter Two

THE GIRL had been inside The Hall only long enough to learn from Hattie Kemp that the new Earl had indeed arrived the previous day and was even now closeted with Mr. Mutter in the Long Library.

"Not for long, I wager," she told the cook with a sniff. "Just as soon as he gathers up the reins of his fortune he'll hie out of here back to Londontown like the Hounds of Hell were nipping at his heels."

"Now Gilly," Hattie Kemp scolded the girl, "you'd not be knowin' iffen his lordship's like that."

Gilly nearly choked on the jam-laden biscuit she was just then popping into her mouth. "The devil I don't! You know as well as I do, Hattie Kemp, that the last time that popinjay was here he took so little interest in his surroundings that he ordered *me* to help him off with his boots. Had me straddle his leg, he did, and then he pushed at my rump with his other foot until, when the boot finally came loose, I flew across the room and landed in the fireplace. And," she continued loudly, to be heard over the cook's laughter, "after all that, all the man wanted to know was if his boot had suffered any permanent damage! Idiot! Lucky for him there was no fire in the grate—I'd have taken out a log and branded him. Why, he didn't even know I was a girl—the man doesn't care two feathers for The Hall or us."

"You was wearin' Lyle's old breeches and your hair all tucked up under Fitch's second-best cap, Gilly, m'love," Hattie Kemp reminded the girl. "His lordship ain't all at fault iffen he mistook you for a lad."

"Hummph!" was all Gilly would answer, wiping her jam-rimmed mouth none too tidily on her sleeve, before she stalked off to get a peep at the new Earl.

* * *

"Let us discuss this dilemma a bit further, Mutter, my good—but just perhaps ever-so-slightly *vague*—man," Rawlings said once Lady Sylvia had retired from the room. "Although I am convinced it must fatigue you, I can only beg your kind indulgence for a space. Please have patience whilst I endeavor to clear my mind of the cobwebs destined to grow when a man's wits are allowed to stagnate in the dull atmosphere of the *ton*, as opposed of course, to being in the company of a man such as yourself who is, I have rapidly come to appreciate, an utter *master* of subtlety, strategy, and understatement." Kevin was under control again, his usual urbane manner reassumed now that he was past the initial shock that had, if the truth be told, very nearly unnerved him when he had heard the lawyer's explanation of the late Earl's Will. His rapid recovery, to continue serving only truth, could be credited as easily to the liberal splash of spirits he had quickly downed as it could to a lifetime of hiding his true feelings.

Kevin's entreaty, the iron fist skillfully hidden beneath the velvet glove, but obvious all the same, was spur enough to send Mutter's treasured gold repeater watch back into its specially designed pocket (sewn on by his wife personally as per his explicit directions) and Mutter himself back behind the desk from which he had risen in anticipation of departing The Hall for the friendlier climate of the village pub. He did allow himself one small show of spirit (more a show of bravado really, as seldom had he been tempted to assert himself outside his own household—witness his long service to the whims of the domineering late Earl). Reassuming his former dignified (he thought) posture, and cloaking his mind in its usual attitude of prepossession (so useful when forced to deal with lesser but nonetheless opposing minds) he intoned severely, "I am at your service, my lord, but I fail to see how I can be more explicit. I believe my explanation was exceedingly clear. Perhaps," he offered more gently, "if you were to tell me the points on which you are unclear, I can guide you through to a place of clear understanding."

Mutter was pleased to see his smile returned by the new Earl—of course he was—so how could he explain the queer shiver that ran down his spine as he encountered Rawlings's glittering, icy blue eyes, which seemed so curiously out of place in his smiling face?

"*Hummph!* Er—*yes* indeed, my lord, as I've said time and time again—just ask my wife or anyone at The Hall or in the village—Henry Mutter's greatest pleasure in this world has been to serve the Earl of Lockport any way I can. Yes indeed, any Earl—any need—you just ask." The man was suddenly gibbering—as surprised at the sound of his own high voice when his words tumbled out over themselves unbidden as the Earl was disgusted (and taking no pains to hide that disgust) by the same.

Kevin waited for the flustered country lawyer to subside, now confident he was the one in the position of power and would no more be treated like a bacon-brained youth or a truant schoolboy. It wouldn't do to have Mutter terrified of him. It was hard enough ascertaining information from the man—upset him further and the lawyer could become incoherent. It sufficed that Mutter now knew who was in charge.

Rising to his not inconsiderable height, his muscles rippling ever so slightly beneath his coat, Rawlings began another leisurely inspection of the room, using his malacca cane to poke and prod at the mountains of clutter that were everywhere. Without looking at Mutter he began conversationally, "I scrawled my vowels all over London these last months, you know, what with setting up my stable, purchasing a suitable curricle and carriage, outfitting myself in the style to which I have always been accustomed but never before felt completely free to indulge in to the top of my bent, and engaging the services of the esteemed Willstone, a man who has made himself quite indispensable to me in our short time together. Ah yes, my dear Mutter, even Willstone was obtained on tick—I owe him nearly two quarter's wages."

Concluding his examination of a particularly repulsive stuffed owl—the bird appeared to be both cross-eyed and moulting—he spun in the direction of the lawyer and with a twist of his wrist turned his cane into a convincing imitation of a judge's accusing finger. "Yes, I say! Even Willstone. I am in debt from one end of England to the other—plus Ireland, North America, and anywhere in the world our soldiers can march or our ships can sail, if my debts *before* inheriting the title are not to be discounted. I stand before you pockets to let—lurched—and on the verge of being screwed up, clapped into the Fleet." Kevin slowly lowered his cane and leaned his clasped hands on the handle as he peered intently at the lawyer. "Now—am I making myself sufficiently clear, sir?"

Mutter could only nod and quickly slide his eyes away from this man who made him feel it was *his* fault the new Earl of Lockport was without funds.

Rawlings pressed his advantage. "You cannot look at me," he sighed, in a patently unbelievable tone of sorrow. "How can I blame you? It is enough to send a fellow to the dogs directly. But I have hope still in my heart, Mutter, for I am by nature an optimistic fellow." He named a sum that brought Mutter's eyes up against his will and forced an involuntary "My goodness!" from his lips.

"Exactly," the new Earl of Lockport concurred genially. "It is a considerable figure, but one I am hopeful is not beyond the estate's capacity to pay."

Mutter was forced to agree that the sum did not exceed the funds on hand.

"Just how much is on hand?" Kevin asked. Mutter told him. Settling his debts would make a considerable dent in the money, but he had no choice. "What additional revenue can I expect in the coming months?" he pressed the man.

Again the answer was disheartening. If the amount was indicative of the depth of the disrepair into which the estate had fallen, large amounts of money must be pumped back into the estate soon or it would be too late. He could not even consider making any but the most minor repairs on The Hall and grounds themselves until the entire fortune was his.

He swung his cane upward to tap it rhythmically against his other hand. "Perhaps the old reprobate kept cash on hand of which you were unaware?" he suggested encouragingly.

Now Mutter indulged himself in a bit of revenge for being so sharply set in his place. "Your great-uncle was an eccentric, sir—not a fool! He kept his money where it is still, in banks and the Exchange. If you had contacted me when first you came into the title, it would have saved you the enormous trip into debt you embarked on—according to the bills I have received to date, and surely I have not received a third of them for their total to be so high—as I would have then told you about the conditions of the Will.

In point of fact, it was nearly four months before I could locate your whereabouts at all," he ended accusingly.

"I was on a repairing lease in the country actually," Kevin responded, admitting that he had employed the age-old tactic of avoiding one's creditors—unavailability.

"This Eugenia," he asked, almost negligently changing the subject as he carefully seated himself on a corner of the desk. "You say she was raised in this house as a servant. I cannot hold out very high hopes of her education or deportment in any event, but I am curious—given the rather bizarre behavior of the servants I have encountered thus far—can I hope the chit is at least housebroken?"

At this Mutter was moved to some small sense of shame, for he had been the only person in any position at all to help the girl over the years, having access to The Hall, unlike the rest of the local populace, and he had stood aside and done nothing to convince the late Earl he was unjustly punishing the child for his own sins.

He cleared his throat nervously and tried to explain the feelings of the community to the man now gazing down at him with raised eyebrows and a skeptical look in his eyes.

"You must understand, my lord, how shocked the gentle ladies of the community were when they learned the Earl had passed his—er—*woman* off on them as his wife. They had welcomed her into their homes when she was a new bride, she being alone since her parents embarked for Italy and a healthier climate just after the supposed wedding and was without other family in the area. You can imagine the ladies' distress when the Earl announced that the quiet ceremony he had explained away as being in keeping with his mourning for his first son and namesake, who had died suddenly at the age of twenty-six, had in reality been a sham he meant to rectify with a secret real ceremony once he was assured Eugenia's mother could provide him with a new male heir. Once the truth was out, no one would have anything to do with the woman or her bas—er, daughter."

"Much evil has been done for the sake of a title or the rights to an estate," Kevin was pushed to remark, although he did not elaborate on his knowledge in this area.

Mutter went on. "Eugenia lost her mother when she was just ten years old and she has since seemed to have forgotten all the many things her mother strove so hard to teach her—manners, unaccented speech, reading, sums, and the like. She has grown a bit wild, my lord, but she is not uneducated."

"You paint a very unappealing picture, sir," Kevin told the lawyer as he rose to pace across the worn carpet. "The child has obviously been badly misused and I can only pity her, but I find it hard to reconcile myself to wedding the unfortunate creature just to give her the name her mother, I assume, thought to be the child's birthright."

"Marriage will give her respectability, it's true, but it may also be true she has been without finer influence too long," Mutter agreed. "She runs the hills like a wild thing, and there are rumors she's a sight too friendly with some of the men in the village."

His mouth twisting in a one-sided smile, Kevin quipped, "My great-uncle was a genius in the art of sweet revenge. He must be, even at this very moment, in the family mausoleum spinning gleefully in his coffin like a child's toy top. His despised grand-nevvy forced into marriage with a half-wild, illegitimate kitchen wench with a penchant for consorting with the lower orders.

"For to what end, I must ask myself, does she seek out the men of the village? Common sense can find but one answer. Not only must I take an unknown person to wife, but I must be denied at least the solace of a virgin bride as well as the security of knowing whether *my* future heir carries my blood in his veins or that of the village rat-catcher. Oh, Great-Uncle Sylvester," he ended, shaking his head and forced into laughter at the absurdity of the situation, "you have outdone yourself. Your Will is a masterstroke!" So saying he poured himself another drink and tossed it off neatly before raising his glass on high. "You sly old dog, I salute you!"

The girl hovering outside in the dark, drafty corridor had heard enough. Her slight chest was heaving under the strain of her heavy breathing (indeed, smoke seemed to be coming from her nostrils) and her hands were balled into tight fists. She had never been so angry in her entire life.

There had to be some way to get back at that top-lofty London dandy who dared make a joke out of her. Who did he think he was to look down on her—he who was no better than he should be—just because he'd had the dumb luck to be born on the right side of the blanket? How dare he stand there and say that he, the mighty Earl, *pitied* her—and in front of that idiot Mutter, no less, who would have it all over the estate by supper that same day.

Her eyes narrowed menacingly. And how dare he assume that she was like the serving maid at the Cock and Crown—a fallen woman who'd lie with a peg-legged blind man for a copper penny piece.

She was *so* angry! Besides, what did he mean about making her his wife? Mutter must be running a rig on him to make the nincompoop believe such a farradiddle. And as to saying it was old Sylvester's idea—why, the man wouldn't give her the time of day (him with a whole houseful of clocks), yet alone arrange for her to be set up as the next Countess. There was something havey-cavey afoot here, that was for sure, and *she* wasn't about to fall for any bill of goods about a quiet wedding in the estate chapel, just to be saddled with a bastard a year later and shunted off back to the servants' quarters.

I'll not stay here and be stared at and pointed out as the Earl's kept woman until it kills me like it did Mama, she told herself. I'll just tiptoe back down the corridor to my room, gather up my belongings, and walk away from here, never to look back.

But she couldn't, and her suddenly slumping shoulders acknowledged that fact. She had nowhere to go, for one thing, and for another she couldn't desert her people—the other servants and the laborers and the farmers. They needed her. She had to stay. Besides—what about Harry and the rest of them? It'll be that sad to run off now, when it had taken so long to get them to accept her in the first place. She'd only been with them for six months, but already Harry said he didn't know what he'd do without her. No. She couldn't run.

So all right. She'd stay. That didn't mean she had to roll over and play dead because the high and mighty Lord Lockport was in residence. No one could force her into a marriage—real or pretended—and Heaven help the man who tried!

"Half-wild, illegitimate kitchen wench with a penchant for the lower orders, is it?" she hissed under her breath. "Gilly, my girl, let's show him you know at least the first rule of polite behavior for ladies—never disappoint a gentleman!"

She unbuttoned her shabby gown midway to her waist and pulled it off her shoulders. (The gown had once sported brown and yellow stripes, but it was now faded all over to a dingy mud color. It was also patched, threadbare, too small by half, missing several buttons on the skirt, and a large section of the hem was ripped loose.) She bent over and rubbed her hands in her hair like she was washing it, before shaking back the wild, tangled, twig-bedecked mane with a toss of her head. Positioning her hands low on her hips, like she had seen the serving maid at the Cock and Crown do dozens of times, she propelled herself into the library by means of a swaybacked, shoulder-rolling, hip-grinding walk so full of movement it would make a seasoned sailor seasick.

"Oho!" she cried out in a strident voice that sounded just like the serving maid's—shrill and more than a little nasal. "Wot's all the ruckus I be hearin' goin' on in 'ere, I'd like ta know."

Needless to mention, all conversation stopped at the first sound of Gilly's voice as two heads swung to observe this rude intruder.

Gilly never wavered in her progress down the long room, slithering and undulating her way even when a stitch in her side threatened to take her breath away. I never truly appreciated that girl's talents, she thought to herself. Perfecting this walk—especially carrying a tray loaded with mugs of ale—is a real accomplishment!

When she had at last covered the length of the room and rolled to a halt in front of the two men, she had to fight hard to keep down a triumphant smile. They both were standing stock-still, seeming for all the world as if they had been pole-axed. Mutter was so red of face she feared he might explode like a Guy Fawkes fireworks display and the Earl—for all his fine London clothes and fancily styled golden hair—looked like he was about to lose his breakfast all over the library carpet.

Gilly chose to ignore Mutter—he was almost too easy a target to make the game enjoyable—and she zeroed in on Rawlings. Keeping her hands on her hips, she leaned forward and then raised her head to stare up into his face. "Wot's the trouble, ducks? Yer lookin' mighty queer if I do say so meself. Well," she prompted, lifting one none-too-clean, calloused hand to chuck him playfully under his chin. "Come on now, me beauty, tell Mama all about it. Wot's the matter, ducks, cat got yer tongue?"

She stuck out her own little pink tongue and wiped it around her lips like she had seen the serving maid do. Perhaps she hadn't done it right—instead of showing all the signs of a thirsty man offered a cool drink—the Earl gave no reaction at all, not even a blink, unless you counted the slight tic that began to work in his right cheek.

Turning to the visibly shaken lawyer—who was just then running a finger around his suddenly too-tight collar—she winked and teased, "Don't ya go gettin' any ideas now, ya randy old goat. I don't walk out with just any Tom, Dick, or Harry—lessen I've a mind to, ya know."

She held out her hands as if to ward the older man off although he hadn't moved. "Ah-ah, no ya don't ya naughty man. Not today." Jerking her thumb toward Rawlings, she whispered loudly, "It's him I'm fancyin' this day, Mutter-Gutter." Turning her head in the direction of her pointing thumb, Gilly trilled happily, "Coo, he's a swell cove, ain't he?" before taking a leisurely walk all around Kevin, eyeing him up and down as she went.

Returning to her starting point, she chucked him under the chin again (the dullard—he was still standing as motionless as a statue) and informed him sadly, "Nope. Changed me mind, I did. Sorry ta be disappointin' ya like that but yer a bit too scrawny for my likin', I be thinkin'! I likes me men with more meat on their bones, I does. Gives me somethin' to hold onta, iffen you know what I mean," she ended, jabbing him a playful elbow in the ribs.

Without a backward glance, she wriggled and bounced (more wriggling than bouncing as there was precious little of her to bounce) back across the room, turning only at the door to wink and blow them both a kiss, before collapsing for a moment outside against the side of the corridor until her heart stopped pounding like it would jump out her throat. She hadn't known being a fallen woman was such hard work, she giggled silently. But it had been such fun! Wasn't she fortunate to have witnessed the serving maid in action so many times? *She* may not have known what the girl had been talking about when she mimicked her words, but the men in the library certainly seemed to understand.

Gathering her skirts about her knees, Gilly ran off down the corridor to the small salon at the back of the Hall to sit and dwell on her small victory.

Mutter took out a large white handkerchief to mop his fevered brow and sweat-beaded upper lip while Kevin, waiting for the lawyer to collect himself, lit a small cheroot from a candle flame and sat down to enjoy the first few tasty puffs.

"I gather that performance was in aid of something?" Kevin drawled at last. "That infant who was just in here pretending to be a hardened whore couldn't be my blushing bride could she?"

"That was Eugenia, my lord," Mutter admitted on a sigh. "But I cannot explain her behavior. She is nothing like that. She looked for all the world like—er—never mind who, my lord."

Kevin gripped his cane near to the middle and used the beaten gold top knob to tap himself lightly and repeatedly at the side of his head. "I think we can deduce that the child was listening at the door—children often do things like that you know—and she heard us talking about her. I expected to see a slovenly doxy, so she, being like any good little girl, eager to please, merely obliged me." He yawned behind his smooth, manicured hand. "Biddable, ain't she? Do you think she could be taught to heel—or fetch my slippers in her jaws? No? Ah, well, one can't have everything. It is enough that she is not stupid as well as ignorant."

Mutter was clearly puzzled. "Aren't they one and the same, my lord?" Really, this Earl made taking care of the old Earl seem like a holiday at the seaside.

Kevin shook his head. "An ignorant person is unaware, unawakened to life and learning. That person can possibly be taught. A stupid person can be exposed to the best deans at Eton and all the top intellects in Society and never learn anything new. Our young Eugenia shows a quick native intelligence. A dullard wouldn't have the wit to try us on with that little performance. I am not reconciled to my fate, but I will allow myself to be slightly heartened."

It comforted Mutter no end that the Earl was taking this so well. Taking a chance himself, he informed Kevin of the Special License in his possession these many months in the assumption his lordship would see the wisdom of complying with the marriage. "There's always divorce, my lord," he offered in the way of comfort.

"Hmm," Rawlings replied, his eyes on the door his bride-to-be had disappeared through, "barring one of us doesn't murder the other one first." He stood up and tossed his cheroot into the stone-cold, bare fireplace. Straightening his waistcoat and pulling down his cuffs, he turned to the lawyer and ordered affably, "Go home, Mutter, and come back at eight of the evening with the license and a parson. As Shakespeare once said, 'If it were done when 'tis done, then 'twere well it were done quickly.' I think it was murder that the character speaking those lines had in mind. Mutter, do you see an omen in that?"

Kevin did not allow himself a smile until the lawyer, looking harassed, had quit the room. "Now there goes a man who will never know the difference between ignorance and stupidity."

Running one hand carefully across his smooth forehead, he pushed back the stubborn lock of hair that insisted upon forcing its will to go its own way on him before picking up his cane and tucking it under his arm.

"The Bard wrote something else, something that should serve as a sufficient spur in the inevitable, inescapable encounter, which I now bravely go forth to face. 'That man that hath a tongue, I say, is no man, If with his tongue he cannot win a woman.' Dear Will, you had such faith in your fellows; but you spoke of a *woman*. Does it take more or less of a man to talk round a green young girl? If I win her, am I a mammoth among men or a colossus among cads? And do I, even in my straitened circumstances, have the right to use this girl to ease my situation and that of everyone on this estate?" He swung down his cane and delivered himself a sharp rap on the leg. "Now you try to rationalize your reasons for behaving like the lowest sort of villain. Shame on you, Kevin Rawlings, shame."

The cane once more tucked under his arm, he walked purposely toward the corridor. Turning in the direction he believed the girl had taken, he set off confidently, a small smile on his face. "You're a wicked, wicked, nasty man, Kevin Rawlings," he chuckled softly. "You could at least have the decency to try not to enjoy yourself quite so much!"

Chapter Three

RAWLINGS WAS correct in his assumption—he found the girl in a small back room he had spied out earlier that day. There were no drapes at the three long windows, and the sun tried its best to brighten the interior with all the sunlight that could succeed in penetrating the age-old layers of grime on the panes.

In the midst of one patch of this muted brilliance stood the girl who had recently tried to pass herself off as a man-mad hussy. Her atrocious gown was now straight on her shoulders, and all the buttons still on the gown were slipped modestly through their buttonholes. There was not, however, much improvement in the riot of disgustingly disheveled-looking hair that, even tangled and matted as it was, easily reached down to her waist, its mixed colors of red and gold turning into a lurid cloak of blazing orange fire about her head.

Titian used just such a shade in his paintings, Kevin mused; perhaps once it's washed and brushed it will look more like Titian's dream than his nightmare. Ah well, he shrugged philosophically, it is only natural to search for some compensation in this farce I am forced to enact.

He inspected the remainder of the girl, at least all that he could catalog with her back turned to him. Remembering the glimpse he'd had of the girl's small, sadly uninspiring bustline, Kevin decided his bride would never need fear his passion for her body would one day overpower him to the point he would take her regardless of her wishes in the matter.

She did have a fairly nice *derrière,* he admitted ruefully, the small of her back being slightly concave before sloping gently outward into tight, firm buttocks and the promise of slim, straight legs. Face it, old boy, he mocked himself, if she was as ugly as a hedgehog and twice as fat, you'd still wed her—you have no choice—much as you'd like to make yourself believe you would whistle the entire business—lands, fortune, and hidden treasure—down the wind if the marriage was altogether aesthetically repugnant.

Earlier, when the girl had been talking, try as she might to sound uneducated and common, he had discerned a quality in her speech that told him she would not have to be taught to speak like a newborn babe, from the beginning. A bath, scrubbed hands and face (would those freckles he'd noticed then be even more painfully visible?), and a decent gown just might work wonders. He didn't expect a miracle, but at least she was still young, claylike as it were, and malleable under his sculpting hands.

Well, he decided, taking a deep breath, the war cannot begin until the opening salvo—the scene in the Long Library being considered only a feeling out of the strength of the enemy.

He took another few steps into the room, the muted sunlight dancing over his shining hair, sparkling jacket buttons, and glistening Hessians. "Eugenia?" he inquired calmly. "I am your distant cousin, Kevin Rawlings. I don't believe we have met during any of my prior visits to The Hall, but I am assured you are aware that I am the new Earl."

There was no answer from the girl standing at the window. Not by the slightest movement did she betray she had heard him. "Eugenia," he repeated, his voice quite unruffled by her show of rudeness.

Without turning the girl at last acknowledged his presence. "My name is Gilly. Do not call me Eugenia."

"Gilly? Really? My, my, however did you come by that name? Your mother's pet name for you as a child? Perhaps you resembled a little gillyflower—or even mayhap a brilliantly colored goldfish in the ornamental pond?" His words were robbed of their sting by his bland tone. Still, Gilly could think of nothing more pleasant than to feed the man to an entire school of "brilliantly colored" fishes—one agonizing inch at a time.

"Gilly is a shortening of my second name, Giselle," she informed him wearily. "It was the best of a bad bunch and I took it. Eugenia is no name for a servant."

Walking in a seemingly aimless way around the room,

Kevin somehow ended up standing face to face with the girl, catching her in a slight jump of surprise. "Gilly Rawlings," he seemed to muse out loud. "Yes, I guess it might have suited you when you were a child. You're a woman grown now, Eugenia, or so nearly so as not to make much difference. It is time to put away childish names. I shall call you Eugenia." He softened these words with a smile that could charm the birds out of the trees.

He might not have bothered. "I am Gilly Fortune; Rawlings is a name I neither deserve nor covet," she gritted, eyeing him coldly. "And you may call me Eugenia until your silvered tongue falls out. *I* shall not answer."

Loathe to reach an impasse so soon, and over something so unimportant, Kevin changed his tactics. "Agreed!" he grinned engagingly, holding out his hand in friendship. "I will call you Gilly."

She lowered her long dark lashes over her huge, innocent, round blue eyes and stared at his hand as if it was a poisonous adder she had come across in the fields. Turning away and walking to the opposite end of the room, she replied crushingly, "You will not. You do not have my permission to call me by the name my friends use."

Swallowing hard on a desire to ring the mulish chit's scrawny neck, thus destroying any hope he had of winning her over with his fatal charms, he crooned back, "You have put me at a loss, child. What then shall I call you?"

"You may call me Miss Fortune. Sylvester gifted me with that surname, just another one of his little jokes, but for the first time it seems quite apt." She spun around to face him, the naked hatred in her eyes looking out of place—almost alien—in those huge blue pools. "I *am* a misfortune for you, aren't I, *cousin* Kevin?"

This was not going well at all. Not only was she standing toe to toe with one of the best verbal duelists in the British Isles, she was making him feel guilty into the bargain.

"I will call you by any name you wish," he put in quickly, as it looked as if she were on the verge of flight. "Only please believe me—I do want to be your friend."

Gilly struck a pose reminiscent of her performance in the library. "Oh, how droll, how very droll," she said with utter disdain. "The Earl wishes to befriend the bastard kitchen wench. How very *condescending* of you, my lord." She looked him up and down and then gave a very ungenteel snort of laughter. "Well you can just go straight to the devil, Kevin, *old sport!*"

Gilly made it almost to the door before a viselike grip trapped her just above her elbow and whirled her around very ungently. In his uncharacteristic kindheartedness Kevin had made a near-fatal mistake. He had allowed his tactics to be guided by Gilly's needs, not his. The irresistible Kevin Rawlings, the man who was the secret dream of every London *débutante,* had always made it a rule not to worry about the finer feelings of any female. It was his cool detached attitude more so even than his good looks that intrigued the ladies.

In the circles in which he traveled, both the very high and the very low, there was no need for kindness. The ladies required no coddling because they were either worldly-wise courtesans, racey society matrons, or well-protected, cherished daughters. Within these groups he found all the feminine companionship he needed, and he studiously avoided unprotected innocents like Gilly.

If Gilly had only been an innocent in the established understanding of the term—an unfledged duckling so to speak—his tactics of flattery and an offer of friendship would have been readily accepted. But Gilly was a curious mixture of *naïveté* and centuries-old wisdom, mixed together in hodgepodge fashion and stuffed inside a somehow tough yet tender exterior.

In short, although unaccustomed to the brand of flattery he had tried on her, she had seen through his smoke screen until he found himself dancing while *she* called the tune.

Well, enough of that! There would be no more guilt-induced mollycoddling of Miss Fortune. Gad, what a ghastly name!

And so, before Gilly could really take in what was happening, she was propelled over to an ancient heart-backed sofa and pushed unceremoniously into it, an action that raised a cloud of dust that nearly enveloped her small frame. As the dust finally cleared, she looked up at her tormentor. With words hovering on her lips no lady of breeding would dream of uttering, she was immediately struck dumb by the face looming down at her. Gone was the insinuating smile. Gone was the twinkle in the blue velvet eyes. Gone was the amiable expression, the pleasant mask Society had taken in with such affection.

In its place was a mouth that was no more than a thin-lipped slash, eyes like two chips of hard ice that slowed the blood in her veins, and a stranger's face—a face that belonged to a warrior, or a king.

"I would strongly advise you to remain seated and listen to what I have to say," the stranger purred softly—menacingly.

Gilly was no shrinking violet—she could not afford to be and still survive. But she was not stupid either. She knew when she was out-gunned. She ceased her struggles and subsided against the lumpy cushions. Stopping just short of total surrender, she dared to say stiffly, "Very well then, get on with it," and refrained from rubbing her sore arm when it was at last freed from Rawlings's bruising hold.

In short, pithy sentences, Kevin outlined Sylvester Rawlings's will, ending with the suggestion that a marriage between them—real, not fake—was the only solution he could envision.

Gilly did not agree and was not hesitant, or tactful, in saying so. "If you had a single ounce of pride, you would reject such a Will out of hand," she told him scornfully.

"Pride is a prop for prigs and a sop for fools," Kevin returned testily. "Besides, I cannot afford the emotion."

"Well, *I* have not the least expectation of complying with Sylvester's warped plans. Why should I saddle *myself* with a frivolous popinjay who would marry anyone, even a by-blow—or worse, even an *Earl's* by-blow—for monetary gain? Frankly," she said on a reluctant gurgle of laughter, "I believe it would be hard to decide just who the biggest loser would be in such a marriage. You, sir, appeal as little to me as I do to you. Oh," she blurted irrepressively, "between the servant-bastard and the society-buffoon, which is the poorest prize?"

The Earl had been courteously inspecting his nails while allowing Gilly to vent her pent-up hostility. Only when she at last seemed to have shot her bolt did he speak again. "I have been saddled with a mewling foundling brat—a rag-tag near-barbarian. Frankly, you obnoxious infant, I am appalled at the very thought of wedding you, especially when comparing you to the women I am accustomed to meeting in Society."

Seating himself in a chair directly across from Gilly, he continued, "Suffice it to say it will not be a marriage of two hearts that wish to beat as one. If there were any way in which we could avoid this marriage, I would be equally as eager to exercise it as you. So it will sadden you to know that even I, who am somewhat respected for my mind and am, in addition, at the moment a very desperate man, can see only this one way to salvation. With just a few moments of reflection, I am sure you will come to the same conclusion, for you are not a stupid girl. We could at least," he offered, "have a marriage of two minds that think as one concerning this estate and the people on it."

Gilly did not look very moved by this eloquent speech. "For a man who took his sweet time showing up to inspect his holdings, your concern now is as overdue as it is unbelievable," she pointed out crushingly.

"I was unavoidably detained on personal business," Kevin returned repressively. "But that being neither here nor there, I am *now* aware of the problems facing The Hall and the complications my great-uncle's Will add to the situation, and I am dedicated to setting things to rights."

"For whom?"

"For the people on the estate, of course."

"Ha! For the sake of your empty pockets more like."

"No matter what my motive, brat, even your prejudiced brain should be able to assimilate the fact that it is the estate that will suffer if you refuse to marry me. Would you sacrifice the entire estate just to thwart me? And I told Mutter you weren't stupid," he ended, slowly shaking his head in disbelief.

"How dare you!" Gilly exploded in fury, falling for his ploy. "I'll have you know I've read prodigiously over the years. I am acquainted with literature, arithmetic, geography, politics, history, and Greek mythology, just to name a sampling of my accomplishments—self-taught though they may be."

The first flickerings of emotion flitted across Kevin's face as he shouted "Hoo! As if that's all it takes to be considered an accomplished person. You are devoid of manners, haven't a whit of style, and possess not a single jot of feminine instinct—and I do *not* count your earlier exhibition of bawdiness a womanly attribute. And now—*now* you tell me you're a damned bluestocking into the bargain! S'faith, the Fleet begins to appeal!"

As if to lend credence to Kevin's belittling description of

her failings, Gilly shouted back, "Oh shut up, you despicable, top-lofty prig!"

He spread his hands in acknowledgement of her outburst. "I rest my argument. Now, if you have done with your hoydenish hysterics, I will state your options to you one more time. You may marry me tonight so that my great-uncle's funds become available within the year, or sooner if we can solve this puzzle Mutter mentioned and find the hidden treasure—of which by the by, I am more than willing to allow you sole ownership for your troubles—thus saving The Hall, the estate, and the hundreds dependent on us for their livelihood. *Or*"—and here he paused dramatically—"you can take yourself off, carrying only what you own and not a stitch or penny more, to beg food and sleep under the hedgerows like any vagabond. Which are you to be—a Countess or a beggar?"

"If I agree to the marriage, you'll not root out the oldsters in the cottages and set them on the road to make way for younger, more productive workers?" she asked, eyeing him narrowly.

"I would not," he replied evenly, hiding a triumphant smile.

"You'll not employ grinding bailiffs or landstewards to make slaves of the tenants and keep them from coming to you with their problems?"

"No grinding bailiffs or—whatever else it was you said," he agreed cheerfully. Surely the chit's resolve was beginning to waver.

"You won't screw down the wages of the laborers or house servants or turn off servants past their prime without an allowance?" persisted Gilly.

"Good heavens child, do people really do such awful things?" he asked in a good imitation of horror. "You must promise to guide me in these things, as you are so conversant with the shabbier practices landowners seem to employ."

"Thanks to Sylvester, I am," she snapped. "Do you agree with giving alms for beggars at the door and allowing visitors to stay at the servants' hall?"

"How could any Christian disagree and still sleep nights?" he asked, tongue in cheek. She was really weakening now, it was just a matter of time. Obviously she cared more for the people on the estate than he had realized.

"No grabbing at waste candle-ends instead of leaving them for the servants to use in their rooms?"

"An inhuman practice!" shuddered Kevin.

"No musty cheese parings substituted for good wheels of our dairy's own best sort?" Gilly pressed him.

"Preposterous to believe a Rawlings would stoop so low!"

"You'll change the straw in the mattresses in the servants' wing twice yearly?"

"Without fail—on my honor."

"You'll replace the millstone?"

"First thing," he sighed wearily, wondering just how long this was to go on.

"You'll keep Hattie Kemp on as cook?"

Kevin took a deep, steadying breath. "I'll replace the millstone first thing."

"But Hattie Kemp—"

"Hattie Kemp has worked long and hard and deserves a rest. I will continue to pay her while reducing her duties and responsibilities. I will even give her a title of sorts so she can hold up her head in the servants' hall. I will finance her tour of China if she so desires. But I will not eat her cooking one more day than absolutely necessary."

If Kevin worried that he had just destroyed all his progress with Gilly, he was to be happily disabused of that notion.

"Good enough," Gilly concluded sagely. "I hesitated to trust your sincerity until you balked at Hattie Kemp's cooking. If you had agreed to that I would have known you had lied about the rest too." She stood up and smoothed down her skirt with an odd, queenlike grace that did little to improve her appearance but went a long way in telling Kevin that this woman-child was no stranger to that frequently painful emotion called pride.

This time when Kevin extended his hand, Gilly took it, her grip firm and her palm dry. "We've a bargain," he stated more than asked.

"The London dandy and the kitchen wench wed tonight—for the sake of the estate," Gilly agreed solemnly, her eyes holding a glint of mischief.

Raising the calloused, chapped, and none-too-clean hand

of his intended to his lips, he quipped, "If today's conversation can be considered a foretaste of what we can expect from our association in the years to come, I can dare to say our union will never be dull. Indeed, that hope has become your prime attraction. Our children should be quite unique, don't you think?"

Gilly's hand returned to her side so quickly she could have been thought to have encountered something hot. "Ch-children?" she stammered weakly.

"I propose to become a husband, not a monk," said Kevin matter-of-factly. "I am after all a man, with a man's needs and desires. I desire children—that pursuit conveniently serves to simultaneously satisfy my needs. Don't be so alarmed, child," he concluded more gently. "I am not an ogre. I can assure you I will endeavor to make the experience as enjoyable for you as it will be for me." Which is not saying much, he added silently to himself.

What was he talking about? Mating, a necessary part of procreation, at least as she had seen it so often between the farm animals, seemed for the most part an exhausting series of physical contortions that looked as impossible to achieve as they were uncomfortable to maintain—quickly begun, just as abruptly terminated, and embarrassingly personal in nature. As for humans—well, like Hattie Kemp said, only men and maybe women the likes of the serving maid at the Cock and Crown actually derived any *pleasure* from the act—and the cook even doubted the serving maid would do it if it weren't for the money that changed hands every time she went off with one of the men.

Children themselves were another matter. Gilly would like to have children. It seemed the natural thing to do—eventually—but was she ready now for such a big step? Nodding absently in Kevin's direction, she walked slowly out the door and down the corridor lost in thought, unaware of his eyes watching her thoughtfully as she went. She hadn't answered him as to her acceptance of their marriage being one that was normal on every level. She'd have to give the matter more thought.

She walked through the kitchens in a daze, never seeing Hattie Kemp, as that woman's brow wrinkled fretfully at the sight of her young Gilly so lost in thought. Once outside Gilly picked her way through the overgrown gardens to sit on a stone bench placed beneath the nude statue of some winged faerie and stare up at the exposed female curves.

Gilly's mind traveled back a few years to the time when her budding body could no longer be concealed, even by binding, and her beloved breeches only tended to accentuate the differences between herself and her young male chums from the estate. It had marked the end of her carefree youth, as even the villagers became careful to keep their sons away from the Earl's bastard daughter now that she was no longer an affable little tomboy but a blossoming adolescent.

She refused to change overnight into a simpering, giggling ninny just because her body had chosen to go all soft and curvy on her—not *that* soft or *that* curvy—but her childish adventures abruptly became solitary expeditions, and she soon became known as a loner. Even when the other girls blossomed, making Gilly once again look undersized with their own more voluptuous curves, she did not seek out her old friends.

Growing up brought loneliness; growing up brought home the shame surrounding her birth. Was it any wonder she rejected the outward trappings of femininity? Was it any wonder she could see no beauty in the female form that could excite men to madness?

"I'll tell him I need more time to get used to the idea," she decided aloud, thereby settling the matter in her own mind. "Surely he could not be *that* anxious to—to—oh, to do whatever it is he is bent on doing!"

Elsewhere on the weed-choked grounds, Kevin was reflecting wryly on Gilly's reaction to his declaration that he meant to share her bed. She was of good, if not legitimate stock, that much he could rely on anyway. But he had no burning desire to bed the brat, especially not before she had been repeatedly and totally submerged in hot, soapy water and rubbed all over with a stiff brush, but it was best to begin as one meant to go on. Once heirs were produced, they could each for the most part go their own way.

Gilly did not really appeal to Kevin physically; considerably less in fact than any of the high-steppers he'd had in keeping in London these months past, and whole worlds less than the *débutantes* he had flirted with in London, with their exquisitely small, soft, and rounded feminine forms.

Yet the longer he put it off the harder it would be to establish any relationship at all along those lines. If he wanted heirs, he would have to bed his wife occasionally, even if he was able to find his real pleasure elsewhere. Mutter's suggestion of eventual divorce left a bad taste in his mouth. He could not abuse the girl any more than necessary. She had been hurt enough already. After all—unlike his closest friend, Jared, who had the Devil's own good luck—he had not been fortunate enough to find a woman like Amanda who could forever blind him to other women while binding him eternally to herself.

So what did it matter if he married Gilly or any other woman? None of them were Amanda.

Besides, all cats were grey in the dark, so they said. He gave a rueful chuckle. "I'll just close my eyes and think of England."

Chapter Four

THE HALL kept country hours, which meant dinner would be served at the ungodly early hour of half past six. This also meant that if Kevin were to have the luxury of a before-dinner drink (a bit of a prop he hoped would sustain him through yet another infamous Hattie Kemp culinary disaster), he must present himself in the large saloon as the hour struck six.

He was in the room scarcely a minute when the hour did precisely that—to the tune of eighteen striking clocks (he later counted them for his own edification). He was, he thought, virtually *surrounded* by the demmed things—ticking clocks, chiming clocks, cuckooing clocks set with paste diamonds, and marble-footed clocks. There were clocks supported by gilt cherubs, clocks draped with reclining ivory nymphs, and one particular repulsive specimen stuck in the middle of the stomach of some overweight, grinning pagan god or other.

"Of all my late great-uncle's hobbies, *this* is far and away the worst," he told the otherwise empty room. "It is also," he added decisively, "the first evidence of his reign at The Hall to be routed out by his successor!" So saying, the new Earl walked over to the clock closest to him (the obese, grinning god) and lifted the bulk with both hands preparatory to disposing of the thing—through the nearest window if no other idea swiftly presented itself.

"Isn't that a bit heavy?" came a voice from the door. "Mutter favors a pocket watch, I've noticed, but perhaps things are done differently in Londontown."

Kevin turned toward his tormentor and lifted one fine brow in disdain. "Careful, brat," he warned, "or I'll order all these demmed timepieces stacked floor to ceiling in *your* chamber—it's as good a place as any other I've yet to find."

Gilly tried her best to look crestfallen (and failed miserably). "Do you mean to say you don't appreciate Sylvester's hobby? How sad. Perhaps you're more taken with some of his other eccentricities—his collection of maps, charts, and such, or, failing that, his voluminous research into ancient mazes and the like. No? Ah," she sighed as a tic began to work in Kevin's cheek, "that's a pity, a real bleedin' pity. Then what shall we do with the end product of old Sylvester's life's work?"

"I suggest a bonfire, if that doesn't offend your sensibilities," Kevin said, then added tightly, "And don't swear."

Just as tightly Gilly retorted, "I *have* no sensibilities—or manners. I am a servant, remember?"

Mutter entered just then, possibly saving the two from coming to blows—no one will ever know—and Kevin disposed of the clock on a nearby table, and in welcome put a purely social smile on his handsome face.

"Ah, Mutter," he said silkily, "so glad you could make it. The clergyman I requested is not with you—was he detained?"

Mutter told the Earl the minister would meet them all in the family chapel at nine, as he first had to visit an elderly lady in the village who was ill, though much improved today, thank your lordship kindly for asking, which his lordship had not.

Kevin then conferred with Mutter as to what he preferred in the way of liquid refreshment, and the two men went about the pouring of drinks, totally ignoring Gilly, who stood watching the scene, a look of disgust on her pinched white face.

Just look at the man would you, she thought to herself. The fellow's a regular popinjay, all decked out like he was being presented at Court or some such thing. She wrinkled her freckled nose at the sight of Kevin's sartorial finery. He looks like a peacock and smells like a rose garden—it's enough to put a girl off her supper.

Gilly may have been untrained in the proper attire for gentlemen, but in this case she was partially correct. Kevin was overdressed for the country—lavishly so. It was mean of him to wish to impress Mutter with his finery, meaner yet to deliberately point out the disparity between the beauty of his own raiment in proportion to the shabbiness of Gilly's faded dowdiness; but Kevin was feeling rather sorely used at the moment, so perhaps his little show of vanity could be overlooked.

By Mutter, that is.

Certainly not by Gilly, whose sly smile, as the inspiration hit her, would have had anyone who knew her shaking in their boots at the realization the girl was plotting some fitting retaliation.

The sly smile turned sweet as Kevin handed her a glass of sherry, causing the bridegroom-to-be to remark to himself that at least the child had good teeth, before dismissing her from his thoughts almost at once as he turned back to catch what Mutter was saying.

"Is Lady Sylvia to join us?" Mutter asked.

"Lady Sylvia was invited by way of a message delivered through one Olive Zook, a peculiar, skittish woman, who returned from her mission holding her boxed ears to tearfully inform me Lady Sylvia attends no social functions unless her *companion*, Elsie, receives a like invitation," Kevin reported facetiously. "I sent Olive back with an invitation for *both* ladies to be present at the ceremony, so perhaps you will see her then."

In her corner of the room Gilly could be heard to give a delicious giggle.

A few minutes later Mrs. Whitebread came in to announce that dinner was ready to be served, if they would all be so kind as to adjourn to the main dining chamber, quickly please, for Hattie did like to have the food arrive hot at the table.

"Ah, a wedding dinner," Mutter mused as he seated himself at his place set midway between Gilly and Kevin, who were soon situated at either end of the long, long mahogany table. "There's nothing tastier than a country wedding feast. I remember mine own as if it were yesterday—beef, fowl, suckling pig, a green goose, some river-eel, puddings, pies, cakes, custards, and of course, plenty of our own home-brewed beer, wine, and syllabub. Fair makes my mouth water, it does."

Kevin looked around the dark, cavernous chamber, which the few brace of candles did little to illuminate, and down the length of the smeared, dust-streaked table, shaking his head in disbelief. "Hold fast to that fond memory,

Mutter. Perhaps it will help you digest Hattie Kemp's sure-to-be-dismal excuse for a nuptial feast."

Long minutes passed and no one appeared from the kitchens. Finally Kevin, who half-wondered at his seeming anxiety over his missing dinner when any man of sense, he told himself, would be better off rejoicing over its absence, lifted the tarnished silver dinner bell at his elbow and rang for service.

From the near-dark at the other end of the table, Kevin heard an indelicate feminine snort. "Fat load of good ringing that tiny bell will do. Mrs. Whitebread will be serving tonight, seeing as the servant hired for the work is herself at table." Raising her voice to near-shriek level, Gilly called, "Hey there—Mrs. Whitebread! My belly's shakin' hands with my backbone! Bring on the mutton!"

While Mutter cringed and Kevin availed himself of another deep drink from his glass, Mrs. Whitebread, Olive Zook in tow, carried in the sum total of Hattie Kemp's wedding feast—jelly pancakes served on priceless Spode china. If he hadn't already known such ridiculousness to be standard fare at The Hall, Kevin might have thought the cook was trying to make a statement concerning her sentiments on the forthcoming nuptials.

As the pancakes congealed (all but Gilly's) untouched on the plates, Mutter raised his glass, cleared his throat, and made a feeble toast. "To your marriage. My condol—er—congratulations to you both."

Kevin reluctantly raised his own glass, as did Gilly. With a good imitation of the men she had observed drinking at the Cock and Crown, she shouted gaily, "Well—easy into the grave!" and tossed her drink at the back of her throat. Luckily, *very* luckily, she then coughed and sputtered for the full minute it took Kevin to beat down his urge to vault up on the table, sprint down its length, and spank his bride-to-be so thoroughly she would be forced to eat her mutton—or jelly pancakes—standing at the mantel for a month or more. Instead, he contented himself with pinning Mutter with his eyes and asking if he was truly *certain* there was no way to break Sylvester's will.

"None, my lord," the lawyer replied in a commiserating sigh.

Peering out from behind wine-fogged eyes, Gilly clucked her tongue at her intended's sad face and tried to boost his spirits. "Poor man. But don't you fret. Unless I miss my guess, you'll be haring off to London or some such place before the ink on the marriage lines is dry, and you'll be able to put all your sordid memories of The Hall and your detested wife out of your mind."

"Oh, no. Oh, no, *no!*" Mutter interjected quickly. "That is not true at all. Could I have neglected to mention that the late Earl's Will makes it mandatory you remain in residence for the full year or until—"

"Until we solve the puzzle and find the jewels," Kevin parroted wearily before Mutter could finish. "How kind of Sylvester, knowing full well my inborn laziness, to have taken care to provide me with an incentive sufficient to turning me into a puzzle-solving fanatic." Rising from the table he added, "I will wish to hear the full particulars of this puzzle business immediately after the ceremony is concluded. Gilly," he called out as the girl made to leave the chamber, "you have two hours to make yourself presentable. I trust you will use that time well."

In way of an answer Gilly paused momentarily at the door—just long enough to pin a wide grin on her face and reply, "Kevin, old sport, you can count on it!"

The Rawlings family chapel was situated in the most ancient part of The Hall. Neither the Hurley oriel windows nor the more recent Grinling Gibbons wood carvings provided sufficient aesthetic beauty to make anyone blind to the generations of accumulated dust that cloaked the dark chamber or to the prevailing damp, cold, dank odor that permeated the place from its stone floor to its high vaulted roof.

Candles placed on the stained marble altar flickered and smoked, but did little to illuminate the chapel, which Kevin, just then standing at the rail awaiting his overdue bride, could only consider a Heaven-sent blessing.

Kevin was being supported in this time of trial by his able manservant, Willstone, who had been pressed into service as the lone groomsman. His slight frame drawn up to its fullest height, the valet was near to preening in his place of honor beside the Earl, and he silently vowed there and then to swear lifetime allegiance to his lordship. That his presence at the altar was a matter more of necessity than a show of returned friendship mattered not a jot to the valet, who felt that at long last, after five generations spent in service to the gentry, the Willstone family had at last "arrived."

Sitting in the raised gallery usually reserved for members of the family were the servants of The Hall—Mrs. Whitebread, decked out in her finest rusty black; Hattie Kemp, her handkerchief already damp with tearstains; Lyle and Fitch, refusing to sit but nervously shuffling their feet in their anxiety to be away to where "they belonged"; and Willie, the groom, positioned some way away and, fortunately, downwind of the rest.

Olive Zook was seated before the huge painted organ that had been made in Holland and, at a signal from the clergyman on the altar, she began to inflict such horrible tortures on the ancient instrument that it belched forth great creaks, groans, whistles, and puffs of dust to the barely discernible tune of Watt's *"Oh, God, Our Help In Ages Past."*

Sitting on one of a pair of gilt chairs placed on the main stone floor of the chapel at her request, Aunt Sylvia leaned over to pat Elsie's death white china hand in encouragement (Elsie, naturally, occupying the second gilt chair) before lifting her voice to sing along with the organ in a high, shrill soprano.

I devoutly hope God has a sense of humor, Kevin smiled to himself. One thing though, he went on to tell himself, regardless how to-let in the attic she may be, Aunt Sylvia at least knows how to rig out her Elsie. The doll looks almost human. I'd let my great-aunt have the dressing of my bride if I weren't sure Gilly would strangle the poor dotty old creature for her efforts.

As Olive began the second verse of the hymn (Kevin hoped against hope the maid would not feel honor-bound to play *all* the many verses in the hymn), the double doors at the back of the chapel opened and Mutter stepped inside the door, dragging a recalcitrant Gilly behind him.

There followed a brief contretemps punctuated by fervent whisperings and one or more foot-stompings before

Gilly at last agreed to place her arm on Mutter's and begin her march down the aisle.

Kevin turned to view his approaching bride and was hard put not to allow his purposely bland features to reconstruct themselves into a visage of fury. He raked her slim, proudly held body with his eyes, focusing lastly on Gilly's mischief-filled face.

Nearer and nearer she came to the altar, at last well within the circle of light thrown off by the candles. Her freckled white skin was alabaster pale against the wild disorder of her orange red curls. The curls were topped incongruously with three high white ostrich plumes that nodded and waved and knocked against Mutter's head with every step moving them closer to the altar.

But neither her white skin, nor her flamboyant hair, nor even her outrageous plumage could outshine Gilly's choice for her bridal gown.

The gown was three sizes too large, nearly slipping off her shoulders as she walked.

The gown was also thirty years out of style, its long full train dragging behind Gilly for a full four feet.

The gown was, moreover, made entirely of satin, a fabric that caught and reflected every bit of light from the candles.

Oh yes, one thing more. The gown was red—bright, vulgar, lurid ruby *red!*

Gilly's eyes met those of her bridegroom as if to say—challenge *me,* will you, Kevin Rawlings?

Kevin raised a hand to rest his forehead wearily against the palm as he shook his head in—what? Disbelief? Disgust? What was he feeling at the moment? Even he was not sure.

Just then Aunt Sylvia, a person whose thoughts at any time did not bear too much deep contemplation, chanced to look up and see Gilly slowly passing by her chair. She reached up and gave her lifelong servant's red skirts a determined tug. "You there—girl—my Elsie is feeling the draught. Go at once and fetch her shawl."

All things considered—the marriage between Kevin Rawlings, Earl of Lockport, and one Eugenia Fortune was not the sort of ceremony to invoke fond memories anytime in the near future.

* * *

"Eugenia Giselle Horatia Dawn Fortune!" Kevin intoned sarcastically once the wedding party (*sans* clergy, servants, and the superfluous Aunt Sylvia) was closeted in the large saloon. "By thunder, Mutter, that's quite an impressive collection to bestow on the result of a casual toss in the hay. Are you *quite* sure the old boy hasn't pulled yet another fast one and my new wife here is indeed the genuine article?"

"Being I was abed with the quinsy when the mock ceremony took place and did not witness it, and being I never saw any marriage lines, I cannot say either way for certain, my lord," Mutter returned. "Even the supposed clergyman involved was a traveling preacher, and once the Earl made his startling announcement over a year later, it was impossible to trace the man."

"And the girl's parents?" Kevin pursued. "Surely she could have appealed to them."

"Even that avenue was closed, my lord, for both became victims of influenza within months of their arrival in Italy." Mutter shook his head sadly. "And they went there to live among foreigners to *improve* their health. There's a lesson there for all of us, I believe."

Gilly, who had been silent so far, could stand no more. "Keep your bloody tongue off my ancestors, Mutter-Gutter, or else I'll be forced to poke you one in the chops!" she warned the lawyer before turning on her groom. "And *you*, you popinjay, how dare you cast stones at my name? If you were shocked when the minister rattled off that string of names I'm cursed with, it was no less of a shock to me when he addressed you as Kevin *Sylvester!"*

Kevin winced. "Please, wife, I wish that to remain *our* little secret. I will refrain from further comment on your names if you will afford me the same courtesy."

"Yes, well," Mutter ventured, "the hour grows late, your lordship, my lady. If I may suggest we—er—get on with it?"

The three settled themselves into chairs, and Mutter shuffled through some papers, at last pulling out one official-looking sheet of fine parchment written on in fine, spidery copperplate.

"Here, then, is the puzzle your great-uncle has set for you, my lord," he said, passing the parchment to Kevin, who then read the thing aloud:

For now, on humble pie you dine—
I give you, girl, an anodyne:
Your Fortune waits with endless time,
Two clues: your name and this wry rhyme.

"Well," Kevin commented when he was through, "Will Shakespeare has nothing to fear. The world was done a great service when m'uncle chose not to become a poet. But what does it all mean—as I trust there is some cryptic message in this scribbling."

Gilly rose from her seat and snatched the parchment from Kevin's unresisting fingers. She paced the room while reading and rereading the puzzle, then stopped and addressed the two men. "The girl in the puzzle is me, don't you think? Other than that the whole thing seems to be totally senseless—just another example of the workings of a twisted mind."

Kevin's left eyebrow rose fractionally. "I know the man treated you shabbily, Gilly, but remember, he *was* your sire."

"So?" Gilly countered, hands on hips. "What do you wish from me—tears, or gushings of gratitude that he at last deigned to recognize me? And how does he do it, eh? By forcing me into an unpalatable marriage and then dangling some puzzle in front of me like a carrot before a donkey!" She tossed back her fiery head and laughed, "Ha! And they call *me* a bastard!"

"Now, now, child," Kevin commiserated as Mutter tried to make himself invisible in his chair, "we must endeavor not to allow circumstances to overwhelm us. Give me the puzzle."

She handed over the parchment as if she were happy to be shed of it and stomped off to plunk herself inelegantly into a nearby chair.

Taking time to sip from his brandy glass before he spoke, Kevin reread the puzzle and then told Mutter he too believed the rhyme was meant for Gilly. "You'll notice the word fortune is capitalized—as if it were the surname he'd invented for his daughter rather than calling her by her mother's maiden name."

"It was a full year before her birth was registered at all, as the Earl forbade anyone from entering The Hall, even the local clergy, and when at last he could be made to have the birth entered, Fortune was the only surname he would allow." Mutter shook his head sadly. "It seems he had this plan for her future even then—how else can anyone explain his Will?"

"Or his dislike—hatred actually—for me, a mere distant cousin, destined to inherit what should rightfully have been his son's."

"Which son?" Gilly snorted. "The drunken fop who was skewered by a cuckolded husband or my brother who never took breath? He had no great love for either, you know. He just wanted a direct blood heir. If I had been born a boy, Kevin my man, you'd still be hiding from your creditors and dodging bailiffs wherever you went."

Gilly was right and Kevin knew it. But knowing they were all victims of circumstance and Dame Luck did nothing to solve the puzzle. All it did was remind Gilly of her grievances and himself of his obligations. Addressing the room at large he ventured, "Could he have trusted his sister with the solution, do you think?"

Gilly slapped her knee in amusement. "And what if he did, you goosecap? Over a hundred clocks in this place and I'd not trust that dotty creature to tell me the time. Lord love a duck," she continued, lapsing into servant slang as she always seemed to do when under stress, "I'd more hope of an answer from Elsie than that old looney."

Kevin laughed in genuine amusement. "You're right of course, infant. I must have let the strain of the past days overwhelm my judgement. That and being cooped up in this cursed pile," he finished, casting his eyes around the dismal room.

"You do look out of place," Gilly concurred wryly. "A fashionable London fribble at The Hall seems about as logical a placement as lace curtains in the stable."

As the newly married couple exchanged heated glances —Kevin angered more than he cared to admit by Gilly's continual baiting of him, and she disturbed by the reminder that this man now standing before her in all his splendor was not only her unwanted husband but a permanent fixture for as long as it took to solve Sylvester's inane puzzle—Mutter mumbled something about the lateness of the hour and slunk away as unobtrusively as he could.

The silence in the room grew uncomfortably long and Kevin at last broke it by suggesting that his wife could better occupy her time by readying herself for bed. "I will be on pins and needles wondering if your night attire rivals your choice in wedding gowns in flamboyance. My heavens," he crooned, "the visions that spring to mind bid fair to unman me. Make haste, my bride. I shall join you shortly."

It had maddened Gilly that her satin gown had failed to discommode Kevin and, even worse, that her planned triumphant march down the aisle had been turned into a farce by Aunt Sylvia. And now, just as if he hadn't been planning it all along, he had finally brought up the subject just to make her appear a complete fool—again.

She stomped past him without a word and slammed out of the saloon, the double doors shutting behind her with enough force to set the chandelier above his head to dancing, bringing down a shower of dust upon his head and shoulders.

"Little tiger cat," he smiled, brushing at the mantle of dust on his coat. "I must take care not to tame her too quickly. Her temper is her only redeeming feature." He downed the last of his brandy and scooped up the half-full decanter to take to his rooms, where Willstone was waiting, he was sure, with a hot tub.

This was his wedding night, he told himself as he eyed the decanter, deciding whether or not the contents were sufficient to his needs. After all, he told himself, You're going to need all the help you can get.

Kevin spent a good hour in the capable hands of Willstone, who interlaced his respectful "If m'lord will raise his foot so I can relieve him of his boots" with bits of gossip gleaned belowstairs—"Olive Zook swears she's carried a score or more buckets of hot water to the Countess in the master chamber"— and one or two more personal comments meant to let his lordship know the valet was cognizant of the great sacrifice shortly to be made by his employer in the interests of ensuring the Rawlings name for posterity.

"You know, Willstone, my friend," Kevin mused, "I begin to understand the great pressure Prinney labored under when first presented with Her Royal Highness Princess Caroline. No wonder the man developed such a fondness for cherry brandy—among other things."

At last, unable to dawdle any longer, Kevin squared his shoulders and inspected his reflection in the clouded mirror. His eyes told him he at least looked the part of a bridegroom—dressed as he was in a midnight-blue velvet dressing gown worn over matching blue silk pajamas. As he stood there Willstone arranged a white silk scarf at his neckline and brushed at some nonexistent lint on the Earl's sleeve.

"All right and tight you are, sir," Willstone assured him, and Kevin exited the room for the long march down the hall to what was to be his new sleeping quarters, the master bedchamber.

The master bedchamber was, as was all The Hall, built along generous lines. Contained behind the massive double doors were an anteroom, a large sitting room, two bedrooms with adjoining dressing rooms and servants' bedrooms, a powder closet converted into a bathroom, and, outside the sitting room, a wide balcony overlooking the West Park.

Locating one slim red-haired girl within this sprawling apartment was no easy matter, but at last Kevin found her in one of the servants' bedrooms, sitting cross-legged on the narrow cot, a rag-tag cotton nightgown on her person and a mulish expression on her face.

She looked up at him as he entered the dim room, her newly washed hair framed softly around her face and tumbling down over her shoulders to her waist like a colorful shawl, unaware of the innocently appealing picture she made, and shot at her husband, "So you ran me to earth, did you? Well, here I am then, your Countess."

Rawlings's eyes narrowed and he asked, "And what, pray, am I to deduce from your presence in this—this *cell?*"

Gilly's chin lifted a fraction. "I didn't think a bastard—even a bastard Countess—belonged in either of those huge beds in the other chambers. It might give me airs above my station."

Rawlings had been through a lot that day—and he had, he knew, a lot more to face in the days, weeks, and months to come. The last thing he needed was more complications. With a muttered curse he swooped down, yanked Gilly from the cot, and hoisted her up and over his shoulder. Marching toward the bedchamber he had already decided to use, he informed Gilly tersely, "I have taken more than I care to take from you, brat. So you're a bastard—so what? You're my wife now, like it or not, and from this moment on you will think of yourself as such."

From her head-down position over his shoulder, half-smothered by her own hair, Gilly shrieked, "I am *not* your wife. It's all a sham, a fraud."

Kevin had reached the wide bed by now and threw Gilly onto it none-too-gently before joining her, positioning his legs across her lower body to hold her down while his hands grasped her wrists and held them above her head.

"The marriage is no sham. Don't you know your own minister?"

"I don't mean it isn't legal—I mean it is just a means to an end, a—*oh,* let me go you pig—you know what I mean!"

Kevin hadn't planned it this way—in truth, he hadn't planned much of anything at all—but the girl's frantic movements beneath him were beginning to stir him. His earlier observations had proved true—hers was a slight but well-proportioned body. As she thrashed her head back and forth, the scent of her newly washed hair drifted to his nostrils, and her wide blue eyes, huge in combined anger and fright, looked like twin pools that threatened to drown him in their depths.

Slowly he lowered his head until he was just scant inches from her face. "I told you ours was to be a real marriage, child, and it is. I am pleasantly surprised to realize at this late date that Sylvester may have erred just a bit in his bid for revenge—as this side of my supposed punishment has suddenly begun to appeal." His voice deepened and he coaxed, "Come now, infant, cease your struggles. I mean to have you and have you tonight. It will be more enjoyable if you do not fight me. As they say—it is best to get over rough ground as lightly as possible."

So saying, he touched his lips to hers and let go her hands. Before he could register more than the surprising sweet softness of her mouth against his, he found himself alone on his back and Gilly standing on the side of the bed, her slight chest heaving in her distress.

"There is another saying, sir—begin as you plan to go on!" she taunted, and then she took to her heels through the door and out into the hallway.

There were over one hundred chambers in The Hall and twenty staircases. By the time Kevin had collected himself, secured a candle, and gone in pursuit the hallway was empty. He turned left and set off, then took the first hallway branching off it, which, he discovered some ten minutes later, was a mistake. He had forgotten what a rabbit warren of a place The Hall was; the corridor he had chosen wove on seemingly for miles, winding and twisting while rising periodically a step at a time, until at last he had climbed a full floor and found himself in a gallery at the very top of the great, high chamber hall.

Halfway back down the corridor the candle stub sputtered out and he was forced to travel the rest of the way in the dark, stumbling and cursing as he went.

When at long last he found his way back to the master bedchamber he was resigned to spending his wedding night alone.

Discarding his dressing gown, he crawled in between the covers and tried to find a comfortable spot on the rock-hard mattress as the smell of damp bedding assaulted his senses. He knew that it was rumored Richard III had slept in this same great bed. And the sheets haven't been changed since, he told himself in an effort to lighten his mood. At least it was better than thinking about his cow-handed bungling with Gilly. He'd be lucky if she ever came within barge-pole length of him again. Even Prinney must have handled himself better, he berated himself.

It was no way to begin a marriage. Especially when just the memory of the feel of Gilly's slim body against his own could so stir his senses.

And where was Gilly while Kevin's rest was being disturbed by the many mental kicks he was inflicting on himself?

She was not abroad in the dark, fleeing from The Hall and her husband. Nor was she hiding deep within the bowels of the cavernous building.

Gilly Rawlings, Countess of Lockport, was once more in the small servant's bedroom, tucked up in the narrow cot, sleeping the undisturbed slumber of the innocent—or was it the victorious?

Chapter Five

BY THE TIME Gilly had a chance to sneak away over the rolling hills late one Sunday morning to visit the graves of her mother and twin brother, the small cemetery alongside the village church was vacant of all but its permanent guests.

She entered the cemetery by way of the wrought-iron gate and, looking around to make sure she had the place to herself, surreptitiously scooped up two bunches of daisies from vases placed on either side of the stone inscribed "IN LOVING MEMORY OF TOBIAS CRANSTON, HUSBAND AND FATHER."

Gilly was sure old Toby wouldn't mind, as he had left behind sixteen children who kept him more than amply supplied with posies.

Walking to the far corner of the fenced-in plot, Gilly sank to her knees in the shade of an old pine tree and placed a bouquet in front of each of the two markers that stood by themselves, some distance from the other graves.

For a time she busied herself tidying the site, removing lose twigs and dead leaves from the mossy ground and dusting the small headstones with the hem of her gown. Then, satisfied that all was well, Gilly relaxed cross-legged beside the graves, in the way she had done all the years she had been visiting first her brother's and then her mother's last resting place.

Over the years she had shared both her happiness and her sorrow with them, and this visit was no exception. "Oh, Mama," she sighed, twirling a long blade of grass between her fingers, "it's been less than a fortnight since I became Lady Lockport, and yet I feel as if it has been a year or more. Oh," she hastened on, "not that I've had any more trouble—Thomas, now don't you listen—like on that first night, but I'll say no more on that head since I've already told you about it, and Thomas shouldn't be hearing about such things.

"No, no," she went on, smoothing down her faded skirts to cover her embarrassment, "the Earl has kept his word so far in that at least. After he discovered me in the servant's bedroom the next morning, he promised he'd give me more time to get used to the idea of our marriage before he would seek—as he called it—his husbandly privileges. I figure," she said, grinning widely, "I should be used to the idea in—oh—fifty or sixty years."

Gilly unbent her legs and rolled onto her stomach in the soft grass. "So, dear Mama, I rest at night undisturbed. But the *days,*" she screwed her face into an exaggerated grimace, "the days are become quite intolerable. The man is impossible to please! First, he orders all of Sylvester's clocks—all but one per room that is—be hauled off to the attics, and before the job is half-done, he orders them back down to be stored in the theatre. You remember, don't you Mama, that horrid drafty cavern with that hideous painted ceiling—I never could abide the thought of all those obese naked angels cavorting just above my head. The stage is near to crumbling, you must understand, and the velvet curtain is in tatters. Even the second curtain, that painting depicting The Hall's east prospect, is smoke-blackened and torn in places. Now to make things worse, the bare board floor is completely covered with Sylvester's clocks, which the Earl has somehow decided must all be kept in working order until he rules out the possibility that one of them is the "endless time" Sylvester mentioned. Olive tarried too long in the theatre last week winding clocks and the hour struck," Gilly giggled. "Poor Olive—for the next two days she was even more deaf than Mrs. Whitebread. Now she refuses to enter the theatre at all, and Lyle and Fitch have been given the job—which is the same as to say only half the clocks are ticking at any one time.

"It was Lyle and Fitch who carried all the clocks to the theatre under the Earl's watchful eyes—and let me tell you *that* is very disconcerting—and the two dears were so rattled they dropped that huge sandglass Sylvester kept in his library. The bottom glass bulb sustained a hole you could put your fist through, and all the sand came pouring out of it and onto the carpet. I was sure the Earl would dismiss them on the spot—or at least as soon as he was through cursing them for clumsiness—but all he did was wink at me, smile, and say"—Gilly tried to imitate her husband's aristocratic drawl—" 'Why do you tarry, wife? Fetch us some pails and shovels so we may commence building a sand castle.' "

Rolling onto her back with a thump, Gilly asked irritably, "How am I to ever feel comfortable with such a man? Only an hour earlier he saw me scrubbing down the stairs in the Great Hall, yanked me to my feet with no ceremony at all, and yelled that I was never—repeat, *never* again to lift a hand to clean The Hall." She pushed her chin toward her chest and quoted in her deepest voice, " 'When in the name of Hell and all the fiends do you think you will be reconciled to the fact that you are no longer a servant in this household? You are *mistress* here, madam, and the mistress of the house supervises the staff—she does not wallow in soap suds with them.' "

Gilly sighed a deep sigh. "But the worst was yet to come, Mama. He grabbed me by the hand to pull me to my feet and immediately started in about the state of my hands." She held them up in front of herself studying them as she explained. "He wanted to know why they were so swollen and sore looking. Of course I told *him* fast enough that chilblains are the badge of honest hard-working hands. He lifted one eyebrow at me—oh, you should see him do it Mama, it's positively *lowering* the way he can cut a person to ribbons with those eyebrows of his, especially since I practiced lifting *my* eyebrows for three whole hours in front of a mirror and only succeeded in looking like I had bit into something vile. Anyway, he lifted that damn—er—dratted eyebrow and looked down that sickeningly perfect nose at me and said, oh, so hoity-toity-like, 'Hands like yours show only that you have a strong back. So does a jackass. For myself, I prefer to find pride in an agile mind.' Then he ordered me to 'do something' about my hands and sashayed away to buff his nails or some other such mind-challenging chore."

In all, Gilly stayed above two hours in the cemetery, going over the events of her days as she had always done. But somehow this visit, like the visit made the day after her marriage, was devoted almost entirely to discussing her new husband. She did tell her mother how Hattie Kemp had, once Kevin had proved himself an honorable man by marrying Gilly, reverted back to her usual style of cooking—plain but wholesome country fare supplemented by supplies the Earl had ordered from the village. When Kevin realized Hattie's earlier culinary disasters had been the result of Hattie's poor opinion of the new master, he raised a royal tow-row that nearly ended with the summary dismissal of the woman, but in the end cooler heads won out and Hattie Kemp was allowed to stay. Mealtimes were no longer to be dreaded, so Kevin was saved the nuisance of having to hunt up both another cook and a face-saving position for Hattie, and only Gilly was not granted forgiveness in the incident.

While her husband-to-be was being starved to death for two days (or, as he had almost believed, been in danger of being poisoned), Gilly had been taking her usual hearty meals in the servants hall with the rest of the staff. And then to make Hattie Kemp's continued position as cook part of her demands before agreeing to the marriage—why, it was the outside of enough to behave so underhandedly Kevin informed her, and warned that he would not soon forget it.

Yet that same man, when he discovered Gilly taking baskets of food to the poor, only smiled kindly and said it was a good thing she and Hattie Kemp were "doing" for the less fortunate on the estate.

Gilly had seen Kevin in the fields astride his spirited bay stallion, directing the workers without seeming the least bit autocratic. He appeared to know what he was about too, and that surprised Gilly, who had thought he'd find it impossible to distinguish vetch from midsummer corn.

With Walter Grey, the estate manager, by his side, the Earl rode the estate from dawn to dusk, checking on everything from the state of the laborers' cottages to the progress of the hop planting, to the maintenance of the threshing machines, to the proper rotation of fields according to the latest edicts of good organic farming.

From believing her husband was not to be trusted out alone for fear he'd topple off a nearby cliff or some such typically foppish act of stupidity, Gilly had gone on to realize—grudgingly—that perhaps the man did know how to run the estate.

The people who depended on The Hall for their livelihood, all of the nearly six hundred of them, seemed to have begun to accept him. As he rode along the lanes the children would curtsy or raise their hats, and the men would nod their respect. The womenfolk—Gilly grimaced each time she was forced to witness it—positively *fawned* over the man, so impressed were they by his dress and manners. And his looks? Gilly unhappily admitted they might also be a part of the attraction.

In the final analysis, it was that rapid shifting of loyalty that cut at Gilly most hurtfully. Oh, Walter Grey was a good enough man as estate managers go, but he needed direction and it had been Gilly's job these past three years to give it to him. Why Gilly? Why not, was what Gilly had thought at the time, being as how the old Earl was well past it, and with the exception of Walter himself, Gilly was the only person who could read and cypher well enough to maintain any sort of records.

If Gilly's mother had been alive, she could have told anyone that Gilly had since her earliest childhood harbored this need to take the whole world's troubles on her shoulders, as if she were responsible for everyone and everything she encountered.

She had made a good job of it too, and it hadn't been through any fault of hers that The Hall had lost its harvest due to the disastrous wet summer of 1811. So had most of the country. The price of oatmeal and potatoes had trebled over the ensuing months, but such prices did little good for the estate that had no goods to be brought to the marketplace.

The workers did not blame Gilly. They knew a combination of Sylvester's neglect and the failed harvest were the cause of their troubles; but if they looked to the new Earl to help get them out of this bind they were all in, it was only to be expected. After all, just how much can one young girl do?

Gilly could only pour out her heart to her mother and brother, telling them how useless she felt now that Kevin had taken over the running of the estate and had forbidden her to continue her duties inside The Hall. Why, if it weren't for Harry and the others she would feel that nobody at all needed her. This she did not tell her mother, as she never mentioned Harry during her visits for fear of upsetting the woman.

At long last, having spent her budget of worries, complaints, fears, and Hall gossip—she had known her mother would appreciate Kevin's comment on Lyle and Fitch, "They are either painstakingly slow or diligently lazy, I cannot decide which"—she rose to return to The Hall.

"Good-bye, Mama. Good-bye, Thomas. Rest well. Thank you again for letting me talk to you. I promise to come back soon and keep you informed of how things are going. Don't worry about me, I'll be right as a trivet once I figure out how to handle that husband of mine."

Only when she was safely on the other side of the cemetery gate did she say under her breath, "Like I told Mama—that ought to take no longer than fifty to sixty years. But what am I to do in the meantime?"

Gilly was right, Kevin was busy about the estate every day from dawn to dusk. And every day he was discovering just how badly needed were the funds Sylvester had dangled before him—how had Gilly said it—like a carrot in front of a donkey.

This particular afternoon he had ridden his horse along the cliffs bordering the Channel—known locally as the Straits of Dover—and he had spied out more than one cave handy to smugglers, with tramped-down grass paths leading to them from the cliffs above.

When Kevin had told Gilly he intended to restock The Hall's cellars with liquors from Bigelow's in London, she had been careless enough to blurt, "Whatever for? The best brandy's right here—" before belatedly clapping her hand to her mouth. Kevin didn't need her to complete the sentence. He was sure the brandy in the area was excellent—as French brandy usually is outstanding.

He was convinced the boats were put out from this very shore on moonless nights, and much as he despised the practice of trading with the enemy, he couldn't hope but wish the enterprise was helping to supplement his tenants' meager incomes.

Tying his mount's reins to a nearby scrub bush, Kevin walked to the rim of the hill overlooking The Hall. From this vantage point he had a clear view of the sprawl of buildings, and he stood for a long time looking at the physical evidence of his inheritance.

The Hall, as he already was aware, was a great, cavernous edifice, rambling as it did up and down the hillside; its many additions tacked on by previous generations willy-nilly until it resembled no style in particular but was a hodge-podge of too much wealth, poor taste, and worse architecture. It was homely in the extreme, so much so as to make itself curiously attractive, he thought, with its brick mellowed by salt and sea breezes to varying shades of silvery pink, depending on the age of the brick in each addition.

The Great Hall, from whence the place supposedly acquired its uninspired name, was constructed in 1360 along with accompanying cross-wings branching out at right angles from either side of the long, tall Hall. The whole business was then encircled by walls and towers some half-century later, and it seemed the primary object of every generation since that time was to extend the original building outward in all directions until every last bit of wall (by then crumbling with age) and every tower were swallowed up whole.

Kevin could see the sun reflecting off windows of all shapes and sizes, which looked out onto the long, curving drive that threaded through the once-formal lawns and partially encircled a large, stagnant lily pond sporting a broken fountain with the stained statue of some forgettable minor Greek god at its center. Weed-choked cobbled walks edged by hedges and rose bushes gone wild ambled in all directions, and to each side of the building lay the remains of terraced lawns and steps overgrown with moss leading up to the debris-cluttered balustraded flagstone terraces.

Kevin's eyes traveled to encompass the once-formal gardens to the rear of The Hall, which were liberally strewn with winding paths meant to entice the casual stroller. At the bottom of the garden—reached by means of a wide stone stairway—was a huge, wildly overgrown, intricate yew maze.

The maze, a product of one of the initial brainstorms of the late Earl, was an exact duplicate of the famous Troy Town maze of Pimperne, Dorset, which unfortunately had been plowed under in 1730. Working from sketches he had unearthed, the Earl had the maze copied exactly, its overall triangular shape stretching to cover two full acres of hedge and pathway, including thirteen entrances, one long way to the center, one short-cut at the left rear, and eleven false entrances. There were no sharp angles in the maze, all the pathways being made up of curves and curlicues, and there were four open areas inside, with a small temple at the very center. The only deviation from the original was that, instead of mounded dirt edging the pathways, the Earl employed yew hedges, which were encouraged to grow to a height well above the average man's head. Allowed to grow unchecked in recent years, the hedges had spread to almost obliterate the pathways, even from Kevin's elevated view, and now all that was left was a jungle fit only for vermin and nesting birds.

Skirting the grounds with his eyes, Kevin looked more closely at the various outbuildings The Hall was dependent upon: the bakehouse, brewhouse, laundries, diary, stables, icehouse, greenhouses, kennels, blacksmith's forge, sawpits, cider mill, and, of course, off in the distance, the gatehouse. Near the dovecot he could see the stew pond, where fish were kept until needed for the dinner table at The Hall. In addition to the many domed temples, free-standing Doric columns, sham fortifications, obelisks, and pseudo-pyramids built for the sole purpose of ornamentation, there was, tucked away in one corner of the park, the family mausoleum, last resting place of the Rawlings family for untold generations. Kevin gave it a jaunty salute before turning away.

All in all, he thought as he sank to his haunches in the grass, The Hall was an imposing piece of work—or at least it had been. But during almost the last twenty years of his life, the late Earl had slowly allowed the buildings and grounds to deteriorate.

It was the same within the walls of The Hall itself. With all but a few of the servants dismissed, the large building had quickly fallen into rack and ruin. Being a very large domicile, the horror of neglect was compounded by its repetition everywhere throughout the building. Having spent the better part of two days touring The Hall, Kevin was well aware of the impact of that neglect.

The chapel and the theatre were indicative of the conditions in all the rooms. The piano in the music room had been allowed to go out of tune, and the harp stood tilted in a corner, several of its strings missing. Two of the large saloons, considered state rooms, were now open only to the weather—thanks to broken panes in the French doors—and sodden leaves covered the Aubusson carpets.

Cobwebs hung from proud noses and strung from ear to marble ear in the second-floor sculpture gallery, and the green baize of the table in the billiard room gained most of its color from the mold that grew upon it.

The orangery served only as a repository for dry, withered plants, and the two formal dining rooms, one of which had been hastily pressed into service for the wedding dinner, had been closed for nearly two decades, their long tables layered in dust.

The Egyptian room on the ground floor was as silent as any pharoah's tomb, and the nursery wing, upstairs in the oldest portion of The Hall, lay behind a solid oak door, nailed shut by the late master himself.

In the armory, the suits of mail had been doomed to rust and discolor, and the Great Hall itself hadn't seen a fire in its huge fireplace for at least fifteen years.

The one hundred chimneys had been denied the services of a sweep for untold years, and the twenty-odd staircases had not a single change of rug and only a few rare and infrequent scrubbings. According to Kevin's calculations, of the hundred rooms in The Hall, forty of them bedrooms, only a half-dozen or so had been used by the Earl. These half-dozen were cluttered and dusty. The remainder didn't bear thinking about.

The late Earl had commandeered for himself the Long Library, the study on the half-landing, his bedchamber, and several of the small salons on the ground floor. In these rooms, he housed his most prized possessions—his collection of timepieces, his countless books, his journals and charts covering subjects and events of interest to—and understood by—only himself, and his account ledgers.

When damp from a leaking ceiling or cold wind through a broken pane intruded into one of his rooms, he had, according to Mrs. Whitebread, ordered his possessions loaded up and moved to another room, locking the door of the unusable chamber behind him as he went.

The few servants Sylvester had retained, now growing older themselves, saw no purpose in trying to maintain any sort of order in The Hall beyond the baize door that led from their own backstairs domain. Besides, they were hard pressed keeping the servants' wing tidy. That area included, in just a partial listing, the boot-polishing room, a candle and lamp-filling room, kitchens, butler's pantry, workshops, housekeeper's room, the servants bedchambers, sitting rooms, and both a large and small dining hall.

In its heyday, Kevin knew, The Hall had been a self-sufficient community, capable of employing two hundred men in the gardens, workshops, and conservatories alone, and another hundred to serve as shepherds, bailiffs, herdsmen, farm workers, rangers, keepers, foresters, masons, thatchers, carpenters, and painters—not to mention the many tenants and their families.

Inside The Hall itself another half-hundred servants had been kept busy in the laundries, dairy, kitchens, and sewing room, in addition to the responsibilities for keeping The Hall so spotless a person would be hard pressed to find a cobweb to wrap around a cut finger, and for catering to the master's guests and their servants. Since it was not unusual to have up to forty house guests and their attendants in occupation at one time, this last was a considerable responsibility.

Now, looking down from his vantage point, it was hard to believe that those days of glory could ever come again. The task of restoring The Hall to its former splendor seemed impossible to accomplish. "I wouldn't even know where to begin," Kevin mused aloud. "It is obvious to me that my first consideration must be to making the estate a profit-producing enterprise once more. The funds on hand, as I shall not pay any more of my personal debts than is necessary to keep me out of debtors' prison, will have to go for tools, stock, and general repairs. Half the tenants cottages must be rethatched, but we can use our own combed straw left over from the threshers for that, thank God. Any money left over, and Heaven knows it won't be much, I will use to hire a few servants at The Hall and to present my ragamuffin wife with both some new clothes and a dresser to instruct her on how to be a lady."

He chuckled as he remembered Gilly's appearance at breakfast only that morning. She was, as usual, attired in a faded kerseymere gown of indiscriminate color and totally lacking in style. Her hair, that lurid cloak of orangey red fire, was scraped back into a tight bun, making her look even more a babe than she normally did, which Kevin was sure was the direct opposite of her intentions.

Even so, Gilly might have pulled it off—this aping of ladylike behavior and demeanor—if it had not been for the egg cup. As soon as the pedestal-based cup holding a whole egg was placed before his wife, Kevin knew she had no idea what she was to do with it.

Presumably, egg cups were not standard table equipment in the servants hall, where Gilly had merely cracked the egg on the side of the table and taken it from there.

But now she was a Countess, and a Countess has her egg served in a fine Spode egg cup. His sympathies aroused by her apprehensive eyeing of the egg as it sat perched in its cup, Kevin cleared his throat and set about demonstrating the proper technique by way of gently tapping the end of his egg all round and then delicately lifting off the top of the shell.

Gilly picked up her spoon and, being careful not to rest her elbows on the table, gave her egg a tentative tap or two. The shell remained solid and Gilly had to try again, her intense young face oddly appealing in the sunlit room.

"Having a bit of difficulty, my sweet?" Kevin could not resist asking as the spoon struck again, more determinedly this time.

"Not a *bit,*" Gilly answered, stressing the last word as she struck out again at the egg. Her spoon succeeded in cracking the shell but may have succeeded too well, thanks to Gilly's forceful tap, for the spoon severed the top of the egg in one blow, sending the small circle of shell and egg white straight up into the air and depositing it on top of Gilly's head.

At the same time, since she had neglected to hold the pedestal, the rest of the egg and its cup parted company, the egg (with its oozing yolk) landing in her lap, and the cup skidding off the table to crash into a hundred pieces on the hard floor.

"A pox on all these fancy dishes and namby-pamby manners!" Gilly exclaimed heatedly, retrieving the egg from both her head and lap and slamming them none-too-gently on the table. "A person could starve to death trying to eat like this. What idiot said we had to look genteel even while filling our bellies? It's downright dumb, and I for one am not going to do it!"

"I appreciate your attempts anyway, child, especially as I had yet to talk to you about your dress or table manners," Kevin put in. "That talk, however, will most assuredly take place soon, as I do strongly desire you to begin conducting yourself according to your station. I do not," he added before Gilly, whose face was flushed with anger, could interrupt, "intend to spend the rest of my days looking down the table at a girl who possesses the table manners of a wallowing pig. You may have a few days in which to decide—either you agree to lessons in table manners and, while we're about it, proper everyday social conduct, or your meals will be served outside in the trough. It makes no never-mind to me."

Gilly's teeth were clenched so tightly she could not utter a word. All she could do was glare down the length of the table at her immaculately groomed, socially correct husband and imagine him with egg yolk dripping down his face and onto his beautiful clothing. She did not dare throw the egg—he could be counted on not to take such an insult lying down—but the temptation was great.

Kevin laughed now as he recalled the look of impotent fury on Gilly's face as she stomped, sans breakfast, from the room. Still chuckling, he retrieved his horse and began the descent to The Hall.

Gilly. What a perplexing child he had wed. Kevin had hoped that by now he would have had a better understanding of the girl who was his wife and at least the beginnings of an idea on how best to handle her. But with each passing day he saw another side of Gilly's personality, and he was forced to constantly reconstruct his mental image of her.

He had heard her dressing down a lazy tenant, warning him he'd be forced to pack and leave if he didn't work harder and drink less, and he had heard her talking to the oldsters, familiar with all their aches and pains and the names of each of their grandchildren.

He had seen her crabbed hand in the estate ledger and records, and marveled at her careful management even while he chuckled over her horrendous spelling.

He had listened while Hattie Kemp, Olive Zook, Mrs. Whitebread and everyone else he spoke with at The Hall praised his wife to the sky, telling him of her goodness, her charity, her concern for the estate and its people.

He had, thanks to Hattie Kemp, learned of Gilly's unhappy childhood and thanked the kind spirit who had allowed her to have been in her mother's gentle hands at least until she was ten years old.

And he had looked deeply into those innocent blue eyes, been warmed by the blaze of her brilliant hair, and felt the stirrings of passion in his loins as he lay pressed against her slim body.

Teaching Gilly the ways of society would be a challenge. Tutoring her on how to speak like a lady, not sporadically, but constantly; how to dress and how to walk; how to hold her fork; even how to tap an egg, would be an interesting struggle of wills.

Ah, but instructing her in the ways of love, *that* would be—he was beginning to believe—a delight!

Chapter Six

IN THE HOPE it might further their still somewhat strained relationship, Kevin asked Gilly if she would like to accompany him on an early morning ride about the estate. Gilly, weighing the plus of having one of her husband's prime horses under her and the minus of being forced into that husband's company, decided to take him up on it.

Kevin chose to dispense with the services of Willie, the groom who usually companioned him whenever he rode out. As they cantered away from the stables Rawlings asked Gilly: "How long has Willie been at The Hall? He doesn't seem the sort to take to such dull country life."

"He was originally a jockey," was all Gilly offered in answer, but it was enough for Kevin to understand at least a bit of the groom's idiosyncrasies; the skin-tight breeches that looked so laughable on Willie's bandy legs, the old jockey coat—once green, Kevin thought—and that ridiculously long, yellow neck scarf the groom affected.

After a moment's reflection during which Gilly considered whether Kevin could be entertaining thoughts of turning the groom off, she decided to unbend enough to explain a bit of Willie's history. "Willie was once a fine jockey," she said of the short, skinny, mahogany-faced man. "He broke his leg at a local meet some three years ago, and I brought him home to The Hall to mend."

"I can't believe old Sylvester welcomed him with open arms," Kevin commented with a grin.

"Oh, Sylvester never knew," Gilly replied innocently. "I hid him easily enough as the Earl so seldom went abroad, and of course there's been no need for secrecy since Sylvester was put to bed with a shovel. Willie's a bit—er—*individual*, but he's a good groom and a good man," Gilly pressed on in hopes of convincing Kevin of the man's worth.

What she did not volunteer was the information that at least one of the groom's least-endearing attributes, his gap-toothed smile, came from an altercation at a local tavern a little over a year ago. When someone saw Gilly and hinted that "the bastard filly looked ripe for her first ride," and he would like to be "first up in the saddle if she ain't yet been broken in by the old Earl hisself," Willie took exception to the man's speech, and although he won the resultant fight handily, it did cost him four of his front teeth.

No, Gilly couldn't relate such a story to Kevin. But she needn't have feared—her husband was an astute man. Obviously the moth-eaten, rank-smelling ex-jockey was important to his wife, and he was not about to turn the fellow off and give the child yet another reason to resent him. He could only be thankful the man was good at his job and grateful he did not have to be within smelling distance of him outside the stables.

Kevin maneuvered his horse alongside of Gilly's. "I would not turn Willie off, child, if that is bothering you. It is enough that you vouch for his honesty."

Gilly laughed then in her amusement. "I never said he was *honest,* Kevin. I said he was good."

"He's not honest?" her husband asked, one eyebrow raised.

"Lord, no. Old Willie's as crooked as a dog's hind leg—but he's a dear man for all that. He'd not nip the hand that feeds him though, if that's what's got you looking so out of sorts."

Kevin looked at his wife for some moments, taking in her heightened color and the dimple in her cheek revealed by her unaffected smile, and it suddenly became quite easy to see the humor in the situation. Soon he too was laughing, and from this shaky beginning the two went on to spend a pleasant few hours traveling over the estate, totally in charity with each other.

They had just decided to turn back toward the stables when they caught sight of two riders on the horizon. As they came closer, a bit of the light seemed to go out of Gilly's face. "It's Mr. O'Keefe and his sister," she informed Kevin in a voice suddenly devoid of enthusiasm.

"And not as welcome as the flowers in May, I gather by your look of distaste," Kevin countered. "Exactly who are they?"

Gilly tossed her head, causing her hair to rearrange itself in a living cloak around her shoulders. "Rory O'Keefe says he's a younger son with no inclination to serve the church. Instead he's set himself up in the village tutoring young boys. Glynis O'Keefe, or so he says, is his sister."

"You don't like them," Kevin added unnecessarily.

"I didn't say that," Gilly countered and then went on as if she could not contain herself. "It's just that they live far too well for the small sum he must earn tutoring. Now, if he traveled with Har—er—well, never you mind. Besides," she added hastily, obviously trying to cover up for whatever she was about to say, "Glynis O'Keefe is an out-and-out snob. Here they come now. Watch how she cuts me dead, like I was made of wood or something."

The two riders were almost upon them now and with their first words Gilly was momentarily shocked speechless.

"Good day to you Gilly, dearest," Glynis O'Keefe fairly gushed. "How terribly pleasant it is to see you again. I was just telling Rory this morning—wasn't I Rory, dear—that our sweet Gilly has had time and enough for her honeymoon, and we would not be considered forward if we came by The Hall for a visit. It's been so long since we've had the pleasure of your company, dear."

At this outright lie, Gilly found her tongue. "Glynis O'Keefe, the last time you saw me you switched your skirts at me and told me to get out of your way before you had me clapped up for pestering decent folks," she accused, her blue eyes narrowing in fury. "Now you come here acting like we're all bosom beaux. Why, for two pence I'd—"

"We'd"—Kevin broke in quickly before Gilly could go any further—"be delighted if you would both be so kind as to accompany us back to The Hall for some luncheon, isn't that right"—he dared Gilly with his eyes—*"dearest."*

"I'd as soon break bread with Boney," Gilly grumbled, but under her breath so no one but her husband could hear her.

The O'Keefes, as Kevin had anticipated, accepted his invitation with alacrity, and he took the time to study the pair as they rode along.

Rory O'Keefe, riding just ahead alongside the stiff-backed Gilly, was a well-set-up looking gentleman, Rawlings mused, of about eight and twenty years. He was handsome enough in a rather feminine, smooth-chinned sort of way, with black wavy locks hanging romantically above his soulful brown eyes. The man had the look of an aristocrat—he sat a horse well, had excellent manners (hadn't he only smiled indulgently at Gilly's ill-mannered outburst?), and had an air of breeding about him. Of course, he also had the definite look of a younger son—his well-cut clothes were frayed a bit around the edges, and he lacked any jewelry save a rather unusual signet ring on the little finger of his right hand.

He shelved his ponderings as he turned slightly in his saddle to listen to Glynis O'Keefe, who chattered inanely as she rode beside him. Now here was a real English beauty. Blonde curls, china blue eyes, small, well-rounded figure—the epitome of all that Englishmen for ages had fought and died for. A shame she talked so much; a greater shame, Kevin mused to himself, that she said so little.

Kevin knew he had displeased his wife by inviting them to The Hall, but he had his reasons for getting to know this pair—reasons he most certainly was not about to divulge to his young bride. Heaven only knew what mad start she would go off on if she were gifted with such volatile information.

Over the course of the next fortnight, the O'Keefes became almost constant visitors to The Hall—much to Gilly's disgust—and soon Kevin had told them of the puzzle and the resultant search to discover the supposed treasure.

To say the O'Keefes entered into the search hammer and tongs would not be an understatement. No one attacked the theatre full of clocks with more fervor, and thanks to their help, it was not too many days before every timepiece in The Hall had been inspected and discarded as having nothing to do with the "endless time" in the puzzle.

Yet all this effort was not wasted. It was Glynis who declared the clocks a definite asset, pointing out their value on the open market and Rory, after astounding Gilly by whisking a small magnifying glass out of his waistcoat pocket and sticking it to his eye, who declared the shiny stones in at least three of the timepieces to be genuine diamonds and rubies.

The clocks were dispatched posthaste to a London dealer and soon Kevin was to witness a rare sight indeed—a *smiling* Mutter. The lawyer was more than pleased with the size of the proceeds from the sale and even went so far as to congratulate the new Earl on his business acumen as well as allowing that, if his lordship so desired, some funds were now available for the Earl's personal use.

"I never thought I'd be grateful for Sylvester's penchant for hoarding," Kevin told his wife as he wrote out a list of what he had called "a few necessities of life."

"Ha! Grateful indeed. Lest you lose your grip entirely and begin to wax poetic over the old goat, let me remind you he also gifted you with *me!*" countered a disgruntled Gilly, who had peeked over his shoulder and seen part of Kevin's list. Along with items such as roofing tile and mattresses, he had listed "dresser for wife" and "wife's measurements for Madame Riche in Bond Street." If he thought he could saddle her with some woman to dress her in satins and laces designed to—no doubt—*his* specifications, he certainly had another thought coming.

At Gilly's irritable tone, Kevin looked up from his task and measured his wife with one assessing look. "Oh-ho!" he observed, taking in her defensive stance—hands on hips, one shabbily clad foot tapping. Twisting in his chair, one arm draped negligently across its back, he said, "One might be excused for thinking that the lady is upset about something. Since it cannot be that she craves my affection so exclusively that the idea of me feeling even the slightest bit in charity with her late father offends her, one must seek elsewhere to discover the source of her agitation. Let me see," he paused to tilt his head inquiringly in her direction. "Now what can have sent my little Gilly into the boughs this time?"

"You know damn full well, Kevin *Sylvester* Rawlings, and don't compound my anger by referring to the old Earl as any kin of mine. He did not choose to acknowledge me when he was alive, and I disown him now that he is dead." She abandoned her threatening stance and advanced to the desk, snatching up Kevin's list only to wave it in his face, threatening his aristocratic nose with violence. *"This* as if you didn't know, is what has upset me. How dare you deign to hire me a—a *keeper?*"

"A dresser is not a 'keeper', infant, although, upon reflection, that idea does have some appeal." Before Gilly could come up with a suitable retort (or, worse yet, launch a frontal assault), Kevin rose and moved a few steps from the desk. "A dresser will only *guide* you as to the proper dress for social occasions and the like. She will not, as if any but an accomplished lion tamer armed with a stout whip could, *dictate* to you. Reconcile yourself to the idea, brat. I warned you this day was coming. As for the rest—and here I mean the other item on my infamous list that pertains to you—my part in dressing you ends with sending a list of your—er—*pertinent* measurements and the facts of your coloring to Madame Riche. It will be up to her to choose your wardrobe. *My* participation in the project ends with paying the bills. All I wish is to have my wife look as lovely as I am sure she is able."

Kevin crossed to Gilly and took the list from her unresisting fingers. "Come now, infant, surely you have some small store of feminine curiosity. Don't you wish to see how you would look if dressed like—say—Glynis O'Keefe?"

Gilly raised her innocent blue eyes to her husband. "Do you really think I could look like her?"

No, Kevin told her silently, not if you were clothed in gold from head to foot. Aloud he soothed into her ear as his breath warmed her flesh, "Of course, my pet. You will be the Beauty of the Age."

Bemused by the soft words and near presence of this beautiful man, Gilly could only give a little sigh of pleasure. Really, her husband wasn't *so* very bad, and she did admit to herself that some slight affection for the man had grown in her over the past month. He was so tall, so strong, so pretty to look upon, and he smelled so good.

So when, moments later, his finger lifted her chin and his warm, firm lips descended to take hers, she found it only natural to respond by pursing her own untrained lips and returning his slight pressure. Somehow, she knew not how, his arms were around her and her own arms—suddenly so achingly empty—rose to clasp her husband about the waist. The sensations aroused by this new contact, as their bodies were now tightly pressed together,

Gilly compared to the giddy dizziness brought on by a lack of food.

Kevin raised his head a moment, smiled slightly at the vision of Gilly's tightly shut eyes and just as tightly pursed lips, before crushing her to him in a kiss as different from his first as was a single burning candle from an entire world in flames.

There in that shabby library, surrounded by moldy tomes and dry ancient scrolls, the afternoon sun raising dust motes wherever it streaked through the gloom, passion was born between the Earl and Countess of Lockport.

The stylishly clad Corinthian and the shabbily garbed young girl, oblivious to the study in contrasts they made as they stood together bathed in a ray of dusty sunlight, trembled a bit at the intensity of their reaction to each other. If the entire Hall were to come crashing down around their ears, it would not surprise them—if they in fact even noticed at all.

Kevin was the first to ease away, his intention not to terminate the proceedings but only to have them adjourned until he could gain his bearings and the location of the nearest wide couch. This, as he was soon to find out, was a tactical error, for it gave Gilly a moment in which to recover herself at least a little bit.

She backed away from him slowly, a hand to her mouth, her eyes wide as she stared at her husband in mingled fear and dawning knowledge. Trembling visibly, she shook her head from side to side and whispered hoarsely, "Oh, no. *Oh, no!*" and ran from the room before Kevin could react.

Left to stare after her retreating skirts, Kevin was silent for some moments, conflicting emotions flitting across his mobile face. At long last he smiled, a rueful, reluctant smile of comprehension. "Oh yes, my dearest goose. It's difficult to believe but, *yes!*"

Gilly did not appear at the dinner table that night, not that Kevin expected her to, nor was she in her small chamber when at last he decided to seek her out close to midnight. She could have chosen to sleep elsewhere tonight, he told himself, not that he blamed her. The first flush of passion could be disturbing enough without the added knowledge that one's more tender emotions might be involved.

Kevin wasn't being arrogant when he thought that Gilly felt some affection for him—and no little amount of it either, judging from the intensity of her response. He had felt much the same way towards her. No longer could he say it was only their proximity and legal bonds that attracted him to her. He had gotten to know his child-bride very well over the past month, and his affection for her had grown alongside his regard for her character.

Odd, he mused, as he returned to the sitting room outside Gilly's chamber, the child is not at all what I imagined for a wife. She's not a bit like Amanda in looks, and although Gilly has much the same spirit and fire, she possesses none of Amanda's feminine refinement. Yet there is something—something nebulous and undefined—that draws me to her like a moth to a glittering flame.

Slowly the combined warmth of the open fire and the brandy he had consumed insidiously lulled Kevin into slumber as he relaxed on a fan-backed sofa placed near the hearth. The hours of the night ticked by, their passage marked by the soft chiming of the delicate gilt bronze mantel clock and the diminishing heat of the slowly dying fire.

Just as the clock finished striking five, the doorway leading from the main corridor opened a crack and a slight dark shape tiptoed stealthily into the room. The figure stopped for a moment, then, seeming to decide it was safe to proceed, began once more to make its way across the wide room. Bent into a crouch and with arms crossed in a seeming self-embrace, the figure appeared to be cold, wet, tired, and—but, what! What was that noise? The figure stopped, tensing—listening.

A small age passed before the figure released its pent-up breath and dared to continue its stealthy progression towards the small door cut into a corner of the room. There were only a few feet of carpet between the figure and safety when a hand reached through the dimness and tapped politely on one hunched shoulder. The shoulder stiffened immediately and the figure tensed as if turned to stone.

"Excuse me if I have startled you, but I cannot help but wonder, this being my chamber and all that—have we been introduced?"

At the sound of the Earl of Lockport's carelessly casual

drawl, the figure whirled about, and a pair of round blue eyes glittered out of the soot-blackened face lifted to confront him. "Damn! Damn, damn and blast you, Kevin Rawlings, you scared me half out of my wits!" the Countess of Lockport accused in a fury.

The Earl stepped back a pace, his shock not in the least bit feigned, as he took in his wife's bizarre appearance. She was dressed head to foot in shabby, dark clothing that, he could tell, was both wet and smelling of sea water. Her face and hands were streaked with the remains of charcoal black soot, and her head was topped by a toque, a pleated voluminous cap banded tightly around her skull.

As Gilly stood staring balefully at her husband, he reached out and gave the toque a tug, releasing a cascade of living fire that tumbled wildly around her face.

Blowing at an errant strand that had settled smack between her eyes, she remained silent as he eyed her unhurriedly from head to foot and back again. "I say," he remarked, as if he didn't know he was just moments from having his eyes scratched out by the fuming tiger cat before him, "if I didn't know better I would believe you had spent the night with The Gentlemen."

Gilly's head flew up at this statement. How did Kevin know that smugglers were called The Gentlemen?

Noting her shock, Kevin chuckled and soothed, "Now, now, my dear infant, although I am aware your opinion of me is not of the highest, even you couldn't believe I can be so green as to be unaware of the smuggling that is rampant from Margate all the way to Bournemouth. What do you use in this area, yawls—or are you more sophisticated and employ, say, a Dutch dogger? Ah, you are amazed! Did you think such things are unknown to us in London? Why, many a friend has regaled me with bits about adventures with The Gentlemen—they do it, so they say, simply for the dash of the thing. Can't see it myself," he added as Gilly stood and listened, her mouth at half-mast.

Look at him, Gilly thought angrily, the great, grinning looby—prattling on like we were sipping tea across a table and exchanging titillating secrets, just as if it weren't his greatest desire to box my ears. Besides, she told herself, any fool can see I'm freezing to death as well—

"But I do run on so," Kevin went on, breaking into her silent thoughts. "And with my poor wife standing there all woebegone and disordered—almost as if she had been forced to take a dip in the sea. Come, wife, and sit by the fire while I add a log to help warm you." He spoke casually, still maintaining an outward air of calm while inside he churned to either throttle the chit or feverishly embrace her, thanking the gods that she was home safe and dry—well, safe at least.

He put out a hand to touch her shoulder, but she dodged under him muttering, "I must change into some dry clothing first," and disappeared into her small bedroom.

After the fire was once again blazing brightly, he gathered a pitcher of water from his own bedchamber as well as some linen to use to clean the soot from Gilly's hands and face. When a few more minutes had passed and she did not reappear, he took up the pitcher and linen, and, refusing to knock to gain entrance to his own wife's chambers, strode purposely into her presence.

Gilly was sitting on the side of her narrow cot, coatless and bootless but still dressed in her damp sweater and leather leggings. Her head came up with a jerk as she said, startled, "What do you want? I'll be out shortly."

"If you don't freeze solid beforehand," Kevin countered, setting down his small burdens and approaching the bed. "Come now, let me help you. I am your husband, you know, though why you think the act of undressing a shivering child should serve to turn me into a beast intent on ravishment, I cannot understand."

So saying he reached for the hem of her sweater and swiftly pulled it up and over her head.

"Oh!" Gilly moaned, her eyes rolling back in her head, before she sank sideways on the bed in a dead faint.

Kevin quickly raised her feet onto the bed and ran to light some more candles. In the brighter light it was easy to see why Gilly had swooned. High on the fleshy part of her left arm was a shallow but nasty-looking graze that could only have come from a bullet. The blood from the wound had dried and stuck fast to her sweater—until Kevin's none-to-gentle removal of that sweater had ripped the wound open once more. Even now dark red blood was welling into the channel cut by the bullet.

At once Kevin became all business. He bathed the wound thoroughly, then bound it with strips ripped from the linen. Once the wound was cared for to his satisfaction, he went about bathing Gilly's face and hands before stripping off her remaining garments and dressing her in a threadbare gown he found in the small clothespress.

All this was done with an economy of movement that bespoke of a man who had dealt with injuries before—as he had more times than he cared to remember during his years at sea with Nelson. Never before, however, could he remember his hands shaking so badly as he worked, nor could he recollect having recourse to constant prayers, as he had the whole of the time it took for Gilly to show signs of recovering consciousness.

Lifting her slim form into his arms, he recalled something that had not escaped his notice even while his mind was occupied with caring for her needs—Gilly indeed possessed the most exquisitely proportioned body he had ever seen, and he had seen more than a few.

The sun was just rising as he laid her in his own wide bed before crawling in beside her. As he covered them both with the quilt, she stirred slightly before turning into his arms, as if unconsciously seeking comfort. With her head on his chest and her right arm wrapped trustingly around his waist, she gave a slight sigh and, he could tell by her even breathing, fell into a healing sleep.

Before he too fell asleep, he lay still for a long time, except for the hand that moved rhythmically, stroking her vivid mane of hair back from her face.

Chapter Seven

THEY SLEPT for several hours, until the sun was high in the sky, and woke slowly, each reluctant to lose the comforting warmth of their snug resting place.

Kevin was the first to open his eyes, and it took him a moment to recall the events of the past night or the reason he had awakened with an armful of warm girl. He then relived for a split second the wrenching agony he had felt when Gilly had fainted before his eyes, and which had only abated slightly when he realized the reason for the swoon. Knowing she was all right may have temporarily eased the clutch of fear that had gripped his heart, but the sure realization of what she had been about that night—and lord only knew how many nights before this—brought back that fear tenfold.

Shifting his position as little as he could, he looked down on his sleeping bride, her head still resting trustingly on his bared chest. Her features softened in sleep, her full lips slightly parted, and a rosy flush on her cheeks, she was the picture of innocence.

Why, she is still such a baby for all her bravado, he thought with a small sigh. Running an estate the size of The Hall almost singlehandedly, taking with it the responsibility for every soul on the place while living in near squalor in the midst of wealth, and burdened all the time by the stigma of her illegitimacy—it was enough to make a grown man turn tail and take to his heels.

But to run with the local smugglers—why it was beyond the bounds of what was believable! Was it for the money or the excitement that she did it—or was it a bit of each? No matter, Kevin decided firmly, she shall not be doing it again, of this much I can be sure!

For a long time Kevin lay still, gazing down at Gilly as

she slept on, until at last his patience wore thin. Picking up a strand of her hair he dangled it above her face, tickling the tip of her nose. Gilly's nostrils twitched a time or two and she screwed up her face in an attempt to evade the annoying tickle, but in the end she was forced to open her eyes.

"Good morning, wife," Kevin amicably greeted her wide-eyed look. "I hope you have rested well, but I must admit to waking you, for my arm—the one now crushed beneath you—is stiff and sore due to having been deprived of movement these last hours. Tut-tut, remember your poor shoulder," he added hastily as Gilly tried to move away and was rewarded for her efforts by a sharp pain in her arm. As she reluctantly lay back down, he soothed, "There now, isn't that much more comfortable?"

Gilly wanted to ignore him—indeed, her teeth were clamped so firmly together her jaw had already set up a dull ache—but curiosity got the better of her. "How did I come to be sharing your bed?" she asked through clenched teeth and then, with increasing urgency, "And how did I get into this nightgown?"

"How much do you remember?" Kevin leered down at her, but at her furious blush he relented and told her, reluctantly leaving out all innuendo and embellishments that might serve to discommode her and repay him for his earlier anguish.

Slowly, careful not to injure her shoulder, Gilly rose to a sitting position, wrapping the comforter about her like the rags of a tattered dignity. "I thank you for your kindness, my lord, but you needn't have bothered. I could have done it myself if I—er—I—"

"If you hadn't fainted dead away and lain until morning only to rise, thanks to your sodden clothes, with a putrid cold or worse?" Kevin offered pleasantly.

Gilly lifted her chin and shot back, "I wouldn't have fainted if you hadn't ripped my sweater away so violently. Besides, even if you did act out of some perverted sense of husbandly duty, I believe your ministrations could have stopped short of carrying me in here to your bed without fear of censure. It was a shabby trick, Rawlings, and well you know it."

Kevin pushed his pillows against the carved backboard and sat himself up before gifting his wife with a wicked (or so she believed) smile. "Do you really think so? I rather enjoyed it myself, as did you if the way you cuddled around me like a limpet can be construed as a way of expressing satisfaction with the arrangement. Now why don't we cry friends, hmm? Give me a kiss, puss, and I'll know you aren't going to hold it against me."

"I don't like kissing," Gilly told him flatly.

"You are, I presume, speaking from the benefit of your vast experience," Kevin said with remarkable sangfroid.

As Gilly's romantic experience before Kevin's advent into her life consisted of one hurried kiss at the hands of a village lad when she was but fifteen, she could only blush and hang her head.

Kevin lifted her chin with one finger and told her kindly, "One swallow does not a summer make, pet. Now, come here and give me my kiss."

With a belated show of spirit, Gilly declared mulishly, "I'd as lief kiss a frog!" and folded her arms across her chest with a snort of disgust.

An unholy gleam came into Kevin's eyes and he sprang up, quoting: " 'A frog he would a-wooing go. Sing heigh-ho says Rowley,' " before capturing Gilly and dragging her down across his chest.

His kiss was begun half in jest but it progressed rapidly until it became an embrace fraught with all the passion the revelations and the worries of the previous night had brought to bear. At first Gilly struggled in his arms, fearful but not repelled by the strange sensations coursing through her body, but soon her struggles ceased and she returned his ardor.

After the kiss ended they lay quietly for some minutes, each intent on their own thoughts, until at last, with his wife still locked within his embrace, Kevin said softly, "You will not be traveling with the free-traders again, will you pet? Loathe as I am to admit it, I aged ten years when I saw your wound and realized what you had been about. Did you run afoul of a revenue cutter?"

Gilly nodded her head, still too shy to look at her husband, especially after his only half-believed expression of concern, and told him, "The surf was running high on the shore with a contrary tide and a fresh blowing wind, so that we did not gain the land until much too late. We were perishing with the cold and wet to our middles, but when we caught sight of the customs officer and his troops on shore, we had no choice but to a man all oars and fight the tide back out to sea again. I heard shots but I didn't know I was hit until later when my shoulder began to hurt while we were sowing the crop."

Here Kevin interrupted Gilly's story to ask the meaning of her last words. "We were carrying geneva tubs and brandy, and luckily already had the tubs strung together with ten feet of rope between them. You must anchor some of the tubs with stones tied to them on other ropes so that everything sinks to the bottom. Tubs float otherwise," she pointed out to her uninitiated husband. "The one tub we don't weight down, the last on the line, floats just under the surface so we can spot it to pick it up later—or harvest our crop, if you will."

Kevin had let Gilly rattle on, knowing she needed time to recover her composure after their rather explosive embrace, but he did not realize how extensive was her knowledge of smuggling, nor, worse yet, that she was more than just one of the onshore helpers recruited to aid in the unloading of the cargo before carrying it to a place of concealment. That she actually went to sea with the smugglers was unbelievable. "How did you get mixed up in all this, infant?" he found himself asking.

She shrugged fatalistically. "Everyone around here is involved one way or the other, either riding the tubs, or manning the shore groups. We need the blunt, you see, especially since the harvest failed last year. At first the men didn't take too kindly to my coming along while they met the delivery boats out in the Straits, but since I can swim and nearly none of the others can, they decided I'd come in handy."

"Who all is involved, Gilly—the leaders, I mean. How many boats do you have? Do you put out often, on a regular schedule?"

He tried to ask the questions in a tone that sounded like he was simply curious about something unfamiliar to him, and Gilly actually began to answer him, "Well, there's Harry, of course, and—" before suddenly clamping her jaws shut tight.

Kevin was idly stroking her hair away from her forehead. "Yes, Harry. I believe you've almost let that name slip a time or two. Go on."

"Why?" she parried, lifting her head to look him straight in the eye. "What need of yours will be satisfied by such information?"

Seeing her narrowed eyes and wary expression, Kevin laughed and said, giving her chin a playful pinch, "Do not look so suspicious, infant. I'm no customs officer, you know—I was merely making conversation. Though now that I think of it, there is something else I can suggest to occupy our time between now and luncheon."

If Gilly meant to argue the point she was given precious little time to mount her objections before Kevin had rolled her neatly onto her back, his lips and hands beginning a gentle assault on her body.

Gilly knew she should fight him, it was wrong—this lovemaking devoid of love. It was insanity, but a gentle insanity, and her resistance melted away with the knowledge that there was at least a little love—if that was the proper definition for the warm feeling that overtook her lately every time she clapped eyes on her husband. She shivered a bit in her effort to keep a rein on her emotions.

She had not known love of any sort since her mother died. Oh, there had been the friendship and affection of the other servants at The Hall, but she was careful not to let anyone get too close to her, become too important to her.

She had loved her mother and her mother had been taken from her. She had loved her childhood playmates and they had been taken from her. Love meant pain. Love meant eventual but sure loss. She did not seek out love any more than she would deliberately seek out ways to inflict injury to her person.

If she allowed her present feelings for Kevin to grow, she would only hurt the more when, once the puzzle was solved and the fortune his, he left her to return to London. But, she argued fiercely to herself, did that mean she should deprive herself totally of this happiness, however fleeting, she was feeling now?

As Kevin nibbled delicately on her ear, his hands soothing her while at the same time filling her with an only recently aroused but still recognizable yearning, she gathered up her courage and asked him, a bit breathlessly, "This exercise in occupying time—how often do you suggest we indulge ourselves?"

Propping himself on one elbow, he smiled down into her

face. "I am a firm believer in keeping a tight rein on my personal indulgences. I try at all times to curb any tendency to do anything to excess."

Gilly tried not to look crestfallen, failing miserably. "Oh," was all she could say.

"Therefore," Kevin continued, still smiling, his hands still gently roving, "I believe once or twice a day for the next forty years should be sufficient without fearing a descent into gluttony."

"Oh!" she exclaimed, unable to hide her blushes. "How—how *comforting* it is to know you are a man of moderation."

Kevin threw back his head and laughed. "You saucy minx," he teased her, delighted by her impudence.

Not even in his wildest dreams, could he have dreamt that he could find such pleasure in the arms of any woman—and especially this woman, his unasked for, unwanted bride. Yet slowly, and (he now realized) inevitably, he had been at first piqued, then attracted, and at last, captivated by this skinny (he mentally substituted the word willowy), flame-headed, freckle-faced girl-woman, until, with the consummation of their marriage at last at hand, he was forced to admit (only to himself) that he loved—truly loved—for the first time in his life.

The love he felt for Amanda Delaney was finally recognized for what it was—the gentle love of friendship and the closeness of troubles shared and trials survived.

He held many of the same feelings for Gilly—the desire to cherish, protect and comfort her; the enjoyment of her conversation, company, and personality; the admiration of her character, honesty, and courage. But there were other feelings that had never been a part of his love for Amanda—this hungry yearning for just the mere sight of her, this intense pleasure at the simple touch of her hand, or this fierce protectiveness born from the knowledge that if Gilly should disappear from his life there would be no reason for him to continue to exist.

Never had anyone roused him to such joy, such passion, and, yes, even such anger. His wife had invaded his heart, his mind, his very soul.

He had always avoided entanglements, choosing his friends carefully but then giving them his lifelong loyalty. Only these few trusted friends, men like Jared Delaney and Bo Chevington, were allowed to see beyond the carefully constructed facade of shallow-brained dandyism to the real man who hid behind those misleading outward trappings. In his own way, Kevin was as leery of emotional involvement as Gilly. He had lost too many friends to the ravages of war, had cursed and cried and suffered too many times, and his nonchalance covered a multitude of scars.

Now Gilly had, unwittingly, breached his defenses, and he was without the weapons to prohibit her from completely overrunning the stronghold of his heart.

Thank the stars, he thought, that she had so far accepted their situation without making any demands on him for declarations of affection. It was too soon, his feelings were still too new, to allow him to voice them aloud. And what if she spurned him, laughed at his weak-kneed capitulation? He could not risk it—not yet. Yet neither could he force himself to keep his hands off her until he felt more comfortable with this advent of love into his life. Fortunately for him, Gilly was ignorant in the art of lovemaking and not likely to recognize the gentle reverence and moments of near desperation he now brought to his caresses as being as different from loveless passion as chalk from cheese.

He wished he had her love, craved it actually, like a starving man craves food, but he tried to content himself for a time with the half-loaf, which was her easy acceptance of this new intimacy in their relationship. He would just have to wait—perhaps love would come.

But that did not mean he could not use some gentle coercion. Now, raining light kisses on her cheeks and eyelids, he murmured throatily, "Oh, my sweet Gillyflower, you delight my soul. Put your arms around me, my beautiful wife, and let me feel your softness."

When Gilly began, hesitantly at first and then with more fervency and less inhibition, to react to his love words, Kevin could resist no longer and groaned, "Ah, my Gillyflower, you are so young, so warm, so—*alive.* I—" before crushing his mouth to hers and there was no more need for words. Together they began to float, then soar, until it seemed there were only the two of them left alone in the world, their bodies locked in an endless embrace as wave upon wave of passion moved them ever closer to the shore.

Gilly cried out but once before they were both caught in the whirlpool that took them down, down, down, to end—miraculously—on some enchanted beach where the sun shone brightly and the world looked as it must have done on that First Day—all fresh and sparkling and peaceful.

These two people—with so much still remaining between them to be resolved—had at last found one form of communication upon which they could agree.

A sennight passed quite quickly, but not uneventfully. While their nights were filled with delights neither of them had ever before believed existed, daylight found them unable to act naturally with each other.

The servants were gifted, or cursed, with seven days of varying degrees of covert, near, and open warfare between man and wife as they engaged in a continual duel of wits and wills, the trading back and forth of insults threatening to shake the ancient Hall down about everyone's ears. This continual sparring, the advances and retreats, was a camouflage they both employed in order to keep their true feelings, their vulnerability, hidden—but neither of them knew the other's motives were similar.

During this trying time, Lyle and Fitch kept away from The Hall, hiding in the gardens, though these gardens did not seem to be benefiting from their presence.

Willie the groom, a witness to more than one verbal skirmish at the stables as the newlyweds prepared to ride out together, viewed the situation from his one-sided loyalty and silently cursed the Earl for his misuse of "such a grand, good girl."

Olive Zook hid whenever she could, Hattie Kemp clucked her tongue and punished her bread dough, while Mrs. Whitebread—thanks to her deafness—was almost as oblivious to the mad goings-on as were Aunt Sylvia and Elsie.

Willstone, his loyalty firmly with the Earl on all matters, wrote to his brother in Chichester that "all would be well once they were back in London and shed of that uncivilized savage" the Earl was, fortunately, only bound to tolerate for a mere twelvemonth or less. He now kept his opinions to himself around The Hall, however, as his chin was still tender from the facer Willie had planted when he was once foolhardy enough to air his feelings aloud.

When he was not busy being totally exasperated by the infuriating chit, Kevin was amused by Gilly's pugnacious attitude that was so at variance with her yeilding passion in the bedchamber. It gave him, for one thing, time to adjust himself to the situation between them, as well as a never-ending stream of insights into the complex person who was his wife.

It was not all so amusing or edifying an experience for his wife. Gilly felt herself to be constantly on tenterhooks, her defenses always in readiness for fear she would unconsciously disclose her true feelings—whatever they were, as they were completely alien to her. She fought a daily battle against her emotions, as she feared Kevin's rejection if she ever let him know how very much he meant to her. Sylvester, her father, for all her declared indifference to him, had always had the power to hurt her—power he recognized and delighted in using. Thankfully, Sylvester was gone.

But now there was Kevin—and he too had the power to hurt her, power a hundredfold more potent than Sylvester's. So far, she hoped, he was not aware of this power.

The question that lay heavy on her mind all day and kept a part of her heart from him during the long nights was: if he were to find out he had this power—would he feel compelled to wield it? As long as their lovemaking was accompanied by overtones of frivolity, Gilly could hide behind their mutual bantering. Just the night before Kevin had commented, after they had made love and were wrapped in each others arms until their heartbeats returned to normal: "What a mutually—if I interpret that soft purring I heard just now correctly—pleasurable diversion this is. As a hobby to pass the time and engross the mind, I do believe it has clock collecting beat all to flinders."

Gilly could only giggle. "Indeed, sir, it would seem to be eminently more satisfying. Now do shut up, I have been run ragged all day hunting down Elsie's silver spoon. I ran it to earth at last in the Conservatory stuck in a dirt-filled pot. I do believe Lyle or Fitch used it as a miniature spade."

"Ah," Kevin chuckled, "that explains it. No wonder they make so little progress on the grounds, if their tools are that limited. And I thought they were merely lazy—how shabby I was to so malign them."

Gilly sunggled more closely against her husband's side. "Do not beat your breast in repentence, for they *are* lazy—nearly somnolent—but they are very good at what they do."

"They don't *do* anything," Kevin was forced to point out.

"Precisely," she replied lightheartedly, "and they're *very* good at it!" earning herself a playful slap that was the prelude to another "mutually pleasurable diversion."

Gilly was in the library reliving the scene in her mind when Kevin came in, the morning post in his hand. "Good morning, wife," he said carelessly, his eyes intent on the letter in his hand.

"Ah, good," he remarked at length. "Rice, my late father's butler who retired to Kent some years back, has agreed to come to The Hall and assist in creating some order in this establishment. You'll like him, Gilly," he told her bracingly. "He's a crusty old character, but he has a heart of gold."

A snort of disbelief was his only answer. The sun was up and so were Gilly's defenses.

Kevin pressed on. "Rice is bringing along an acquaintance he met some time ago, a—let me see, ah, here it is—a Miss Bernice Roseberry. She will serve as your dresser."

This statement was not acknowledged at all, and Kevin dropped the subject after informing Gilly the two would be traveling post and should arrive any day soon.

Sifting through the remainder of the letters, he stopped, examined a heavy folded sheet and exclaimed, "Oh, ho! Here is a letter from Jared Delaney—you remember my speaking of Lord and Lady Storm, don't you, infant? I spent a good bit of time with them at Storm Haven last year until their twins were born."

Gilly remembered. She also remembered how Kevin's eyes had lit up when he had mentioned Lady Storm a few days after their marriage, and how his voice had warmed when he said "Amanda."

Unaware that Gilly's temper—a shield against the pain of rejection—was rapidly coming to a boil, Kevin ripped open the seal and began to read. "He jokes that he cannot believe I have finally been caught in a parson's mousetrap.

Ha! Earl's mousetrap more like," he joked as Gilly's hands clenched into tight little fists.

"Oh, good grief!" Kevin groaned, his mouth twisting into a grimace of dismay. "It wanted only that. Listen to this, brat," and he quoted from the letter:

> . . ." '*Amanda had the happy notion to visit you and your new bride and Bo and Anne have already agreed to accompany us. The twins have kept Mandy fully occupied these past six months and I believe some time away from them would benefit her, not as if I could gainsay her decision to visit you if I tried, as you should well remember my sweet wife's determination in getting her own way. I am, as always, putty in her hands. We depart Storm Haven the first of August and should reach you within two days, weather and roads permitting.*'

"He goes on a bit on some other matter, but the finer points of field drainage pale before his other news. Good God, how can we possibly have them staying under this roof? The place is so derelict I find it difficult to believe there are two decent bedchambers other than our own left in the entire establishment."

As Kevin began to pace, Gilly, who hid her trepidation at coming face to face with any of Kevin's friends, especially Amanda—or Mandy as her husband called her—said with an attempt at nonchalance, "Then write back fobbing them off."

"And *why* shall I say they can't come?" he charged in return.

Gilly shrugged. "Tell them the truth, it's a valid enough reason."

"Ha!" barked Kevin. "If I were to be so foolish as to forewarn Amanda of my plight, she would not hesitate to drag Nanny, Aunt Agatha, Tom, Harrow, the twins, and half the staff of Storm Haven clear to Sussex and encamp until she had The Hall completely renovated to her satisfaction. No, I'll not tell her the truth; I'm not such a cabbagehead."

Kevin's outburst gave Gilly the impression that his precious Amanda was an overbearing, dominating female and she became, if it were possible, even less enchanted with the idea of having the woman at The Hall.

But when Kevin spoke again, Gilly's anger and resentment was to mushroom a hundredfold.

"Thank the gods Rice and your dresser will be arriving soon. Now listen, infant," he instructed severely, "and I want no arguments from you on the subject. I will expect you to conduct yourself with propriety while my friends are in residence. Let your dresser guide you—your gowns should be here any time soon. Remember—you are mistress here now. I'll brook no sweeping of grates, slopping of hogs, or—most definitely—consorting with free-traders. You are the Countess of Lockport and my wife. You will behave accordingly."

Gilly sprang up from her chair in a flaming fury. "The devil take your bladder, Kevin Rawlings. Who are you to dictate so to me?" She strode across the expanse of carpet, her too-short muslin skirts kicking about her ankles, and stopped just inches from colliding with his chest. "I am not ashamed of The Hall and I'm not ashamed of honest work. Mayhap if you spent less time preening yourself like some popinjay and more time with a broomstick than a hairbrush, The Hall would not look so shabby."

"And mayhap if I had a magic wand I could turn dust into gold!" Kevin shot back sarcastically before cutting more firmly into her tirade. "And another thing, wife. Although I understand outbursts like 'the devil take your bladder' to be innocent parrotings of a child overexposed to such cant, my friends may not be so broadminded, especially Anne, Bo's wife, and a very sheltered creature. Learn to guard your tongue or I shall be forced to take measures to correct you."

Gilly struck a belligerent pose and opened her mouth to spout a phrase of two that would *really* set the high and mighty Earl's ears to burning but was cut off by her husband's next words.

"I know this is a lot to ask, pet," he began somewhat nervously, "but my foolish pride demands that I speak." Taking a deep breath, he went on: "Vain popinjay that I am, I would wish, although I have already written Jared about the reasons for our precipitate marriage, to convey the image that ours is a happy union. In other words, while my friends are here, I would like us to exhibit some signs of affection between us while in their presence. Is that too much to ask?"

Gilly's heart took up a painful throbbing in her breast as she took in Kevin's earnest expression. Surely she had been right—Kevin *was* in love with this Amanda. What other reason could there be for him to be so concerned over putting a bright face on their marriage?

Nodding her head in assent to his request, her former anger now forgotten in the face of her newer, more painful reaction to the realization Kevin's heart belonged to another, Gilly slipped from the room, her husband's eyes following her woebegone figure in puzzlement.

That night when he entered their bedchamber, Gilly was nowhere to be found. There was a full moon, so he knew no smugglers were out, but he was at a loss to locate her.

When she appeared at breakfast the next morning, her eyes suspiciously red-rimmed, he asked her where she had slept.

"That is none of your concern, my lord," she told him coldly. "I'll be your lapdog all the day long once *your* friends arrive—it's the least I can do to help a man so fraught with insecurities as yourself—but don't expect me to be your pillow at night. I've no time to spare for mewling babes—and less desire to share a bed with a man so embarrassed by his wife's conduct he only seems able to approach her in the dark."

Kevin sat back in his chair and applauded softly. "That was quite a speech, wife; undoubtedly a well-prepared one. But as Shakespeare said: 'Since maids, in modesty, say "No" to that which they would have the profferer to construe "Ay," 'I do believe you protest too much."

"And I believe you are a low-down, filthy—"

"Ah, ah!" Kevin broke in hastily, and Gilly, her face white with fury, rose and stomped from the room.

Kevin's laughter followed her but there was no humor in his face as he spent that night too very much alone in his huge bed.

Chapter Eight

AMANDA DELANEY was a beautiful woman. From her coal black hair and eyes the color of old gold coins, down to the tips of her dainty feet (not too great a distance as, although softly rounded, Lady Storm was just a little dab of a woman), she fairly oozed charm and femininity from every pore.

Amanda, by her mere presence, made Gilly (even clad as she was in one of her new gowns the recently arrived Miss Roseberry had coaxed her into wearing) feel flashy, cheap, clumsy, plain, and jealous. Jealous of her beauty? Her charm? Her bearing? Definitely all those things, Gilly admitted to herself, but mostly—hard as it was to acknowledge—jealous of Kevin's obvious affection for the woman.

From the first moments of introduction and exchanged greetings, Gilly had felt out of her element in the midst of these four (five, counting Rawlings), and could only long for the anonymity of the servants hall. These people inhabited a world she had only dreamed of—a world she had only wished for in her wildest fantasies.

Now, as they all sat in the newly cleaned but still shabby large drawing room sipping Mrs. Whitebread's special herb tea and munching Hattie Kemp's honey-topped scones, Gilly sat back and let the babble of conversation flow over her head as she observed Kevin's friends.

Jared Delaney, she had seen at once, was obviously a personage of some consequence. Not that he was straight-backed or top-lofty in any way—but there was an air of confidence about the man, an aura of quiet authority as it were, that clung to his figure like a velvet cloak. He was, thought Gilly, as handsome as a Greek god to boot, what with his great height, jet black hair, and startlingly vivid blue eyes.

Together, he and his wife made a devastatingly handsome couple, and she concluded, after only a few minutes spent observing them, a couple very much in love with each other. Whether it was the way Amanda laid her hand on his arm when she spoke or the frequency with which his eyes sought her out, Gilly's general impression was that, if her idea about Kevin's affections were true, her poor husband was whistling at the moon.

Somewhat relaxed by this knowledge, Gilly examined Bo and Anne Chevington, a pair very dissimilar physically from Lord and Lady Storm. Where Amanda was beautiful, Anne was pretty—pale, blonde, and unassuming. Bo, unlike the physically impressive Jared, was short, a bit round, and the recipient of hair even more carroty than Gilly's. He seemed shy, and spoke in tight clipped sentences—almost as if he was in a rush to become silent once more.

I think I like them all well enough—heaven knows they are a far cry from the posturing, preening O'Keefes—but, she told herself depressingly, that does not mean they will like *me* in return. After all, I am not one of them. She felt sure all of them—and most positively Amanda—held definite thoughts on the sort of woman Kevin should marry. That this could not possibly include an unmannered bastard kitchen wench took no great burst of insight on Gilly's part.

Well, she mentally shrugged, that was all just too bad wasn't it, for like it or not, they were all stuck with her! So thinking, Gilly made an effort to listen to the conversation that had so far focused on the poor state of the King's highways and the advisability, to quote somebody's Aunt Agatha, of taking along one's own sheets when forced to make use of wayside inns.

"How is dear old Aggie?" Kevin broke in with a feigned grimace. "Still frog-marching everyone about like some line officer intent on keeping all in order?"

Amanda laughed, as again her hand went out to her husband who quickly took it and lifted her fingers to his lips. "Thanks to my sweet wife's forethought in producing twins, both my aunt and Nanny—you remember her, Kevin, that fire-breathing creature with the heart of a lion—are so endlessly occupied that we sometimes go entire days between er—*domestic crises.*"

"Remember, dearest, what happened when little Beau cut his first tooth?" his wife interjected. Amanda then turned to speak directly to Kevin and Gilly, who sat at either end of a small sofa. "Nanny, you see, wished to put powdered cloves against poor Beau's gums but Aunt Agatha insisted a few drops of brandy would be more the ticket. In the end," Amanda had to stop to giggle, "they decided to try the remedies out on themselves first—with the results that Nanny's tongue was so numb she couldn't speak and Aunt Agatha imbibed so much brandy she fell asleep at table and snored all through Sunday dinner."

"The vicar was visiting," Jared added, a chuckle escaping his own lips. "He was quite nonplussed."

Now Gilly relaxed in spite of herself as they all enjoyed the joke, and when Kevin sat down close beside her after replacing his teacup on the tray, she did not shrink away from him.

"So, Bo," Kevin addressed the chubby redhead, "what have you been up to since your marriage? You've been quiet since your arrival, even for you."

It was Jared who answered. "Ah, Kevin, do you not remember the saying—'The deepest rivers flow with the least sound.' And our Bo certainly is a deep'un. Why, they've not been married but three months and already Anne is with child."

As Bo and Anne both turned a deep red, Amanda poked her husband in the ribs, admonishing him for upsetting Anne.

"What—more babies?" cried Kevin with mock incredulity. "Is the whole of England then out to reproduce itself? Keep this sort of thing up, gentlemen," he admonished his two friends, "and soon there will be no room left at all and we shall all topple into the sea."

At this Amanda spoke up. "Kevin Rawlings, you have not changed a whit since the day I met you. First, you complain that your friends have deserted you by marrying and now you accuse us of trying to usurp your land with our offspring. Yet after bemoaning our actions you have, at least in part, emulated them. Already you are married—and sooner or later you too will be a parent, as it most naturally follows, you know."

Anne blushed at such frank speech and only whispered, "Amen."

"Quite jolly right," Bo added.

"Trumped your ace," Jared pointed out.

Topping it all off, Amanda remarked, "And it will probably be the making of him, although Aunt Agatha has said innumerable times that our Kevin is beyond salvation."

Gilly was incredulous a moment, listening to this good-natured attack, but then joined in the laughter at her husband's expense.

Kevin looked about the room as if crushed by this assault by his bosom chums. "The treachery of one's friends is depressing to say the least, but that my bride chooses to side with my attackers fair bids to unman me. Wife," he said turning to face Gilly, who was suddenly quite sober, "say I beg you, that you are not already planning to gift me with a miniature replica of myself."

"No, my lord," she replied softly, "I am not."

"Thank the gods!" her husband responded, raising her hands and pressing kisses on both palms. "I want you entirely to myself for some time to come, dearest. You are too precious to me to begin to think of sharing you with another."

Gilly colored hotly at this speech, knowing Kevin's friends, who could not see the laughter in his eyes, were likely to take the impression that she and Kevin were deeply in love. They could not know how tightly he held her hands so that she could not pull them away and slap that inane look off his handsome face. She knew he wanted her to make an answer of some sort that would support his impression of a loving couple, lost to the people just now avidly watching this touching scene.

"And you know, *dearest,* of the depth of my affection for you," she at last replied, satisfying their audience and succeeding in wiping Kevin's expression clear of any trace of humor.

A rapport of sorts had been established in the group by the time the small party broke up in order to dress for dinner. Indeed, Gilly was beginning to look forward to the chance of getting to know Kevin's friends better, and they, in turn, seemed to like her well enough. But she still, as she had done this last fortnight, held Rawlings at arm's length.

She did allow him to keep his arm about her waist as

everyone mounted the stairs, but as soon as their own chamber was reached she shook him off and ran for the sanctuary that was her own bedchamber.

Once safe inside, she was greeted by the dresser who had arrived on the second day of her new estrangement from her husband. "Bunny," she called out now, "it was just as you promised it would be. Nobody stared or said anything in the least bit cutting. I really think I like them all quite a little bit."

Bernice Roseberry raised her head from the latest copy of *Journal des Modes* she was just then perusing and replied calmly, "Of course you do, child. I never did harbor any great fear that they would descend on you like a pack of rabid wolves crying out for your blood. Now stop fidgeting about like a skittish colt while I help you out of your gown."

The arrival of Bernice Roseberry into her life in mid-July had marked the beginning of great changes in Gilly. Prepared to dislike the woman on sight, Gilly had been somewhat taken aback by the dresser's frank, open speech and no-nonsense way of looking at things. Besides that, the woman was unflappable. She never so much as blinked an eye when she was first presented with her rag-tag charge and told, by the impeccably groomed Earl no less, to "do what you can."

Obviously Miss Roseberry delighted in a challenge, for she plunged headlong into a campaign to turn her new mistress into a young lady of fashion—whether that mistress liked it or not.

Gilly's resentment and arbitrary behavior was met with an unflinching obsidian stare—not to mention a scathing flow of sarcasm that even Kevin at first could not and latterly deigned not to even try to counter.

Added to this forceful personality was a physical presence that was more than a little daunting. Although of only average height and quite thin (her flat chest was the woman's one secret regret), she gave the impression of being larger than life.

About five and thirty, Miss Roseberry made no push to beautify herself in the way she wore her hair (a tight bun, smack on the top of her head), or in the clothes she wore—and her face was always devoid of paint. There was no softening frame for her features—her flat brown hair and flatter brown eyes were hardly likely to take anyone's attention and turn it from noticing her fierce, straight brows, jutting chin, or long, needle-thin nose.

As for her wardrobe, it seemed to consist of interchangeable high-necked dark gowns, with her only jewelry consisting of a string stuck with pins always hanging at her breast, a small pair of scissors dangling from a ribbon on her wrist, and a huge watch (her late father's) strung around her neck by a heavy gold chain.

Moments after her arrival, Kevin, leaning down to whisper into Rice's ear, commented, "Now there's one I wouldn't care to encounter in some dark alley."

Miss Roseberry, having keen ears, overheard and promptly stage-whispered to Gilly, "It's a comfort to know the Earl is a prudent sort who knows when he is both outmanned and out-gunned." Gilly's resentment—although she still felt honor-bound to put up some show of disliking Miss Roseberry, if only to thwart her husband—had begun to fade at that moment.

Armed with the Countess's new wardrobe just arrived from London, and laboring under precise orders from the Earl, Miss Roseberry set out to civilize Gilly. Table manners, the proper way to pour tea, the intricacies of social conduct, and more were lessons that filled their days.

Yet it was only when, with their guests due in less than a week, Gilly dared to ask the dresser timidly, "Do you think you can make me even passably pretty?" that the top-lofty Miss Roseberry set aside her consequence, gathered the young girl into her arms, and crooned, "There, there, child. Don't you fret—Bunny will help you."

When Kevin overheard Gilly calling Miss Roseberry Bunny some time later, he laughed and asked where on earth that singularly inappropriate handle had come from.

"Bunny says her father used to call her by that name as a sort of endearment," Gilly answered him defiantly. "And don't you say another word, Kevin Rawlings. Bunny has not had an easy life since her father's death—he was a schoolteacher, you know, and could not leave her well-fixed, even though she is of gentle birth. Otherwise *nothing* could have induced her to become a dresser. She has high principles—why, she left her last place of employment because her mistress wore so many jewels and so much paint on her face that Bunny told her she refused to work for a tart."

"My, my," said Kevin incredulously, "it would appear Miss Roseberry has a staunch supporter in her new mistress. How very droll."

The Earl wasn't quite so amused, however, when the evening after an aborted attempt to reestablish his former nocturnal rapport with his wife, he found Miss Roseberry asleep on a pallet outside the entrance to Gilly's bedchamber.

And so it would seem Kevin's plans had succeeded much too well. Gilly had been made much more than her wish of "passably pretty," thanks to her new gowns and Miss Roseberry's talents, and she had also gone a long way towards becoming a well-behaved young lady. But his plans had not included his wife's dresser-cum-mentor exceeding her duties to the point of becoming a dragon in the chit's defense. Lord only knew she had a surfeit of those already. At his latest tally, he had only Willstone and Rice to list on his side of the ledger, and everyone knew the valet and the aged butler were not exactly forces to be feared.

So Gilly slept alone—and Kevin slept alone—and Miss Roseberry slept midway between them on the floor of the sitting room.

Gilly had once been dowdy, ill-kept, unmannered—and accessible. Since Miss Roseberry's invasion, Gilly was surprisingly pretty, faultlessly groomed, prettily polite—and totally beyond his reach. It was a bleeding pity—that's what it was—and if his friends ever got wind of it, he doubted he could bear their jokes.

Now, while Gilly quietly submitted to Bunny's ministrations, Kevin, having rushed through his own toilette with an uncaring air that brought tears of frustration to Willstone's eyes, was pacing back and forth across the sitting room like a caged tiger impatient for his daily ration of raw red meat.

At long last his wife appeared, Miss Roseberry in tow, and he begged a word with his bride in private.

"Can I trust his lordship not to pounce on the poor defenseless child the moment I turn my back?" asked Miss Roseberry silkily.

Kevin bit down hard on a fitting retort and unbent enough to ask Gilly—very humbly for him—to please grant him this small favor. "I promise I'll behave," he added sincerely.

"Hummph!" Miss Roseberry sniffed. "Believe that, my girl, and you'll believe anything. The man doesn't have it in him—just ask Rice, who's known him from his cradle."

Gilly, seeing the tic that had begun to work in Kevin's otherwise expressionless face, forestalled any recitation of her husband's past sins by patting Miss Roseberry on the shoulder and assuring her she was more than capable of holding her own with her own husband.

"Believe her, woman," added Kevin earnestly. "She can you know—and I have the scars to prove it."

Gilly blushed a bit, knowing he referred to his last attempt to enter her bedchamber, an event that left him with a large bump on his forehead thanks to Gilly's accurate aim and a nearby vase used as ammunition. The sound of the vase shattering on the floor (only after inflicting its damage on Rawlings's blonde pate) had brought Miss Roseberry at a dead run and saved Gilly any retribution at the hands of her husband. He had had no further opportunity to be alone with his wife since.

Once Miss Roseberry reluctantly withdrew from the sitting room, Kevin approached Gilly. "You are looking quite beautiful tonight, puss."

This was no empty compliment—Gilly did look beautiful. Miss Roseberry may have declined to rig herself out with any style, but she was a perfect genius when it came to making the most out of her mistress.

Tonight, for instance, Gilly was dressed in a cunningly cut gown of the lightest bronze shade, with an overskirt of sheer spun gold net. Her creamy shoulders rose above the low neckline and her hair, now cut quite short and artfully groomed to cluster about her small face in a cap of loose curls, revealed Gilly's long, graceful neck while turning her pixielike face into a heart-melting vision of pert nose, enchanting freckles, and enormous blue eyes.

Byron would swoon at the sight of her, Kevin mused now and had to tear his eyes from her before he fulfilled Miss Roseberry's fears and pounced on his wife like the love-starved man he was. Instead, he allowed himself only a single self-pitying smile before turning away, saying, "You made me proud today, child, very proud. My friends are all quite enamored of you already."

"I like them too," she replied softly, barely restraining the hand that longed to reach out and touch the man standing with his back to her.

They were both silent for some time, each feeling the tension between them as keenly as a knife in the breast.

"Gilly, I—"

"Kevin, I—"

They both burst into speech at the same time, then stopped upon hearing the other.

"You were about to say?" queried Kevin, relieved that Gilly was willing to speak to him.

"No, no, you go first," she stammered nervously, for she was no more sure of what she had been about to say than was he of what words he would use.

There was another small silence before Kevin smiled, the smile making deep slashes in his cheeks and sending sparkles to dancing in his eyes.

"Ah, Gilly," he whispered huskily, shaking his head, "I have missed you, puss." The smile left his face, and his eyes darkened to indigo as he reached out his arms to his near-to-trembling bride.

"I-I've—missed you t-too," Gilly stammered before putting out her own hands and meeting her husband halfway in their rush to be in each other's arms.

Later that night, after a dinner that was marked by an all-round feeling of camaraderie and friendship, the Earl and Countess of Lockport gave their excuses and bid their guests an early good-night.

Miss Bernice Roseberry passed the night in her own bedroom.

Rice (as far as Gilly was aware, he possessed no other name) was all that a butler should be: stuffy, condescending, laughably correct in his manner and bearing, unflaggingly loyal, and, most improtantly, more than willing to surreptitiously guide Gilly away from any potential social *faux pas.*

He seemed to regard his new mistress as a child who had somehow strayed from the nursery and inadvertently acquired a Countess's coronet through no fault of her own. Because of her extreme youth and readily apparent *naïveté* —and abetted by the story of her past gleaned from members of the staff—he felt an instinctive sympathy for the child. He also was aware that she had been literally blackmailed into marriage, and although he believed the very sun to rise and set with his own Master Kevin, he also believed Gilly was too much the innocent to be married to such a man of the world.

So far Rice's sojourn at The Hall had been most pleasant. He was happy to be back in harness, as it were, having found retirement after Kevin's father's death too uneventful by half, and thoroughly enjoyed having a staff to bully once more.

He patrolled the corridors, his tall (very), thin (extremely), brittle-looking form encased in proper black—his white gloves occasionally inspecting a table for dust—the scourge of the three young village girls who had recently been added to the housekeeping staff. The Hall might be shabby, but with Rice in charge, the accumulated filth of two decades was rapidly being swept away.

With an apron tied about his middle, he supervised the polishing of silver or instructed the very-insulted Hattie Kemp in the fine art of French pastry-making.

Olive Zook, whom he secretly believed to be a lame-brained lunatic, although a harmless enough sort, he left to her own peculiar devices.

Mrs. Whitebread was the only real cloud on Rice's horizon. The woman greatly admired the butler and followed him about the whole day through, looking for all the world like a tongue-lolling puppy, answering all his inquiries with exasperating misinterpretations of his questions. By the end of each day he was hoarse from shouting at her as well as increasingly more certain the daft woman had designs on the bachelorhood he had clung to so doggedly these five and fifty years.

Gilly also believed the housekeeper was nursing a *tendre* for the butler, which heartily amused her as Rice was not exactly Gilly's idea of handsome. Not only was he painfully thin, he had, at her last count, exactly a dozen outrageously long grey hairs spanning the top of his head (carefully cultivated from a slightly thicker side and back growth) in hopes, thought Gilly, of deflecting the sheen reflected from the chandeliers off his otherwise bare skull, and thereby not blinding anyone.

Gilly did find Rice's face interesting. He had soft, baby-like skin that was creased with a fine web of lines, crossing and recrossing each other like veins on a dry leaf, and he possessed the bright rosy red cheeks of a choirboy. Yes, Gilly mused reflectively, there *was* a certain something about the man that would appeal to a woman like Mrs. Whitebread.

Yet it was Gilly who longed to kiss the man's wizened cheek moments after he had come into the main saloon to announce that Mr. O'Keefe and his sister had arrived on an afternoon visit. Rice had only met the pair twice before, but he had already formed an opinion about them that even his proper manner could not hide.

The Rawlings and their houseguests were all together in the room, commiserating with each other that the rain that had begun that morning showed no sign of abating and allowing them outdoors. The men all rose politely as the O'Keefes swept into the room.

"I shan't take your hat, sir," Rice pronounced in stentorian tones, "as you musn't worry you'll be expected to stay on past the usual quarter-hour alloted such unannounced visits."

Gilly's spirits, which had sunk a little at Rice's first announcement, were remarkably lifted, and to show her appreciation, she (deciding that actually kissing the man would be a bit too obvious) shot Rice a dazzling smile and a wink of thanks.

Rory O'Keefe, looking his usual handsome storybook-prince self, did not seem to be insulted when he was left standing, hat in outstretched hand, watching Rice's retreating back. He merely shrugged his shoulders before laying the hat on a nearby table and advancing to shake hands with his host.

"Fella's a popinjay," Bo whispered into Gilly's ear before turning his eyes on Glynis and inquiring, "I say, Gilly. Who's the ladybird?"

Gilly bit down hard on her knuckled fist to keep from laughing out loud. As the introductions were made all around, Gilly watched her new friends carefully, happily surprised at what she read in their faces.

Anne looked at the pair of beautiful creatures with the same sort of flustered surprise she might have shown had two exotic peacocks just then strutted in from the gardens.

Bo, as if his pithy comments had not been enough, was eyeing the O'Keefes up and down, his chubby-cheeked face extremely solemn as he seemed to be trying to assure himself they weren't about to lope off with the silver.

As Jared Delaney rose to shake hands, towering over Rory and by his own dark handsomeness making the latter look more like a copy than an original, Gilly saw his keen eyes assessing the newcomers. His greeting was civil but restrained, and he was careful to keep himself next to his wife rather than offering his seat to Glynis.

It was left to Amanda to pick up the conversational ball, complimenting Glynis on her gown and asking Rory how he liked tutoring young boys, as Kevin had mentioned during the introductions.

The O'Keefes are being pumped for information, Gilly thought to herself, and Amanda is so masterful an inquisitor, they don't even know it.

"Gilly, dear," Glynis said, interrupting Gilly's amusement, "how terribly—er—*charming* you are looking today. Whatever possessed you to cut off your hair?" The woman gave a delicate shudder. "I don't know if I would have the nerve to be seen in public with hair as short as any man's, but then with yours being such a very *odd* shade, I guess you felt the less there was of it the better, hmm?"

One swing, swore Gilly silently, just give me one clear swing at her and I'll wipe that condescending smirk off her face.

Luckily, whether for Gilly or Glynis it is not known (as coming to cuffs in the midst of a social afternoon would have repercussions for both the attacker and the attacked), Amanda broke in chattily, "Didn't you know, Miss O'Keefe? Short curls are all the rage in London, thanks to Byron. Have you by chance read his *Childe Harold's Pilgrimage*, Cantos One and Two, which have been published just recently?" Before Glynis could answer, Amanda launched into a short recital of some of the more popular lines, giving Gilly's temper some much-needed time in which to cool.

When Glynis spoke again, it was with the knowledge that any further attacks on the upstart Countess would not be allowed to go unanswered, as these people all, if their momentarily hostile faces upon hearing her comments on Gilly's hair were to be used as an indication of their feelings, were actually prepared to stand allies to the chit. Since she could not indulge in veiled sarcasm, she fell back on her most reliable ploy, that of being an empty-brained little widgeon who wouldn't harm a fly. She spent the remainder of her visit chattering happily about all manner of trivialities, and pointedly ignoring Gilly, while the four men discussed politics and the wars that were now raging on two fronts, Europe and America.

When at last the O'Keefes had taken their leave—the object of their visit still undisclosed unless Glynis's innocuously put-forth queries as to how the fortune hunt ("such a lark for all of us, you know") was at the heart of the matter—Jared asked Kevin point-blank how much he had told the O'Keefes.

While Gilly blushed furiously Kevin informed them that the O'Keefes knew Sylvester had set them a puzzle in his Will, but he had not been such a skipbrain as to let them think his marriage to Gilly was anything but a love match.

"Which, in direct opposition to my late great-uncle's hopes, it is. Isn't that right, darling?" he said to Gilly encouragingly as he lifted her fingers to his lips.

His wife merely nodded; if she had dared to speak aloud, she knew she would have been unable to keep from blurting: "If only it were!"

"Well, I'm relieved to hear you haven't let them in on your private business, not that I really believed you would, close-mouthed creature that you are—but I wonder, am I imagining it or did I see an avaricious gleam in Miss O'Keefe's eyes when she said the words fortune hunt?" Jared went on as he rose to pace the room.

"She's a pretty woman," Anne ventured timidly, "but there's something about her that sends prickles up and down my spine."

"Funny," Amanda volunteered. "She made me feel something too, but it was more like an itching in my palm as if I wanted to strike that sickeningly sweet smile off her face as she got done insulting poor Gilly here."

The object of Amanda's concern assured the company at large: "Don't worry about me. I can give as good as I get—lord knows I've had plenty of reason to practice at it—but I thank you all anyway for jumping in as you did, never allowing our dear Miss O'Keefe the time to toss any more of her poison darts. It was really quite diverting watching you all guiding the conversation away from me each time she tried to steer it back in my direction."

Bo leaned over and patted Gilly's hand. "What friends are for, ya know. Blonde, pretty, don't mean she's an angel. Fella's havey-cavey. Don't know how-so, but a slippery piece of goods, I say."

"Huh?" was all Gilly could muster in return.

Jared broke in then, first explaining that Bo felt both O'Keefes to be other than they appeared to want everyone to think them to be, and then went on, "I've seen O'Keefe's sort before—so smooth and agreeable. I believe if I had said the sun rises in the West, he would have gone right along with me. A toadeater of the first water if ever I've seen one."

After listening to his friends, Kevin ventured, "You know, I am surprised at you. Gossiping about our neighbors like a bunch of old tabbies over their saucers of cream. Glynis is just an ordinary female, a bit envious of my wife's good fortune, but only a harmless female indulging in a little friendly dig or two as females are prone to do."

"Blanche, a female too. Harmless as a vial of poison," interjected Bo, wagging a finger in Kevin's direction.

"Who's Blanche?" asked Gilly.

"She was a creature from my husband's chequered past who tried to make a bit of mischief after our marriage," supplied Amanda serenely.

"Mischief? Ha! Murder, more like," blustered Bo.

"Be that neither here nor there, Bo dearest, I believe Kevin is right about one thing," said Amanda, as she busied herself smoothing the pleats of her skirt over her knees, "we are carrying on like common gossips. I say we stop right now—just as soon as I say that Glynis O'Keefe is a born mischief-maker; and as for that brother of hers, why if he had just a drop more intelligence, I truly believe he could serve as a tolerable doorstop. Now," she smiled sweetly as everyone else in the room stared at her openmouthed, "let us change the subject and talk of something more interesting. Kevin—tell us more about this puzzle. Perhaps we can spend the rest of this dreary afternoon on a treasure hunt."

Kevin went to the library and came back with a copy of the puzzle, telling them of the success to date in tracking down the endless time mentioned in the rhyme. "There we were, acting like a bunch of confirmed lunatics—chasing about like dogs after their own tails—peering into clocks."

"Anodyne? Haven't the vaguest," piped up Bo, as he took his turn reading the puzzle.

"It's from the Latin, dearest," replied Anne, surprising everyone into looking at her as she explained, "In Latin it's *anodynus.* It's much the same in Greek—*anodynos*—but the meaning is the same."

"Anne, you never cease to amaze me," chortled Amanda. "I imagine you have an explanation for us on just how you have come by this marvelous knowledge."

The young woman bowed her head shyly. "You know how I love flowers and plants and things? Well, many of the names are Latin and, as before I met Bo I was often alone, I began studying the language as a—a *hobby* of sorts."

Jared shook his head at his wife. "Tsk-tsk, pet. And to think your only hobbies are such mundane things as sketching and watercolor painting. For shame, you slacker you."

"How would you like to be sketched in the style of one of our famous caricaturists—I particularly like the way they draw a person to resemble an animal. In your case, a grinning jackass comes most readily to mind," Amanda answered.

Kevin handed Jared his refilled glass of brandy, remarking silkily, "It would seem our Mandy has been too long with your Aunt Agatha, sport. She's beginning to rattle off set-downs with all the old gal's fire and verve."

"Ah, me, friends, no one shall ever know the trials I must endure," Jared agreed gloomily before brightening, and winking broadly at his wife, he said, "Yet with it all, married life still holds its compensations. Doesn't it, Mandy?"

It seemed to Bo that his question had been forgotten, and judging from the way Amanda and Jared were making calf-eyes at each other, it was time he brought them all back to the subject at hand.

"Sweetings," he directed his words to his wife. "Anodyne. Explain it. Deuced bothersome; not knowing, that is."

Anne patted her husband's hand sympathetically. "It means to relieve pain—like with a medicine, I suppose."

Kevin took up the puzzle and read aloud, " 'I give you, girl, an anodyne.' It would seem, if the girl is Gilly, as I believe her to be, that he means for this rhyme to be a means to easing some pain."

"She don't look sick," Bo ventured blankly. "Don't complain." He shook his head. "Brave girl, pluck to the backbone."

Laughing, Gilly retorted, "I'm not in any pain, silly. I think Sylvester meant another type of pain entirely."

"Of course," cried Amanda, clapping her hands in glee. "He means *heartache!* Oh, Gilly, suppose the fortune is your mother's marriage lines—that would have to be the pain, your poor mother's sad trial—wouldn't it?"

"Not to mention the heartache of growing up under such a cloud as that of illegitimacy," Anne put in earnestly.

Could it be? Was it possible? But why would Sylvester have hidden the truth all these years, for what reason, to what end? Gilly shook her head sadly. No. Sylvester, if there *had* been genuine marriage lines, would have destroyed them long ago. He certainly would not make some grand gesture from beyond the grave—not unless he thought the truth, coming nearly twenty years late, would *inflict* pain, not ease it.

While Gilly was examining and discarding her reactions to the idea Amanda presented, Kevin was struck by an awful thought. If Gilly *were* legitimate, it meant Sylvester could have raised her in the lap of luxury and left her with a private fortune that was one of the largest in the land. He seethed when he thought Gilly might have been spared those long, hard years of isolation and servitude, but he felt the first flutterings of panic when he realized that if Sylvester had recognized her at birth, she would have had no reason to wed Kevin at all.

She wouldn't have been left destitute and at the mercy of the whims of a twisted mind, and she surely wouldn't have been forced into a marriage she hadn't desired for the sake of gaining a surname that had in reality been her birthright.

If Gilly were proved to be legitimate by this so-called fortune, it would raise problems between them that he felt were better left buried. How could he ever again look her in the eye, knowing that she had been forced into marriage? She couldn't help but resent him, God knew she'd have ample reason, and he'd feel honor-bound to offer her a divorce so she could take her title and her money and her birthright and seek out a life of her own choosing.

"Kevin—I say—Kevin, you're looking rather queer. Something wrong?"

"Huh—oh, Jared, no, no, nothing's wrong. I was just thinking of something." He rolled up the parchment he was holding and suggested they all adjourn to the Conservatory so that Bo and Anne could make some suggestions as to how to set that neglected chamber to rights.

"Oranges, of course, and pineapples," he chattered on, leading Anne from the room by her elbow. "Some pretty greenery too, and some flowers, roses I think, don't you?"

The rest followed on behind, silently wondering what had occurred to dampen Kevin's usual good spirits. He was hiding something, that was clear enough, but what was it?

In the time they had known him they had come to believe they could tell his every mood, no matter how well he hid his real thoughts from the rest of the world. But they were at a loss to recognize his sudden withdrawal in the main saloon, the cloudiness that had invaded his eyes, and the bleakness that had marked his smile. Yes, he had covered up almost immediately, as he was a past master at that. But even if they had been privy to a longer glimpse, it is doubtful they would have known what he had been feeling in that unguarded moment.

They should not have felt badly about their lapse. After all, before that moment in the saloon, he had never once in his nine and twenty years been so careless as to let fear show so plainly on his face.

Chapter Nine

FOR A WEEK and more, Bo and Anne had been disappearing immediately after breakfast, reappearing only for meals and for a short time after dinner in the red drawing room before making an early night of it.

Being lovers of plants in most any form—indeed, it was their shared interest in the subject that had first attracted them to each other—the neglected gardens at The Hall attracted them like bees after honey. Early in their visit Bo and Anne corralled Lyle and Fitch and, amazingly, seemed to have very little difficulty in getting them to do their bidding. The Chevingtons didn't realize how very odd the sight of Lyle and Fitch bending their backs to any sort of labor was, and they most certainly were unaware that this burst of industry was caused by their fear of Bo.

Anyone who was even minimally acquainted with Bo knew he was the most docile of men, but his clipped speech (a defense against a childhood stammer) frightened the gardeners, who believed the red-haired cherub to be slightly off in his upper stories and therefore liable to turn on them if they angered him. This assumption was based on their experiences with the village butcher, Quiet Dick Turner, a man of few words who nonetheless expressed himself quite eloquently with his meat cleaver whenever someone or something was so foolhardy as to arouse his volatile temper.

Kevin, knowing a good thing when he saw it, promptly assigned ten foresters to temporary duty under Bo's directions and almost miraculously the gardens began to be reclaimed.

But the pseudo-Troy Town maze was Anne's first love. From the moment she clapped eyes on the overgrown tangle, she itched to see the two-acre sprawl restored to its former glory.

For three days, Lyle and Fitch and a few more hapless fellows commandeered into the effort chopped and clipped and lugged heavy branches until, at dusk of the last day, a bonfire was lit to dispose of the small mountain of debris taken from the maze.

Kevin decided to treat the bonfire as an event to be celebrated. That night there was quite a crowd of merrymakers singing and dancing about the blaze; the mead, cowslip, and home-brewed beer flowed freely.

Gilly was standing a bit away from the crowd when Amanda approached her and handed her a mug of delicious but extremely potent honey-sweet mead.

They watched the festivities in silence for a while, seated on an ancient stone bench under the trees, sipping at their drinks. Finally Amanda spoke, her question so unexpected that Gilly could not hide her dismay. "Am I right in thinking, no matter what the circumstances of your marriage, you have developed more than a little affection for our friend Kevin?"

"*Affection!* Amanda, how many mugs of this mead have you had? How could anyone feel affection for that impossible man?" Gilly jumped up from her seat and paced back and forth in front of Amanda, the picture of outrage and frustration. "First he complains about my chilblains and orders me to do something about my hands. But when I put goose grease on them like Hattie Kemp said to do, he made me take a bath—at midnight—before he'd allow me in bed, because he said I smelled like a barnyard."

Gilly didn't hear Amanda begin to laugh, as she was really getting the bit between her teeth now and her words fair tumbled over themselves in their hurry to be said.

"He smiles at Anne when she comes in all grubby and stained from the garden, but has refused to allow me to work around the farms or even help in The Hall. When I confronted him he said what Anne was doing was 'different' but when I demanded he explain how it was different he shouted at me, 'I don't know, it just is' and stomped off.

"There's no pleasing the man. It's gotten so I'm afraid to do anything, because I can't tell which way he will jump when he hears about it. I used to take my troubles to my mother—she's buried in the church graveyard—and by the time I'd get through telling her about them, an answer would present itself. I guess maybe thinking out loud helped, but there is no help in understanding that arrogant, pigheaded creature I'm shackled to.

"Affection for Kevin, you say?" Gilly fumed impotently. "I don't care a button for the man. I-I—oh, no! I think I'm going to cry. I can't cry. I *never* cry!" So saying she slumped down on the bench, put her head in her hands, and began to give a very credible impression of a female dissolved in tears.

Amanda put her arm around Gilly's shoulders, patting her soothingly until Gilly was once again in control of herself. "I'm pro-prodigiously sorry, Amanda," she hiccupped at last.

"There, there, dear, it's quite all right. My goodness, I didn't realize Kevin and Jared are so very alike. Perhaps all men are so unpredictable and hard to understand. My experiences with Jared in our first days together were measured in highs and lows—there never seemed to be a safe middle ground where we could meet and understand each other. These adjustments take time, Gilly, so don't needlessly tear yourself down. All you need is a little direction and you'll have him brought neatly round your thumb in no time."

"You'll pardon me if I find that a trifle hard to believe," Gilly quipped before taking a good deep drink of mead.

"Kevin is a man used to hiding his true feelings behind a mask of foolish banter," Amanda told Gilly. "Jared says it has ever been so; I guess he is just a very private person. I do know this—Kevin doesn't give his affection often, but when he does it is given for life. I believe you are extremely precious to him. After all, I've seen how he looks at you when he believes no one to be watching; but he will try his best to keep this knowledge from you until he is convinced you won't rebuff him.

"As for the goose grease or his ideas on the division of labor among females, I challenge you to find a single man in England, indeed all the world, who has the slightest grasp of common good sense. Oh, no, they are too busy starting wars and building fortunes to bring any consistency into the everyday realities of life.

"That is of no matter—we cannot change them—we must simply learn how to ignore their little lapses and go on as if they never occurred. Once you have children you will, in raising them, find many similarities in the methods used to get them to do what you know is best. It seems to be a woman's destiny to go around behind a man sweeping up after him and keeping some semblance of order in his life. Why else did God feel it so necessary to create an Eve if He had not already decided Adam was making a shambles out of Eden left on his own?"

Amanda's voice had been becoming more slurred and sing-song as she went on with her impromptu homily, and by the end of it, both women were sitting arm in arm, their empty mead cups dangling from their fingers as they were enveloped in a pleasant fog of *bonhomie.*

"All right, O Wise One, I shall in future try to overlook Kevin's ridiculous outbursts, but how do I get him to admit he—er—*likes* me, if indeed you are correct?"

"*Loves,* dear, the word is loves," Amanda scolded mildly. "The answer to that is simple. Make him jealous!" she crowed triumphantly.

"Jealous? Of whom? Rice? Lyle? Fitch?"

Amanda leaned over and whispered in Gilly's ear, "Rory: *r—o—r—y,* Rory—that's the one. Just bat your eyelashes at that pretty-boy a time or two and watch Kevin fume."

"But the fella's revolting," Gilly argued.

"All the better," Amanda trilled. "Kevin will be furious if he thinks you prefer that brainless jackanapes to him. I guarantee it, you'll have Kevin declaring his love for you on bended knee within a week. Just like that." She tried to snap her fingers, succeeding on the third attempt, and then rested her woozy head on Gilly's shoulder.

Gilly thought for a moment and then declared, "Your plan is deceitful, low, dishonest, underhanded, and totally des-des-des*pic*able—I'll do it!"

Completely in charity with each other and indeed with the entire world, Amanda and Gilly catnapped as they sat, rousing only when Glynis, who with her brother had somehow inveigled an invitation to the celebration, shook Gilly by the shoulder saying, "Wake up sleepyhead, I have a message for you."

"W-What is it?" mumbled Gilly, who was finding it hard to return from a dream in which Kevin figured prominently, finding him in scene after scene rescuing her from dragons, evil knights, and wicked sorcerers before carrying her off on his snow white charger.

"Clemmie Jenkins asked me to find you and tell you her mother's time has come."

Gilly came instantly awake. "Oh, my stars, and me half in the bag from Granny Swithins's mead. Amanda—wake up. I've got to go to a birthing."

This news served to delight Amanda, who insisted upon accompanying Gilly to the Jenkins cottage at the far end of the estate. "This is Peg's eighth in as many years and the babe will come fast," Gilly told them. "We'll have to hurry or we'll only be in time to congratulate the proud parents. Glynis, would you please find Kevin and Lord Storm and tell them where we've gone? I'm sure Clemmie's brought up the wagon I've let them keep at the ready at the cottage these weeks past, and we will have no trouble managing on our own. Tell them we'll be back as soon as we can."

"Of course, I will, Gilly dear, you know you can count on me," Glynis promised fervently.

As they drove away from the light of the bonfire, Gilly remarked to Amanda, "I do know I can count on Glynis—I just am not sure *what* it is I can count on her to do."

The sun had been up for more than an hour before the rundown wagon creaked its way up the circular drive in front of The Hall to be met at the steps by the Earl, his guests and half the servants.

"Where in bloody Hell have you been?" Kevin roared without preamble.

"Glynis didn't tell you," Gilly said in a voice devoid of surprise.

"No, she didn't tell me," Kevin parroted sing-song. "*What* didn't she tell me?"

Jared Delaney, who had been married longer and had been heir to more than one of Amanda's impulsive starts, remained silent and only walked quickly to the side of the wagon to assist his wife in stepping down to the driveway.

"I asked Glynis to tell you, though I had my doubts that she would," explained Gilly, as Kevin hauled her unceremoniously from the wagon seat and deposited her none-too-gently on the stone drive.

"Why did you ask her then, you idiot?" bellowed Kevin. "You have to be the most thoughtless, ramshackle, cotton-headed creature in Nature. I am all out of patience with you!" Not daring to say more until he got himself back under control, Kevin stomped some paces down the drive and searched his pockets for a cheroot.

"Is this a sign that he cares?" Gilly could not resist asking Amanda in a whisper.

"If it is, I believe I would strive to seek out actions that produce such signs to less dangerous degrees. For a moment there, I thought he'd have an apoplexy," giggled Amanda irrepressibly, earning her a stern look from the love of her life.

Gilly merely shrugged. Really, she thought, she just couldn't see what all the fuss was about. Jared seemed calm enough, just as Amanda said he would be, and, as for herself, Gilly had been responsible only to herself for so long it had not occurred to her that Kevin could be seriously worried about her welfare.

She had asked Glynis to tell him more as a courtesy than anything else. After all, hadn't she been running the estate freely all her life? What harm could possibly befall her in Peg Jenkins's cottage? Really, Kevin was just behaving like a man again—flying off the handle over the silliest thing. Did he think she was some helpless babe not to be trusted off leading strings?

"If anyone is interested," she at last announced to the group around her, "Peg has come up with a second girl after six straight boys. Mother and child are fine and everything went smooth as silk."

Kevin whirled about, his unlit cheroot dangling from his slack mouth. "What did you have to do with Peg Jenkins's baby?"

"I delivered it, of course," she returned levelly. "Amanda helped me, although Peg, bless her, did most of the work. That makes fifteen babies for me now, seven of them all by myself since old Mrs. Yorby died. She was the midwife," she added unnecessarily.

"You have no business any place near a childbed," Kevin accused her hotly. "You're not much more than a babe yourself. It's indecent—that's what it is."

"*Indecent*, is it! *Babe*, am I," Gilly shrieked back at him. "Why for a penny piece I'd black your eyes for that!"

As the two appeared about to come to blows, Amanda plucked at Gilly's sleeve and whispered, "Remember,

Gilly, we must guide them through these unsettled moments. It's our duty. Watch me," she said, and winked at her before turning to go back to her husband.

Grasping her husband's arm with both hands, Amanda pressed herself close to his side and looked up at him with her molten gold eyes. "Oh dearest, I'm so sorry Glynis neglected to tell you where I was. You must have been *frantic* with anxiety. I don't know how I could have been so thoughtless, but I was *so* caught up in the excitement of being there to see a new little baby come into the world that I just didn't think straight." Tilting her head to one side, she pressed on, "Can you ever forgive me? I promise never again to be so bacon-brained, really I do."

Jared looked down at his wife's woefully contrite expression and, enjoying all this attention quite enormously, answered hesitantly, "I don't know—you did give me quite a scare, you know. I didn't sleep a wink all night. We were just about to launch a search party when you drove up. Why should I forgive you so easily?"

"Oh, you poor darling!" his wife exclaimed with a voice full of concern. "I didn't sleep at all either. Perhaps if we retire at once to our chamber, we can both rest a bit. Lean on me, dearest, and as we climb the stairs perhaps I can think of a way to make it up to you for all you have suffered."

Halfway up the steps they both turned their heads towards the couple still on the drive, Amanda directing an impish wink at Gilly, and Jared just gazing toward the courtyard absently, a fatuous grin on his face.

So that's how it's done, mused Gilly as she watched the retreating figures and fought down the urge to give Amanda's performance a round of applause. Oh, well, she decided, shrugging, I may as well be hung for a sheep as a lamb—here goes!

"Kevin, dear," she cooed, wrapping her hands around his sleeve. "I cannot begin to express my remorse for not having informed you of my whereabouts last night. How totally selfish it was of me not to realize you would be concerned for my welfare. How can I *ever* make it up to you?"

"I know just the way," Kevin told her in a voice soft as velvet.

Gilly smiled happily and took one step towards The Hall, only to be hauled backwards, lifted off the ground, and deposited rump up over Kevin's raised knee as he half-knelt on the drive. He administered three hard smacks to her posterior before she could even gain her breath to mount a protest, and three more smacks that caused three separate cries of pain to pass involuntarily past her lips.

Once on her feet again, and painfully aware that her embarrassment had been witnessed by everyone from Rice down to the young tweeny, she rounded on her husband and informed him indignantly, "I will never forgive you for that, Kevin Sylvester Rawlings—*never!*"

Smiling broadly and looking at his ease for the first time since he had discovered his wife was missing, he told her amiably, "I don't doubt that a bit, brat. Yet, considering the amount of satisfaction I derived from the act, I feel it to be but a small price to pay for *my* forgiveness of *you.* I find that I am no longer the least bit angry, in fact, I do believe I'll go out riding. Do you care to join me?" he asked her as she could not resist rubbing at her throbbing posterior. "Ah, no, I guess not. And perhaps not for several days."

He chucked her under her chin, which she immediately turned away from him, and, a springing lilt in his walk, he mounted the steps, passing through the servants, who had parted Red-Sea-like before him, awe on all their faces.

Bernice Roseberry and her pallet returned to their sentry station that night, which was only to be expected; but, though she and the master of The Hall both passed restful nights, the same could not be said for The Hall's mistress, who wavered between schemes designed to wreak a mighty revenge on her husband and possible ploys aimed at making him fall hopelessly in love with her.

Kevin was dressed for an early morning ride—having invited Jared along to help him exercise some hunters in the upper fields—but even the most disinterested observer could see that the Earl's heart wasn't in the project. As he sat slumped at table in the morning room, an untouched plate of kippers growing cold in front of him, Jared thought his old friend to be the picture of Romance Gone Wrong.

"Still by yourself in your cold, lonely bed, old chap?" Jared asked, reaching for a crusty roll.

From his reclined position Kevin queried nastily, "Still peeking through keyholes, sport?"

Lord Storm only smiled as he laced his roll with some honey, fresh from The Hall's own bees. "I plead not guilty. I heard it from my man Harrow, who had it from Willie, who overheard Miss Roseberry, who was speaking with —oh, you know the way of it belowstairs, I doubt I need go on."

"No, indeed," Kevin replied with the ghost of a smile. "Perhaps I should ask Harrow if I slept well or if I kept all the servants awake—what with my weeping and gnashing of teeth and all such sundry turmoil."

His friend laughed at this sally but then turned serious. "Things are not going too well, are they Kevin, but then you didn't really think that spanking would blow over in a puff of smoke, did you? You know," he went on, changing the subject a bit, "we were all quite concerned when first we read your letter telling of your marriage—as if you didn't know Amanda's suggestion we visit you wasn't purely to give her some respite from the twins—but upon our arrival we thought the two of you to be getting along quite well."

"Famously. Quite the cooing turtledoves," Kevin cut in sarcastically.

"Playacting, Kevin?" Jared deduced astutely. "Why?"

"It was a marriage of convenience, remember," supplied Kevin flatly.

"If not even expedience," added Jared, remembering the terms of the Will. "So why the charade?"

Kevin lolled further back in his chair, raising the two front legs off the floor. "Amanda," was all he said.

"Amanda? What on earth—Oh-ho! I understand now. *Amanda.* Of course! If she had sniffed even a scent of something amiss, she'd have had no rest—and neither would you—until she had come up with a scheme to make you and Gilly fall upon each other's necks pledging love everlasting." Jared shook his head in mock terror. "Gad, man, I cannot blame you for trying to put us on. But if I know my wife, and I think I do, she'll have ferreted out the truth by now, and you, my dear boy, are in for a veritable *siege!*"

Wiping his hands on his napkin, Kevin sighed self-pityingly, "I am open to suggestion. What think you—a midnight escape to London? Or perhaps I should buy back my commission and return to the Continent—God knows I'd rather face Boney than your matchmaking wife."

Jared, having finished a hearty breakfast (much to the disgust of Kevin, who had not been able to force a single bite past his own lips), lit a cheroot and leaned back at his ease. "This disenchantment—is it both mutual and total?"

The conversation had gone further than Kevin liked—had he any say in the matter, it would not have taken place at all. Jared was much too astute. "I admit to being fond of the child," he admitted at last.

"*Fond* of her!" Jared exploded. "What a bag of moonshine. Your eyes follow her everywhere."

"Of course they do," countered his friend. "I wish to see what trouble she'll land herself, and most probably me, in next. You have no conception of the power to disrupt that is harbored inside that one small girl."

Jared's eyes narrowed as he assessed his friend. "Then the girl is repugnant to your finer instincts?"

"Don't see why. Ain't as if she's toad-faced. Not humpbacked either. Pretty, actually. Why don't you like her Kevin? I do. We all do. Ain't that right, Jared? We do, don't we?"

"Oh, good grief," Kevin groaned theatrically as Bo, his cherub's face screwed up into an attitude of bewilderment, stood in the doorway of the morning room. "This is all it needed to make the farce complete. Come in, my friend, take a seat why don't you, and if you please—and I'm convinced you will—join Jared here in lecturing me on the ins and outs of peaceful marital coexistence. It seems only fair, after all. I do recall you and I badgering Jared when it looked like the only result of *his* marriage was to send the poor fellow into a sad decline."

"Kevin," cut in Jared pleasantly.

"Um?"

"Shut up."

Bo looked from one friend to the other and, deciding a third person—a referee of sorts—might be a welcome addition to the assemblage, sat down, reaching for a roll and the honey pot.

For a few minutes Kevin and Jared sat quietly, as, even years into their acquaintanceship with Bo Chevington, the seeming ease with which the man disposed of enormous quantities of foodstuffs without ever giving the appearance of gluttony never ceased to amaze them.

Once Bo's appetite, no paltry thing, was appeased, Jared suggested a way to heal the breach between Lord and Lady Lockport:

"Arouse her romantic soul—all women have one."

"Do you suggest I should compose odes to her charms?" sneered Kevin. "She'd laugh me clear out of Sussex. The chit has been running hot and cold ever since I met her. I'll be damned if I'll pledge affection to the brat and make a complete cake of myself when she tells me to peddle my poems elsewhere."

"No touch of spunk, our Kevin," remarked Bo, licking honey from his fingertips.

"Oh, come now, Kevin," Jared said bracingly. "Correct me if I'm wrong, but aren't you the man who has had more damsels tossing hankies in his direction than any other ten men in England? Surely you have some small insight as to the depth of your power to lure the gentler sex. Gilly's not indifferent to you, I'm certain of that. All that remains is to make *her* aware of her feelings. And the best way to do that is to make her believe *your* interests may lie elsewhere."

"Splendid! A ruse! An intrigue! Jolly-good sport, heh?" piped Bo, earning him killing glances from the other men.

Kevin rose and walked to the window. Looking out over the East Park, he said quietly, "You mean Glynis O'Keefe, of course."

"Egad! Never say he's to suck up to that straw damsel," Bo grimaced painfully. "Don't like her. Don't like her above half. O'Keefe too. Cod. Man's a complete cod." When Bo's indignation finally caused him to choke on a bit of the peach he had been eating, Jared slapped him on the back and told Kevin to pay the man no nevermind.

But Kevin's brow was puckered in concentration. "You don't like them, Bo? I can't say they are of the first water, but are they really that repugnant to you?"

Bo, his face still beet red from his exertion, could only nod vehemently while Jared laughed and asked him if he was afraid of mice and butterflies as well.

Still Kevin refused to join in the joke and only reminded Jared, "Remember that it was Bo who warned us against your conniving cousin Freddie, and we laughed then. As it turned out *we* were the fools in that one. Maybe our friend

Bo here has some powers we are ignorant of but would do well to heed. No," he ended quite seriously, "I'll not dismiss Bo's intuition quite so nonchalantly this time."

"But you will flirt with the woman?" pressed Jared. "Lord knows Gilly won't swallow the bait if you start making calf's eyes at Miss Roseberry, who is the only other eligible female within miles."

Although it went against the grain, Kevin agreed to the plan. Heaven only knew it would be easy enough to get the chit to play—wasn't she already so obviously casting out lures in his direction? And with the pair of them constantly underfoot anyway—or so it appeared to Kevin—there would be no end to his opportunities to make Gilly jealous enough to invite him back into her bed. Once he was there, he told himself, a positively devilish smile twisting his handsome face, the rest would be as simple as snatching sweets from an infant.

Noting their host's withdrawal into himself, Bo decided to bring him back to reality. "Noise last night, Kevin. Frightened poor Anne no end."

"What—oh. Oh, yes, the noise," said Kevin, coming out of his beatific dream. "For the past few weeks we've been disturbed more than once by such noises. Miss Roseberry suggested we search the family tree for a likely ghost—you know, things that go bump in the night. I've occasionally set Lyle and Fitch to patrolling the corridors at night, but so far they've succeeded only in ferreting out Olive Zook in the pantry filching fruit tarts and frightening the poor simple soul half out of her head. I apologize if our 'ghost' has disturbed your slumbers."

Now Jared's eyebrows went up. "Could you have thieves about?"

Kevin exploded with laughter. "Whatever for, my dear man?"

"Rich now, Kevin. Like Golden Ball."

"Bo, I hesitate to tell you that you are mistaken, as I have just gotten done defending your intelligence to Jared here, but unless manure has replaced gold as currency since I left the City, may I remind you that until the so-called fortune is found I am land rich but cash poor. *Very* cash poor."

That was true enough, but the word fortune set off an idea in Jared's head. Someone else could be interested in

Kevin's so-called fortune. Someone greedy enough to risk conducting a private search for it at night. He mentioned his idea to Kevin.

"But who?" queried Kevin, beginning to pace up and down the worn carpet. "Only a few of us are even aware the fortune exists—if it really does."

"O'Keefes!" Bo ventured boldly, then more softly, "Gilly?"

"Gilly!" Both men turned on Bo, one with interest and the other in fury. But at Bo's solemn nod, both men were forced to agree with this deduction. Gilly could have reasons to want to find the fortune—especially if, as Amanda suggested, it held proof of her mother's marriage.

All thoughts of a morning ride were abandoned as Bo's words made Kevin's suggestion they all adjourn to the Long Library and the decanter of wine that they knew they would find there most appealing.

Whether it was in order to change the subject or because he felt it was time and enough he let his friends in on what was going on at The Hall, Kevin was soon telling them about the smuggling going on in the area.

"How comes it you've been able to glean so much information in the short time you've been here?" asked Jared shrewdly.

In way of an answer, Kevin said: "Have you ever noticed my valet, Willstone?"

"Willstone? Can't say as I have," replied Jared. "What about you, Bo?"

"Nope? Should I?"

"Exactly, my friends," Kevin grinned. "Willstone is a real treasure, one of those rare individuals who is so completely nondescript that he makes absolutely no impression. It is impossible, even after meeting him several times, to remember anything about him. This has made him very useful, as he can visit the village tavern and glean information without raising any suspicion. Then, of course, there's Gilly."

"Your wife? What has she to do with it?" Jared asked, confused.

"Smuggling's not for the ladies. Good works, that's the ticket," Bo pointed out.

"Not my Gilly," corrected Kevin, not without a bit of

pride. "Rides the boats, no less—at least she did until I found her out and put a stop to it."

Jared chuckled, then sobered. "Heaven help us, don't let Amanda get wind of it. She'll be dead set on coming along for the ride."

Kevin, having already searched Sylvester's collection of maps of the area, spread out a detailed map of the coastline near The Hall. The three men leaned over the table as Kevin pointed out the most likely spots for boats to land along the shore. "Here, here, and here, gentlemen. I have already been to these areas and seen evidence of boats putting in. The surrounding hills are cut through with trails and the cliffs are honeycombed with caves.

"Sylvester's charts and journals mark these caves clearly as they were used long ago for food storage, places of refuge, and even for religious ceremonies. Since some were used by our ancestors to prepare for death by closing themselves for a time in the dark chambers and contemplating the—says Sylvester—'state of future being,' I am surprised local superstition does not keep the villagers away, but obviously their need for money outweighs their fears."

"This is all very edifying, m'dear," interrupted Jared, "but unless you mean to turn your own people over to the revenue officers, I fail to see your interest in the subject. Or are you planning to join The Gentlemen in order to gain a bit of the ready?"

Kevin rerolled the map and then checked the door to the main corridor to be sure it was locked. Returning to his friends, he told them quietly, "Neither. I hesitated to bring you into this my friends but—as long as you're here anyway —how does a bit of spy-catching appeal to you?"

"Oh, jolly good!" piped Bo, always eager for a bit of action, earning himself a tolerant smile from the other men.

Jared poured himself another glassful and sat back facing Kevin. "Is this on your own initiative—a hunch from something Willstone overheard along the way—or have you orders from London?"

"The latter of course. Just before I set out on my journey here, I was called to the Admiralty. You remember Peter —served with me at Trafalgar—he is based in London now, and it was he who told me the Ministry is sure information is being leaked to someone who crosses to France from these beaches. While they seek to plug the leak from their end, Peter, thinking I may be bored in the country, suggested I fill my time doing a bit of digging on my own—strictly unofficial, you understand."

While Bo entertained himself with dreams of derring-do, Jared considered Peter's reasoning. The plan was brilliant—Kevin was the ideal man for the assignment. After all, who would suspect a fashionable London dandy like Rawlings of harboring any thoughts in his brainbox more weighty than the most flattering way of arranging his golden locks?

Just as the friends were done agreeing to assist in the search for the spy who could quite possibly be making use of the local smugglers as a means of transport between Sussex and Calais, there came a loud rattling of the door latch followed by a fierce knocking at the door.

"Let me in, let me in at once! I *must* find her, you hear, *I must!*" came the shrill screeching of a near-hysterical female voice.

Kevin slapped his hand to his forehead. "Aunt Sylvia. Drat the woman, what is she about this time?"

Getting up from his chair and crossing to the locked door, Jared said with a ghost of a laugh that it sounded like Kevin's aunt had misplaced her doll Elsie once again.

"Among other things—like her wits," Kevin groaned, wondering yet again what sin he had committed to have been punished so with seemingly endless burdens.

"Oh, come now, sir," Jared scolded good-naturedly. "I seem to recall Lady Varsey's sister—the daughter of a duke no less—went everywhere with her pet monkey on her neck."

"Least Elsie don't smell bad," Bo added helpfully, then exclaimed, "I have it! Earl hid the fortune in Elsie! Sure of it. Deuced clever of the man, what?"

Jared stopped dead in his tracks at this and turned to look at Kevin. "Is it possible?"

As the pounding on the door grew in intensity, the three men ransacked the room until Elsie was discovered behind the doors of a Sheraton wine cabinet.

Holding the grinning, wide-eyed doll at arm's length, Kevin eyed it warily while Bo and Jared walked around and round, poking under Elsie's dimity skirts and tapping at her china limbs to test their solidity.

"Rip her open. Crack her head. Only way you know," ordered the bloodthirsty Mr. Chevington.

"Are you run mad?" exploded the Earl. "A whacking great rumpus that would cause, you idiot. I can hear it now—Aunt Sylvia running the halls screaming 'Murder! Murder!' whilst we work frantically with glue and a needle hoping to stave off arrest by restoring the deceased to some semblance of order."

Lord Storm's lips twitched appreciatively as he conjured up a mental image of the scene Kevin described. "Give her—er, *it,* to me," he suggested.

Elsie was laid face up on a nearby table as Jared made a thorough search of the doll's body, stopping just short of dismemberment. "Gentlemen," he pronounced solemnly at last, "I can find no evidence of secret compartments, pockets, or the like. The china head is quite hollow, and in case you were concerned, the maiden's virtue remains intact." So saying, he unlocked the door and delivered Elsie into Lady Sylvia's outstretched arms.

"It was only an idea. A hunch. So sorry," apologized Bo as Kevin glared at him balefully. "Could have been," he added defensively.

Kevin continued to stare at his chubby friend for a long moment, and then, letting out his pent-up breath in an exasperating sigh, he said, "I need a drink. All this fortune-hunting nonsense is making us act like Bedlamites."

Jared and Bo agreed with nods of their heads, holding out their glasses to their host for refills.

"Could have been," Bo muttered once more under his breath before, wisely, holding his own counsel. Kevin wasn't any fun anymore. This fortune business was taking all the humor out of him. Even the adventure of a possible spy operating in the area wasn't enough to put the spring back in his friend's step.

While Bo lamented his friend's loss of humor, Jared eyed Kevin closely, noticing yet again a rather haunted look about the man's eyes. Good God, Lord Storm thought suddenly, if that's how I looked when Amanda and I were first married, it's no wonder Kevin took me to task. Ah, love—it has its pitfalls as well as its benefits.

"Let us drink to the successful capture of the Lockport spy," toasted Jared, adroitly shifting his friends minds back to their earlier discussion, and until luncheon the three stayed closeted in the library devising a scheme to apprehend the man.

Chapter Ten

THE HALL was all in darkness, with only a few candles in the corridors and the light from the dying embers in the fireplaces casting weird flickering shadows against the walls.

Everyone was, it being well past two in the morning, tucked up in their beds fast asleep.

Anne Chevington, the picture of contentment, was snuggled up against her husband's shoulder, as he lay softly snoring, an open copy of *The Compleat Gardener* resting on his ample belly.

Down the corridor Lord and Lady Storm also slept in each others arms, having completed a discussion of each other's matchmaking schemes, a conversation that had engendered some lovemaking a little closer to home.

All alone in her wide bed slept Lady Lockport. No contented smile softened her features, just as no masculine chest served as her pillow. She tossed and turned, as if some dissatisfaction troubled her even in her sleep, and more than one sigh was heard to escape her lips.

Behind the door on the opposite side of the Countess's sitting room resided the only occupant of The Hall who was not yet abed. Not that Lord Lockport had not tried to sleep—heaven only knew he craved a few hours in the arms of Morpheus—but it was not to be.

Kevin Rawlings paced the floor of his chamber, his mind unable to let go the scene enacted earlier in the large saloon. "She clung to that popinjay like a demmed barnacle," he gritted aloud as the picture of his wife and Rory O'Keefe deep in discussion in a corner of the saloon came back to haunt him yet again.

Oh, yes, he had been sitting in Glynis's pocket the whole

evening long himself, but even though he did it on Jared's advice, his heart wasn't really in the thing.

You're jealous, old man, his inner voice told him. "You're damned right I am!" Kevin agreed aloud before downing a half-glass of burgundy and pouring himself another.

In the act of bringing the wine to his lips he hesitated a moment, thinking he heard a noise in the corridor. After a moment he shrugged, dismissing the sound as just the natural creakings of an ancient building, and took a small sip from his glass.

There! He heard it again. Not settling of old timbers that, and no ghost ever succeeded in making a sound like breaking glass. Chains dragging or deep groans, that's what ghosts sounded like, he was sure.

Putting down his glass, he moved stealthily toward the sitting room and tiptoed past Miss Roseberry's pallet to the small door leading to the dresser's bedroom. Silly woman, he half-smiled, did she really believe he was such a slowtop that he was unaware of the door that led from that bedroom directly into his wife's chamber?

He had to know that Gilly was abed and not, as Bo suggested, skulking the corridors at night seeking the fortune.

He approached the bed slowly, unable to resist the temptation of a lengthy observation of his wife's slumbering form.

Should he wake her? Did one take one's wife along on midnight searches—especially if they could prove dangerous? No, one did not. But if one did, and caught the burglar, wouldn't it be nice to have one's wife witness such a feat of derring-do? Kevin decided, considering himself more than a match for any thief, that one did.

Putting a hand across her mouth as a precaution, he leaned down and whispered into her ear: "Gilly-girl. Psst! Gillyflower—wake up."

Two huge round blue eyes flew open in mingled astonishment and fear; those emotions replaced rapidly, as those same blue orbs narrowed, by a mingled outrage and accusation that were truly eloquent.

Look at him, she shrieked inwardly, standing there grinning like the village idiot. What is he about anyway?

Gilly's mental question was soon answered when he

hissed, *"Listen!"* and, pinned down as effectively as she was, having no other option open, she did. Sure enough, there was within a few moments something for her to hear—a sound, muffled but still audible, coming from the main saloon beneath her chamber.

Kevin brought his mouth to within a hairsbreadth of her ear and asked her if she would promise to keep still if he removed his hand. Not knowing if it were his hand, his mere proximity, or his warm breath fanning her ear that most upset her heart rate, and not sure if it was indignation or anticipation that had so accelerated that same heart rate, she vigorously nodded her head in the affirmative.

Once released, she sprang up from the bed, and slipping on the sky blue satin dressing gown that had been draped over a nearby chair, she whispered, "What are you waiting for—reinforcements? Haul yourself over to the door to the corridor and let's get going. If you want to catch a thief, Kevin, you must be prepared to do more than listen to noises and take ten years off your wife's life by half-smothering her with your great oafish fist."

The Earl smiled ruefully and shook his head. "Ah, Gilly, you are a treasure. A veritable pearl beyond price. Some women would swoon, then again some would cower under the counterpane while sending their husband's off alone to investigate—possibly to their deaths at the hands of some fiend intent on some nefarious mission. Even others would, upon awaking to hear such a noise, fail entirely to understand the significance of such a 'bump in the night.' But not my wife—no indeed. That Amazon, that Boadicea —oh, no, not she. Not only does she comprehend the situation, she launches herself posthaste into the fray. I say, wife, do you wish to take up the poker or shall I?"

Gilly let out her breath in an exasperated sigh. "If you have done with your speeches and your histrionics, perhaps we can *get on with it?"*

Yet as Kevin made for the door another thought occurred to Gilly. "Wait!" she hissed. "I have a better plan. Come with me."

So saying, she tiptoed barefoot to the wall beside the bed, and pressing on a wooden rosette decorating the massive clothespress, she stepped back as the press swept silently down the wall for the space of two feet, revealing a dank, cobweb-hung flight of stairs that sank down into the darkness below.

"What?—"

"Shh! This staircase leads directly to the main saloon." Snatching up her night candle, Gilly led the way down the curving stone staircase, the flickering flame raised on high causing her orange gold hair and satin robe to send off starbursts of light as Kevin followed two stairs behind her, holding her hand.

"Where do we come out?" he whispered, the poker he had mentioned jokingly now cradled firmly in his left hand.

"There is a small hinged door behind the curtains in the deep window embrasure. We can enter the saloon with no one the wiser *if you will but put a muzzle on your yapper!"* Gilly returned in a fierce undertone.

It took Gilly a few moments to find the spring that would release the door and when she did at last locate it, the door opened inward with a loud screeching noise reminiscent of the uproar a pig makes when caught in a grate.

"We could have had a fanfare of trumpets instead—they would at least have been more harmonious," Kevin groaned.

The screech had no sooner subsided than another noise, that of running feet, could be heard, and by the time Kevin could bodily displace Gilly and take up the chase, all that was left for him to do was to close the glass doors to the garden that had been left swinging in the intruder's wake.

"So much for that," he commented tightly as Gilly joined him at the door.

"I'm sorry, Kevin, truly I am. I guess the spring needs a bit of oil. I should have thought of it sooner but it has been years since I've made use of that particular passageway," apologized Gilly earnestly.

Together they went round the large saloon lighting candles until they could see well enough to ascertain what the trespasser had been doing in the room. There was no sign of any disturbance of Rice's well-ordered housekeeping, none at all, which was unusual, as thieves are not normally known for their fastidiousness in the midst of burgling.

As nothing was missing, not even the chased silver snuff box encrusted with a circlet of rubies Bo had left in plain view on a small end table, the intruder's intention did not seem to be robbery. After all, he had certainly had time and enough to pocket the snuff box and much more before he was interrupted. It could only be deduced that the person had been looking for something specific and had taken great pains not to disturb anything and thus alert the residents that he had been there at all.

"In case he did not find what he was looking for and wanted to return for another visit," crowed Gilly, gratifying Kevin by her quick understanding of the situation.

Even more gratifying was the dawning realization that Bo had been wrong in his assertion that Gilly could have been secretly hunting out the fortune herself in a bid to be shed of Kevin once and for all.

Yet as they climbed back up the stone stairs to Gilly's bedchamber, Kevin was hit with a disquieting thought. "Is this the only secret passageway or, Heaven forbid, is The Hall honeycombed with false walls, trap doors, and hidden rooms?"

"There are several, located all over The Hall. Why do you ask?" Gilly questioned, hunting out any stray cobwebs by running her fingers through her short mop of curls (now sadly flattened from sleeping, although Miss Roseberry, by means of an artfully applied curling wand, would refurbish them in the morning).

"Because, you delightful ignoramous," returned Kevin, who had decided he would be damned if he'd spend the rest of the night alone now that he had gained entry to his wife's bedchamber, "*if* there are hidden passageways, *and if someone besides ourselves has knowledge of them,* we are open to any number of visits from our midnight prowler. Just the *thought* that he could enter my own wife's chamber and accost her while she sleeps here—*alone*—fair makes the hairs on the back of my neck stand up in dread."

Gilly chuckled at this show of sensibilities. "That's laying it on a bit too thick and rare, don't you think, Kevin, even for you? I am perfectly safe—that is a one-way passage. After spending a near-lifetime prowling all over The Hall, I can guarantee you that this particular passage at least opens only from *this side* of the clothespress."

"How greatly you relieve my mind," mumbled Kevin, clearly crestfallen. "But what about the *other* passageways? Do any of them lead outside? Of course they do—

what is the sense of secret entrances and exits if they do not lead outside!"

Gilly admitted there were such secret exits, although she had failed to locate them, and even told him of one of Sylvester's strangest projects—that of ordering mammoth tunnels dug from the stables outward in a honeycomb fashion so that he could actually drive a curricle and two around parts of the estate *underground.*

Kevin nodded. "I have heard the Fifth Duke of Portland did much the same, and his underground warren included, besides the drive, a vast amount of rooms in which he could indulge his love of privacy. Strange lot, our countrymen. But," continued Rawlings, now strategically seating himself at the end of Gilly's bed, "the questions remain—how accessible are these underground tunnels? How many do they number? And, Heaven forbid, who all knows of them?"

"They do present a danger, don't they?" lamented his wife, sitting down beside him. Then, it being quite late, she yawned and rested her head on his shoulder.

Kevin took this opportunity (as he was no slacker when it came to making the most of any breach of defenses) to slide his arm around Gilly's shoulders. They remained thus for some minutes, Kevin being reluctant to rush his fences. But soon he tired of the game and made to turn Gilly towards him to deepen the embrace.

She was asleep! The silly chit was fast asleep! Kevin's light kisses on her eyes and cheek did nothing to rouse her, but only caused her to sigh once in contentment before burrowing her face more closely to his chest.

What a dratted coil. If he woke her—if he indeed could wake her, for she was, in his mind at least, almost comatose—she could be counted on to order him from the room or, failing that, call for her dragon, Miss Roseberry. Yet, if he slipped her gently into bed and crawled in beside her, there would be the devil to pay in the morning. Besides—how could he possibly lie in the same bed as Gilly without going mad with wanting her?

In the end, Kevin was forced to acknowledge that he would be best served to deposit his wife back under the covers and take himself off to his own chamber. Perhaps a slower seduction was in order. But in the meantime he knew he had to put as much distance between Gilly and himself as he could, or else he might destroy all—indeed, the heat of his passion was at the moment so intense he was surprised the bedclothes were not aflame.

And so the dawn found Lord Lockport slumped in a chair in his chamber, his dressing gown still tied about him, a half-empty glass dangling from his fingers.

If this was what love did to a person, thought Willstone as he removed the glass from his master's slack hand, I'll take steak and kidney pie, thank you anyway.

"Ghost walked again last night, Jared. Hear it?"

"Hmm?" Lord Storm replied to Bo's query absently, his mind on other matters.

Kevin had requested the two men to meet him in the library before dinner (having not seen his friends all day due to a minor crisis on one of the farms), and Jared was more than a little concerned that their friend had news of some gravity to impart.

"Noises. Heard 'em. Anne heard 'em. Anybody could. Going deaf, Jared?" Bo went on heedless of his friend's introspective mood. Just then their host tardily (as usual) entered the library looking resplendent in his finery (again, as usual), and Bo asked without preamble, "You hear it, Kevin? Screeched to wake the dead. Banshee, you think?"

Lord Lockport was not blessed with the ability to read minds, but it took no great insight on his part to decipher Bo's codelike speech. "Not banshees, friend. Hinges, more like," he told Bo as he poured himself a glass of burgundy.

That statement demanded an explanation that Kevin rendered happily enough—only leaving out the ignominious ending to the adventure.

Jared pondered the tale for a moment and then asked the question that had risen in his mind. "Why drag your wife along on such a potentially dangerous mission?" As Kevin opened his mouth to protest, Jared held out his hands and went on, "I know, I know—you wanted to assure yourself that *she* was not the intruder. I would have done the same myself. But, after easing your mind on that head, why wake the girl? If you felt the need for companionship, wouldn't Bo or I have been a better choice?"

"Peacocking," muttered Bo, his nose stuck in his glass.

"What?" asked Jared. "Oh—*peacocking.* Of course, Bo, how dense of me not to have thought of it myself. Our

Kevin meant to show off in front of the lady. Still a bit of the schoolboy left in you, eh, Kevin?"

The Earl self-servingly sought to ignore these barbs from his astute friends. He had no great desire to be made the butt of any more jokes. Perhaps if he had succeeded in getting back in his wife's good graces—not to mention back in her bed—but he hadn't, and he needed no reminders of that sad fact.

"I discovered something last night, gentlemen," Kevin announced. "Aside from the passageway Gilly pointed out, there are any number of other secret panels, stairways, and passages in The Hall."

"Priest's hole?"

"Yes, Bo, I'm sure there's one of those as well," Kevin assured the interested man. "But it's the underground passages *outside* on the estate that really bother me—tunnels large enough to drive a curricle through, and the vastness of the network is unknown. If any of the tunnels open into The Hall, and if our intruder has knowledge of them—well, I don't imagine I have to spell it out for you."

"Indeed not," agreed Jared, his brow wrinkled in concern.

"Adjourn to the cellars? Tap on the walls?" Bo suggested amicably. "Hold the candles. Bring the bottle. What, ho? Shall we?"

The eager redhead was half out of his seat before Kevin's barked "Sit down you idiot!" caused him to fall back into the chair with a disappointed sigh. Clearly, if there was any adventure to be had concerning the tunnels, it was not to begin that evening.

Just then the dinner gong sounded and the men went off to join the ladies and their guests for the evening, Rory and Glynis O'Keefe. Ever since Lord and Lady Storm had separately gifted the Lockports with much the same advice, the O'Keefes had been invited to The Hall with, if Bo Chevington's opinion had been asked for, nauseating frequency.

After an interminable meal, during which Rory made calf's eyes at Gilly and Kevin outdid himself in his attentions to the openly preening Miss O'Keefe, the ladies adjourned to the recently refurbished music room, while the men remained behind to relax over their port and cigars.

"How charming you look in that gown, Gilly dear,"

Glynis simpered sweetly once they were settled in the room. "You will wear a prodigious amount of green, won't you? La, never mind. After all, what other choice do you really have with that hair?"

"Oh, I don't know, Glynis *dear,*" Gilly returned wide-eyed. "I know Kevin also likes me in black, although he protests that I'm much too young to wear such a matronly, funereal shade."

As Glynis almost invariably wore stylish black (as she was doing at this moment), Amanda and Anne were hard put to cast their eyes elsewhere lest they look at each other and burst into giggles.

"Blondes usually look extremely well in black, I've always thought," Anne felt bound to put in politely, favoring Glynis with an admiring smile and effectively diverting the woman away from delivering a second sugarcoated insult (that would no doubt be taken up again by Gilly with who knew what dire results).

Long minutes passed in painfully correct civility and the tension in the room rose accordingly. Before armed hostilities could break out, the gentlemen came in, Rory still busily trying to reiterate his agreement with anything his companions had talked about over their drinks.

Gilly could not help but compare the differences between Rory and her husband as they strode into the room side by side. Kevin's Brummel-like attire won hands down in any comparison with O'Keefe's neat but tired jacket and darned waistcoat.

The bodies beneath their clothing were both well formed, but there was something subtle—some catlike grace of movement that gave hint to a lean but powerful physique—about Kevin that made the other man look soft and weak.

Kevin was intelligent, Gilly thought, while Rory was decidedly a man who should devote more time to listening rather than opening his mouth when he had so little to say. Kevin was polite; Rory was fawning. Kevin had a sense of humor; Rory had no sense at all. Kevin was real; Rory was artificial. Kevin was—oh, sighed Gilly quietly, Kevin was everything she could wish for. Kind, thoughtful, gentle, considerate . . .

Gilly shook her head at her folly. She knew what Kevin was. He was a two-faced, debt-ridden, fortune-hunting, pleasure-mad opportunist. He married her saying he wanted to save the estate, knowing full well it was only a means to secure the old Earl's fortune in a year's time. Not content with that, he is seeking more gain from the jewels Mutter thinks make up the hidden fortune. He even seems eager to learn about the smuggling, most probably because he sees a way to make some money from that. But how—by joining the group, or by turning them in? How little she trusted him! As further proof of his selfish interests, she went on doggedly, he demands his marital rights until he can get back to his paramours in the city, at which time he'll conveniently forget his countrified bastard wife.

Ah, thought Gilly, sipping heavily at her wine, if he hadn't shown himself to be an utter glutton by chasing Glynis O'Keefe, I might have allowed myself to be fooled and come completely under his spell.

Well, she decided as she reached out her hand to draw the willing Rory down beside her on the sofa, it's time I showed my husband that he can't count *me* among his acquisitions. Flirting with Rory may have been Amanda's way of getting Kevin jealous, but I shall use it to make Kevin believe that my interests lie elsewhere.

Any flirting Gilly may have done with O'Keefe up until the moment he joined her on the sofa was to pass as nothing, as she now fairly drooled over the man, so marked were her attentions.

Asking if anyone wanted to hear a song, she directed O'Keefe to bring her the ancient lute that stood in a glass case in the corner.

"Oh, no," Glynis cried, "Not those *ancient* songs again! What a shame your piano is so out of tune or I could play and sing for you, Kevin, rather than for you to endure Gilly's sad repertoire."

"I like her songs," Kevin defended, forgetting his role of flirting male for a second, thus causing Glynis to scowl fiercely, before recovering quickly and succeeding in looking crestfallen, repentant, and lovely at the same time.

"I like them too," piped up Rory (who swore he liked everything) as he bowed over Gilly and presented her with the instrument.

Kevin pretended to gag but everyone ignored him.

The lute was difficult to keep in tune, and Gilly worked for several minutes until she seemed satisfied. Then she began playing random snatches from a merry tune written by Henry VIII, as Bo, who lost all his inhibitions at such times, ably sang the words telling of the Monarch's lust for the good life.

Kevin had heard Gilly play before and was, as usual, proud of the way she performed the old songs and airs. Hattie Kemp had informed the Earl that Gilly's mother had taught her to play the lute using songbooks they found at The Hall, such as Thomas Campion's *Third Book of Airs.* It may have first been published in 1617, but it was the most recent material available, as the late Earl's tastes hadn't expanded to include music.

With Gilly's talent for the lute, Kevin mused, it was a pity the harp and other instruments were so sadly in need of repair. As soon as there are any funds to spare, he resolved, the harp must be mended. He—who had made her a lifelong prisoner of The Hall—owed it to Gilly to at least provide her with some forms of amusement.

Damn, but it wasn't fair! Kevin seethed when he thought of how his contemporaries in London would cut Gilly dead if they knew she was a bastard—which it wouldn't take them long to discover. Even his popularity wouldn't be enough to spare her such humiliation by Society, which had destroyed so many people before her. Only royal by-blows and legalized bastards like the Harleian Miscellany, who might all bear the same surname but who could none of them be sure were sired by the same father, were accepted in Society. Maybe when she's older, less startlingly beautiful (oh, how Kevin's original opinion of his wife's looks had altered), the *ton* could be made to tolerate her. But until that day, there was nothing for it but to keep her here, at The Hall, where she had friends and loyal servants to protect her.

She could have gone anywhere she liked, done anything she wanted, if only she could have half Sylvester's fortune (the least she deserved) and the freedom to leave The Hall and her past behind her. With enough money she could have set herself up in Ireland or somewhere and lived in luxury, married a man she loved, and raised a half-dozen red-haired little babies.

But no, Gilly couldn't do that; she wasn't free to do that. She was married—chained to a man she would only give herself to in the dark—never in the sunlight. A man she tolerated but did not love. Damn his uncle. Damn the Will. Damn The Hall. Damn everything. I damn them all, Kevin swore to himself, because they have damned my love for Gilly to live and die unrequited.

For a while, he mused further, I thought she was beginning to care for me—really care for me—but too many things keep interfering: the spy, the smugglers, our house guests, the fortune and its midnight seeker—not to mention the O'Keefes. Now Kevin's mind was bringing him to the heart of his current unhappiness—Rory O'Keefe. Kevin had noticed Gilly's flirtation with the man already—as he was intended to have done—but never before tonight had it been so pronounced, so *blatant*.

The harder Gilly flirted with Rory (by means of small girlish smiles, giggles, and shameless eyelash batting), the more Kevin retaliated by flirting with Glynis (by means of artful compliments, meaningful glances, and one or two playful winks).

Like watching a shuttlecock flying back and forth across the net, the other four people in the room looked from one couple to the other, as enthralled as an audience watching an exceptional performance at Covent Garden.

Once Bo tried to intervene, easing the charged atmosphere a bit when he begged Gilly to play the lively tune *Now Is The Month Of Maying*, and while everyone sang the choruses, Bo backed them up with a hearty *fa-la-la-la-la-la*.

As a diversion it was a laudable try, but when Amanda begged for another tune, "something soft and possibly sad," Bo wished he had suggested a few hands of cards instead, for Gilly began to play one of Campion's more plaintive airs:

Shall I come sweet love to thee
When the evening beams are set?
Shall I not excluded be
Will you find no feigned let?
Let me not for pity more,
Tell the long hours at your door.

As she sang, her eyes never left Rory's face, so near to her on the sofa. Then she turned slowly towards Kevin and sang the second verse directly to him:

But to let such dangers pass
Which a lover's thoughts disdain,
'Tis enough in such a place
To attend Love's joys in vain.
Do not mock me in thy bed
While these cold nights freeze me dead.
While these cold nights freeze me dead.

While the first verse had been sung in a seductively pleading voice, the second, a quite suggestive bit of poetry actually, was sung in a voice somehow suddenly gone hard, as if she was conveying a between-the-lines message to Kevin.

He received the message with a look of fury on his face. Gilly was letting him know she felt their lovemaking to be a mockery, that she—and he—would freeze dead before they'd share the same bed again.

Well, enough was enough, and too much was just too much. So thought Kevin Rawlings. His usual cool urbanity for once completely gone, he determined to get up from his seat, go over and grab Gilly by the scruff of her neck, and march her up to their chambers where he would either strangle her or bed her.

He actually had risen to his feet, as had Jared, who was reluctantly about to restrain his friend, by force if necessary, when the glass doors opened with a force that set them crashing back against the inner walls, and a man stumbled into the room.

"I-I've . . . been . . . sh-shot!" Kevin's estate manager, Walter Grey, gasped between ragged breaths before sliding gracefully to the floor.

Kevin and Gilly were the first to reach him, Kevin turning the man onto his back while Gilly's hands went straight to Grey's shoulder, that was dark and sticky with blood.

Anne ran to the bellpull and yanked it, pulling the length of rotted velvet down around her ears.

Amanda raced into the corridor and loudly called to Rice to bring two footmen.

Bo and Jared trotted out into the garden to see what they could see, which was not much.

Glynis and Rory never moved.

Within moments, Walter Grey was laid upon a long sofa

with Gilly deftly removing his left arm from his leather jacket and gently tearing away his homespun shirt.

"Rice," barked Kevin, "have Willie ride for the doctor."

"Whatever for?" Gilly exclaimed heatedly. "Rice, send for Mrs. Whitebread. Tell her Walter's been shot. She's to bring along whatever's necessary and meet us in the blue bedroom. The first thing we must do is remove the bullet while poor Walter's still unconscious."

When Rice didn't move, debating in his mind whose order to obey, Amanda came up behind him and gave him a slight shove. "Get on with it man; go fetch Mrs. Whitebread." Obviously Lady Storm couldn't doubt Gilly's ability to handle the situation and, after all, thought Rice, that lady had seen the young mistress deliver a baby. Rice bowed and went off swiftly.

The men waited downstairs while Willie, who had been called for by Mrs. Whitebread, assisted the ladies. Anne, pleading fatigue, had already gone off to bed.

The O'Keefes had taken themselves off within minutes of the disturbance, Glynis's ploy of declaring herself faint at the sight of blood earning her nothing but a sneer of disgust from the man who had minutes earlier been fondling her fingers, while Rory, who usually had to be pried out of The Hall, seemed for once to be in a mighty rush to depart.

"Who could have shot Grey?" questioned Kevin. "He's such an inoffensive creature. Did you know he so abominates violence that he has removed all the traps in the home wood and only allows the foresters to thin out the rabbits and other small game when we are nearly knee-deep in vermin."

"Been to his cottage," contributed Bo. "Overrun with creatures."

"I've seen the man riding about the estate in a pony cart," said Jared. "Isn't that a rather odd way of traveling for an estate manager? Horseback seems much more convenient."

Kevin chuckled and explained that Grey was a notoriously poor horseman. Gilly had prevailed on Kevin to purchase the pony cart to ease the manager's ever-stiff hindquarters. "It was a nice change to see the man sit down when he came into my office. For a while there, I was convinced his knees didn't bend."

Amanda came in just then and held out a square of

white cloth for the men to inspect. In the middle of the cloth sat a small, round metal ball, lately extracted from Grey's shoulder by Willie.

"No poacher uses that size shot," Kevin declared. "It looks like it came from a large pistol. Has Grey been able to say anything yet?"

"He was taking the night air near the maze when he heard something moving in the shrubbery. When he went to see if an animal was stuck in the thick branches, he was shot. That's all he remembers." This information came from Gilly who had just reentered the room.

"Sounds like he stumbled onto something he wasn't meant to see," offered Jared, lighting a cheroot after Gilly and Amanda nodded their permission. He thought better with a cheroot in his hand and, after taking a few puffs, declared that Grey had stumbled on one of three likely suspects: the intruder, a smuggler, or a spy.

"A spy!" cried Amanda and Gilly in unison.

"Oh, come now, Jared," scoffed Kevin in an attempt to discount his friend's words. "Surely spies have more pressing things to do than hang about The Hall. We have no military secrets here."

"Too right. Spies in London. Not here," agreed Bo, seeing the wisdom of diverting the ladies from the idea of a spy operating in the area, a careless slip of Jared's tongue that had already set martial lights to glinting in both women's eyes.

"No, no," disagreed Amanda, standing up and beginning to pace. "This area is prime for spies, what with being right on the coast and so near to France. Of course it was a spy. He probably had a rendezvous set up with someone he hired to take him across the Channel."

"The Straits," Gilly corrected automatically. "We call it the Straits around here. It makes sense of course, this theory of yours, Jared, except for one thing. No one around here would help a spy—we're all loyal citizens here."

"There are the local smugglers. Surely the spy, if there is one, which upon reflection I seriously doubt"—he said in deference to the withering looks he was receiving from Kevin and Bo—"might have offered them a chance to earn some extra blunt carrying messages, or even the man himself, to and from Calais."

"Well, the constable will come tomorrow to question

Grey once he's feeling more the thing," Kevin pointed out. "Until then, gentlemen, ladies, I suggest we try to keep our imaginations in check. Gilly," he prompted, holding out his arm. "It has been a long day. I think we might all follow Anne's example and make an early night."

The others agreed and soon Gilly found herself in the sitting room of the master chamber. Once there however, Kevin dropped his pose of affable husband and turned on her to declare, "You made a spectacle of yourself downstairs with that lurid song. I know you were trying me on, but I warn you, wife, one of these days you'll go a step too far. Only Walter Grey's arrival on the scene saved you this time, although I am not at all sure I should not take you over my knee right now and save myself some aggravation."

"Try and I'll do you a mischief," Gilly countered. "Besides, it's *I* who should be dealing out punishments if the way you drooled over that simpering Glynis O'Keefe all night long, listening to her silly prattlings like they were priceless pearls of wisdom, hadn't made me so sick to my stomach I have no energy left with which to box your ears."

Kevin stormed across the carpet to confront his wife. "And what of her brother? Talk about nauseating scenes—why I waited with bated breath, sure you would leap into his lap at any moment and begin to purr."

"My behavior does not signify," sniffed Gilly, "as it pales beside your truly embarrassing pursuit of anything in skirts. I must say I find your taste in women, if Miss O'Keefe can be used as an example of your preferences, to be most disappointing. I thought even you beyond finding the weak attractions of such a silly widget appealing."

"Ha! And I suppose you're to be commended for flirting with a toadeating pest like *Mr.* O'Keefe? I beg to differ, my dear, as I believe it shows only that you are very green indeed. No *real* woman would look twice at such a pale imitation of a man. You do yourself no credit, Madam, if such as he could be your ideal."

All at once Gilly had enough. Stamping her foot in fury, she exploded, "I think the man is an ass, a complete and total *ass!* I only played up to him in an attempt to make you jealous. It was Amanda's idea and there hasn't been a sorrier notion since I once fleetingly believed I could come to care for such a hardhearted womanizer as you."

"Is that right!" Rawlings shouted back, his anger at Gilly's deception making him temporarily blind to the fact that he had tried much the same tactic as his wife—again at a friend's suggestion. That Gilly had let it slip that she had once found him appealing did not register at all.

By the time these facts did strike him, he was alone in the room, Gilly having clapped one hand to her betraying mouth and run for the safety of her bedchamber and her protector, Bunny.

Kevin stood stock-still in the middle of the sitting room for some moments, a decidedly silly grin upon his face, as he realized they had both been playing games to see if they could strike sparks off each other. But his face was near to splitting with his elation when he recollected Gilly's last admission and her resultant consternation at letting it out in the heat of the moment.

"She is *not* indifferent to me after all," he exclaimed happily to the empty room. That put an entirely new light on the situation between them. Now that there would be no more smoke screens between them, as neither needed to keep up the pretense of flirtations with the O'Keefes, perhaps they could begin to rebuild their relationship on a more solid base.

Miss Roseberry opened the door of Gilly's chamber, nodded curtly to Lord Lockport, and laid down her pallet outside the threshold in preparation for another night of guard duty. Kevin knew the doors leading to Gilly's bed from the servants' room and the corridor were surely locked after his intrusion of the night before, and he saw no choice but to give up any idea of seeing Gilly that evening.

In his campaign to win his wife's affections, the first barrier to be breached, thought Kevin, was the routing of the redoubtable Miss Roseberry. He went to sleep still thinking of a way to overcome that determined lady's defenses.

Kevin had just dismounted and was walking his horse slowly back to the stables when Willie came running towards him waving a scrap of paper as he forced his bowed legs to hurry.

"What's forward?" the Earl asked quickly, thinking

about the shooting the night before and wondering if Walter Grey had suddenly taken a turn for the worse.

The local constable had come and gone early this morning; a sad excuse of a man, who spent more time mumbling and scratching his head than he did checking the area around the maze for possible clues. That was why Kevin had ridden out this morning—to do a little clue hunting of his own, with very little results. The trail down the grassy slopes to one of the caves did look to have seen recent use, but there was no path from anywhere in that area that led towards The Hall.

But Willie, after stopping in front of Kevin and pausing to catch his breath, shook his head in the negative to his master's unvoiced question and just shoved the paper he held under Kevin's nose.

"Easy there, man, easy. You're likely to take a slice out of me with that thing. Here—give it to me," Kevin ordered.

Quickly Rawlings tore open the sheet and read its contents aloud: " 'Come to the center of the shrubbery at noon. Do not fail. It is a matter of life and death!' " He then turned the sheet over and said curtly. "There's no signature. Who gave this to you?"

"I finded it jammed under a stone on the mountin' block," Willie panted, still a bit breathless.

Kevin shrugged, his tan buckskin hacking jacket straining across his shoulders. "Well, as it bears no salutation as well as no signature, this note could be for anyone—from anyone," he reasoned. "But you did well to bring it to me, Willie. I thank you. Did you show it to anyone else, or tell anyone what it contains?"

Willie colored under his swarthy darkness, kicked once or twice at the loose stones under his feet, and admitted, "I doesn't read, yer lordship."

"Sorry," was all Kevin answered, trying to ease the groom's embarrassment. Putting a companionable arm around Willie's thin shoulders, he, with a few well-chosen words, managed not only to relax the man but also enlisted his aid in keeping the contents of the note a secret.

"I'll just go and change out of my dirt" (not the least of which had lately come from his close association with Willie's dusty coat) "and be off to a *tête-à-tête* with the author of this melodramatic piece of nonsense."

A few minutes past noon Kevin was to be found sauntering nonchalantly through the gardens on his way to the maze—undoubtably the "shrubbery" mentioned in the note. He was (as he certainly appeared, dressed in impeccable "gentleman-taking-his-afternoon leisure" attire) in no great hurry to discover who had sent the note, which he did indeed think to be a hysterical bit of exaggeration. The handwriting was definitely masculine, but the crabbed hand was unrecognizable to him. Who could have written it? Who was it meant to summon? And to what purpose, what end?

He took a better hold of the malacca cane he had tucked up under his arm. If Willie had somehow uncovered a note from some secret admirer meant for Gilly, Kevin was sure to get a little exercise swinging that cane a few minutes from now.

Just as he was about to descend the wide stone stairway to the lower gardens, he saw Anne Chevington rushing out of the maze, her full skirts hiked above her ankles to ease her flight. His cane at the ready, Kevin bounded down the steps to catch Anne, whose head was turned as if to look for possible pursuers, and placed her behind him and out of harm's way.

"Oh, Kevin! Thank God it's you!" Anne cried distractedly. "Come quick! *It's kidnappers!* We must stop them! Told me to run—to save myself. I didn't want to leave, really I didn't, but I had to think of the baby, so I ran for the shortest exit from the maze. Someone followed for a bit—I could hear him crashing through the shrubbery—but he must have given up. Oh, do hurry, Kevin. We must summon some help!"

Instead of racing straightaway into the maze, in which he knew he would surely become lost within seconds of his entry, he propelled Anne to a nearby bench and sought to make some sense out of what she was saying.

Once Anne had taken a few deep breaths and wiped her eyes, she told Kevin that some masked men—anywhere from three to six of them—she was too frightened to take an inventory—had come upon them as they sat talking on a bench in the middle of the maze. "They demanded to see you, Kevin, but when they were sure you weren't about, they said they would take us instead. They said we were to be the 'bait.' " Anne grabbed Kevin by the shoulders and implored him to understand. "I didn't want to desert her, really I didn't, but she insisted. And then she launched herself on two of the men, kicking at their shins and everything, and I was able to get away."

"She!" exploded Kevin, leaping up from the bench. "I thought you were talking about Bo! Who is it—Gilly or Amanda? Speak up, Anne, for the love of Heaven. *Tell me who it was!"*

"It was your wife—Gilly!" sobbed Anne, burying her head in her hands.

Heedless of his fine clothing and uncaring that he was unfamiliar with the twisting paths and dead-end avenues of the maze, Kevin plunged into the shrubbery, his cane at the ready.

He was back within a few minutes, time enough for Anne to have flagged down a passing servant, who had summoned the rest of the house party from the morning room where they were awaiting luncheon. "There's no sign of Gilly," he told his friends, "but from the look of things she wasn't taken without a bit of a struggle."

"Anne told us the whole, Kevin," Jared said, patting the distraught-looking husband on the shoulder. "Don't worry, we'll get her back."

Kevin angrily shook off his friend's hand. "That's not enough," he said angrily, as he raced towards the stables with Bo, Jared, and all the available male servants. "It's *my wife* who has been taken!" Then this most unflappable of English peers astonished all his listeners by giving vent to an impressive string of curses (for the entire length of time it took to reach the stables) without ever once repeating himself.

Chapter Eleven

"WELL, a whacking great thing this is, if I do say so myself. First I'm dumped head down in a smelly old bag. Then I'm carried off willy-nilly over someone's shoulder like a sack of meal, only to end up here, sitting in a puddle in the bottom of this leaky old scow, being stared at by a bunch of dead fish and all you idiots I thought to be my friends. Good God Harry—are you and your fellows in your cups or have you simply all just lost your senses?"

"Now, now, Gilly-girl, don't ye go gettin' all bent outta shape o'er a little mistake," admonished the middle-aged swarthy fisherman named Harry as he took in the sight of Gilly Fortune and repressed a shudder when he recognized how close she was to losing her temper entirely.

Oh, there'd be the devil to pay for this day's work, he was sure, thought Harry. If Gilly didn't skewer him first, it was a sure thing the Earl wouldn't settle for less than drawing and quartering the lot of them.

"A little mistake?" Gilly's screech interrupted Harry's thoughts. "*A little mistake!* Ha! Don't say you didn't recognize me, Harry, seeing as how it was straight on noon and the sun right above us, so that you couldn't help but know it was me standing there."

Harry gratefully grasped at the 'out' Gilly had handed him. "Well, with yer fine duds and—and yer hair all chopped off shortlike . . ."

"Bull feathers, Harry," Gilly cut the man off mid-excuse. She looked around her at the half-dozen men she had sailed with time and again on the tubs. To a man, they were dressed alike in the dark, nondescript clothes of the fisherman, their faces blacked as if they were about to set off on a smuggling run. "What were you doing skulking around the maze like a bunch of thieves?" she asked the group at large, a tingle of apprehension running down her spine as the seriousness of the situation was brought home to her.

She was not in fear of her own safety—nobody here would hurt her, she was sure, but these men were obviously upset about something. "Come on, Harry, 'fess up. You weren't there to pick daisies—what's going on?"

Knowing from past experiences with the chit that she would persevere until she had the truth (hadn't her bulldog tenacity gotten her a seat in the tubs?), Harry sighed deeply, pulled off his black knit cap, and hunkered down in front of Gilly to look her in the eye.

"It be like this, missy," he began earnestly, and Gilly, her legs curled up under her damp and stained spriggled-muslin morning gown, listened with growing alarm.

Her friend told her about the disappearance of two of their last three smuggling hauls—the one she had herself helped sow the night the revenue officers nearly caught them, and another one since she had left the group. Once they had harvested that first crop of sunken kegs, the men had stashed the stuff in the usual shoreline caves to await the overland gang, which would transport everything inland the following night. But when night and the overland gang arrived, the booty was gone—vanished without a trace.

The second haul disappeared just as mysteriously. One lost load could be attributed to the King's men discovering the stash, but as the second haul had been hidden in different caves, the chances of the revenue officers possessing either the brains or the luck to discover *two* hidey-holes so quickly were so remote as to be impossible to believe.

Besides, Harry went on reluctantly, word had come to the gang that the new Earl needed money—and needed it badly. Hadn't his man Willstone been nosing around the Cock and Crown asking all sorts of queer questions? And hadn't the Earl suddenly found the blunt to start making some repairs on the estate? And wasn't Gilly Fortune wearing brand-new gowns—the same Gilly Fortune who knew just where every cave was situated and the probable nights when her old friends were most likely to set out their tubs?

Oh, yes, the evidence was damning. Except to explain the source of Kevin's funds—from the sale of Sylvester's collection of clocks—Gilly was at an impasse as to how to refute the gang's accusations. Harry's claim that she might have been a party to the betrayal she refused to dignify with an answer.

"Who told you that my husband *the Earl* was strapped for funds?" Gilly asked Harry, who was looking very embarrassed, for he knew his speech had not contained a single deferential 'milady' or other outward sign of the rank she just then so neatly reminded him she now bore.

"I—I'd druther not ta say," he hedged before adding, "M-milady."

"Milady my sainted mother!" snorted the Countess of Lockport. "A minute ago it was just plain Gilly. What's the matter, Harry—have you belatedly remembered that you're talking to the enemy? Now, keeping in mind that you have accused my husband, and, unbelievably, myself, of a truly infamous deed, and keeping in mind that I'll have your liver on a spit if you cross me—and you know I do not threaten idly—I'll repeat my question. *Who told you?*"

It all came out then. The way Harry had taken on a silent partner, so to speak, some months back—a man who said he could get a better price for any goods Harry and his gang could set ashore. In return for a bit of the profits, this man had set Harry up with an overland gang that had indeed paid prime money for their kegs of brandy and bolts of fabric and lace—nearly twice the amount Harry had gotten from his other contacts.

"Love a bloomin' duck, Harry," yelled Gilly, all her fine speech deserting her as she turned on her friend in a fury. "Did it never occur to you to wonder *why* this overlander was willing to pay so much?"

Gilly's quick mind had taken two and two, and she was sure she had come up with a very dangerous four. Jared had spoken of a spy, and although Kevin had pooh-poohed the idea, Gilly had thought at the time that her husband had tried too hard to divert everyone's mind from the possibility there was a foreign agent in the area.

"Did this man, your recent benefactor, ever ask any *favors* in return—besides his cut of the money?" she asked now, her eyes narrowed into slits of intense blue fire.

"Er-uh, well, mebbe he did and mebbe he didn't," Harry delayed. "Wot's it ta ya?"

"He did! I can tell by the way you're shifting your great hulking feet and looking everywhere but at me. Come on, Harry, give over."

"Onc't in a while we carried a man for him, only one way each time. But he wuz only some Frenchie takin' money and food to his kin left behind when this Froggie bolted on account of the Revolution. He's a harmless enough sort," Harry almost whined as Gilly moaned theatrically and threw up her hands in disgust.

"A spy, Harry. You've been lugging a great, ugly *spy*, that's what you've been doing!" she accused, sending the half-dozen brawny men into a babble of fear.

"We none of us knowed," one cried.

"Never say that, milady," another begged.

They were obviously convinced their young friend was right, and they were very frightened. But Harry was not their leader without a good reason, and his mightier brain soon snapped back into working order. With a few well-chosen words he silenced his men and turned to Gilly.

"There'll be no more Froggies on our tubs, milady, I promise ya that!" he announced firmly. "We're all good Englishmen here, and we doesn't wants English blood on our hands."

"That's all well and good," replied Gilly, "But that leaves us still with problems to solve. It is not enough to stop carrying the spy; the maggot must be captured and turned over to the authorities. Since your mysterious benefactor introduced you to the spy, it follows he has to be a traitor himself. I ask you again, Harry. A name, man. Give me a name!"

Harry mumbled something under his breath.

"What?"

"I says I doesn't *know* his name," repeated Harry, shamefaced. "We only met the onc't, when he waylaid me one night and put his plan to me. After that I only talked with the Frenchie."

"Well surely you saw him that first night," Gilly prompted.

Harry shook his head. "He stood in the shadows like, and I ne'er see'd his face. I heared him tho," Harry said more forcefully, "and he were one of the gentry sure as check."

"And on that damning evidence you have convicted my husband?" Gilly sneered.

Harry reluctantly told her that gossip in the village—he steadfastly refused to say from whom—had provided them with the idea that the Earl was their man. They believed he had decided he wanted more than his share of the profits—he wanted it all. The note sent to The Hall and the plan to abduct the Earl for a "chat" concerning the whereabouts of the missing booty naturally followed.

"One more thing, milady," another of the smugglers piped up. "Two nights past we caught up a fella on the estate, a fella a-carryin' one of our kegs. He talked like a City man, not at all like one of us, but he loped off afore we could find out who he wuz workin' fer."

"Damning evidence indeed," breathed Gilly with a worried frown, "but you forget—Kev—er—the Earl didn't arrive at The Hall until late June. Harry, you said you were first approached some months ago."

"He coulda come down here afore then, surrep—er—surrep—"

"Surreptitiously," Gilly ended, realizing the truth of that statement. Kevin had been the Earl for some six months before showing his face—six months he was reluctant to speak about.

"All right, fellas, what do you want me to do?"

Gilly had been gone a little above three hours, hours Kevin (and therefore his friends) spent traveling mentally through several different levels of Hell. Rawlings's first impulse—to mount his horse and speed off after his wife's abductors—was aborted when he realized he had not the slightest idea as to which direction his search should take.

It was left to Jared to calm his distraught friend and suggest the three men begin their search at the point of the abduction—the large, open center of the maze. It was apparent at once by the evidence of an overturned bench and a scattering of leaves freshly ripped from the shrubbery that Kevin had been correct in his assumption that Gilly had not gone quietly with the men Anne described.

More evidence was found along the pathway leading to the left rear entrance of the maze, showing that this was the exit the men had used, but there the trail ended.

Bo was all for sending for the constable, until Amanda

reminded him of that man's recently demonstrated remarkable lack of intelligence.

Willie was summoned to The Hall and told to question all the outside servants (meaning Lyle and Fitch who, he later found sleeping under a bench in the Conservatory), while Rice grilled the household servants to find out what they knew.

The two men had just reported back to those gathered in the main saloon, ashamed to admit that their exhaustive questioning had produced nary a single clue, when there was a sound on the flagstones outside, and Gilly burst into the room through the French doors.

"Heyday! It's Gilly!" exclaimed Bo unnecessarily.

Brushing down one dusty sleeve before wiping her grimy hand across her forehead (adding one more slash of dirt to an already woefully begrimed face), Gilly retorted acidly, "Of course it is. Who else were you expecting?"

Kevin dashed his wine glass to the floor and raced across the room to take his wife by the shoulders and examine her critically—rather, thought Gilly resentfully, as if she were a mare he might consider purchasing. Then suddenly she was tight in his arms and shocked into returning his embrace as he whispered hoarsely, "Ah, Gilly. My brave, headstrong little Gillyflower, I thought I had lost you."

"Don-Don't be silly," she found herself soothing him. "You'll not be rid of me that easily." If this was a show put on to convince his friends of his devotion, Kevin certainly was a consummate actor, for even Gilly half-believed he was truly shaken by her disappearance.

By this time everyone was crowding around them, and Gilly hastily disengaged herself only to be embraced again, this time by a visibly worried Amanda Delaney. "Oh, my dear, I cannot tell you what a pucker we were all in, wondering what on earth could have happened to you."

"Indeed," Jared added, "and Kevin here was not the least of our worries either. Why, he's been twitting about here these last seemingly interminable hours like an ancient cockerel who has lost his only pullet." Hard on Jared's heels Bo entered the conversation, pumping her hand up and down between his two beefy fists, thanking her for sacrificing herself to save his beloved Anne, as Anne stood apologizing for turning coward and agreeing to leave Gilly there alone.

All this commotion was fast setting up a fierce pounding in Gilly's temples, as it was well past noon and she hadn't eaten since breakfast. Her struggle with the smugglers, combined with the disquieting news they had imparted to her, had taken a large toll on her reserves of strength, and as she smiled and made meaningless sounds of agreement with anything that was being said, the last of her stamina deserted her and she was hard-put not to succumb to the yearning to relax against the arm Kevin had kept draped protectively about her waist.

Just when she thought she would sink to the floor in a swoon, something she had only once before in her life done, but was convinced she was about to experience for the second time, Miss Roseberry—not one to stand on ceremony at the best of times—bustled purposefully into the room in her rusty black gown and took command of the proceedings.

Within moments, Gilly was extracted from the company, who had begun to ask pointed questions as to where she had been, and was being whisked upstairs to a hot tub. "Sal-volatile, that's the ticket," Miss Roseberry declared bracingly as she propelled Gilly along in front of her.

"Actually, dearest Bunny, I'd rather a brandy," Gilly coaxed in return, earning herself a haughty sniff, before her dresser-cum-nursemaid told her, in a voice that brooked no arguments, that Gilly was to have a leisurely bath, a soothing draught made from Miss Roseberry's special recipe, and, lastly, an early night.

Gilly had been submerged almost to her neck in the steaming bath long enough to have been washed and her hair shampooed. She was just preparing to rise when the door to her chamber opened and her husband barged in unannounced (as well as uninvited and unwanted), sending Gilly back down into the bubbles in her search for cover. Kevin suppressed a grin as Gilly clutched her large bath sponge to her breasts, and only allowed himself to raise one speaking eyebrow in her direction before advancing on Miss Roseberry, who was hovering beside the tub, warmed towels at the ready.

"You may go," he told the balefully glaring woman.

"*You* may go," Gilly shot over her shoulder at her husband.

Miss Roseberry, naturally, stood her ground. She would

defend her charge to the death—and the belligerent set of her shoulders stated that fact most eloquently.

Kevin saw this and changed his tactics. Shrugging as if to say it mattered little what the woman did, he turned to the bath, and while Gilly stared at him like a cornered hare might eye a hungry fox, he plucked the sponge from her nerveless fingers and drawled, "It is so depressing, is it not? The human body is a true miracle of engineering, yet, for all our dexterity and built-in mobility, it remains impossible for any of us to comfortably wash our own backs."

Even as he spoke he was dipping the sponge into the sea of bubbles and dribbling streams of warm water down Gilly's exposed spine. Miss Roseberry's discomfort grew by leaps and bounds as the Earl's application of the sponge became more and more personal in nature (Gilly—caught between enduring this torture and rising from the tub to stand before him clad only in a layer of very revealing bubbles—was for the moment incapable of deciding which was the worse humiliation).

When the naughty sponge found its way up and over the creamy rise of Gilly's left shoulder and began its descent down the other side, Miss Roseberry could stand it no longer—she deserted her mistress without a backward glance, completely dismayed by her unspinsterly reaction upon viewing such a scene.

The sponge was now being drawn in lazy circles over Gilly's upper chest, circles that seemed to dip lower and lower with every passing second.

"You have no right," she choked at last.

"I have every right," came the amused reply.

The sponge continued its travels, dipping into the warm water before surfacing to run over Gilly's wet skin, now grazing the upper curve of her breasts, now sliding into the slight cleft to massage, to stroke, to linger.

"I wish to get out. The water is cold."

"Ah, but are you sure you are thoroughly clean? I believe I have missed a place or two." Using the sponge to demonstrate, Kevin went on, his voice now a husky murmur, "Such as here . . . and here . . . and . . ."

Gilly fairly jumped to her feet, the water in the tub splashing all over her tormentor and anything else within three feet of her, and in a few quick moments she was standing on the rug, a large towel clumsily wrapped about herself.

"The game is over you big bully, so why don't you go away now and leave me in peace," she declared, her breathing rapid and shallow.

But instead of leaving—the gentlemanly thing to do, he mused ruefully—Kevin picked up another towel, wiped himself dry, then steered Gilly onto the bench in front of the dressing table and used the towel to briskly rub at her wet hair.

When he was done, the feat accomplished with Gilly all the while glaring at him in the mirror, he threw down the towel, took up a comb, and began to arrange Gilly's short mop of fiery hair into a smooth cap that—he thought privately—made her look like a wood nymph, or perhaps a particularly fetching pixie. What a singularly vast storehouse of willpower I must possess, he mused, not to throw her on the bed this instant and kiss those pouting red lips until she is senseless.

Flicking the last locks into place, he at last broached the questions that had been burning inside him ever since the abduction.

"Do you remember me speaking of Harry?" she replied for openers, deciding to go about telling her story her own way.

"Your smuggling friend?" he returned. "*He* kidnapped you? What did you do—take a keg for yourself from the last run? Was this the 'matter of life and death' he mentioned in the note? By the by, tell Harry shrubbery has two *b*'s—and no *i*'s at all."

"Will you be serious, please, if it doesn't overtax your mind?" Gilly scolded wearily before telling him pointedly that *she* had only been Harry's second choice—that it was Kevin they had originally come to see.

"Why me? I have nothing to do with smuggling. Surely if they wanted to sell me some brandy or some other contraband, there were easier ways of going about the business. Was such high drama really necessary?"

Gilly took a deep breath and stood up, turning to face her husband. "Two of Harry's last three hauls have been stolen. He wanted to find out if you had taken them."

Kevin had been racking his brains to come up with a reason for *anyone* in the district to wish him ill, but his ideas hadn't even come close to this. "Good God, woman, what would I want with the bloody stuff?" he demanded angrily.

"Harry heard you needed money. When you sold the clocks and used the funds to start fixing up the estate, Harry thought you had stolen and sold his goods," she informed him reluctantly.

She watched Kevin as he began to pace the room, his right fist slamming into his left hand. "You corrected him, I trust?"

"I did."

The pacing went on uninterrupted. "Who told the estimable Harry I was in need of funds?"

"It was gossip overheard in the village; he refused to say who. It's really not important." Taking a deep breath, she went on fatalistically. "Harry's been carrying a Frenchman on his tub occasionally. I just found out about it today."

The pacing abruptly stopped and Kevin whirled to stare closely at his wife. "I want the rest of it—the *whole* of it—*now!*"

While Kevin had been intent on his assault on the threadbare carpet, Gilly had seen her chance to covertly slip on her dressing gown. Now, feeling not quite so vulnerable, she too began to pace—slowly, hesitantly giving Kevin the information he wanted.

There was a long silence in the room when she had finished, broken only by the ticking of the mantel clock. Just when Gilly thought her nerves would surely break from the tension of waiting and watching as conflicting emotions came and went in her husband's expressive eyes, he spoke again.

"This Frenchman—he's a spy of course," he stated flatly.

Gilly nodded her agreement. She then told him that Harry had been unaware he was carrying a spy in his tubs until she pointed it out to him, and she knew that Kevin believed her. She had no desire to see her friends hung on some gibbet as traitors to the Crown.

"And this mysterious *gentleman*, Harry's benefactor—the man who introduced him to the seagoing Frenchman—who do *you* suppose he is?"

Gilly colored hotly and looked down at her bare toes.

"My God! *Me!* You thought it was me! Not only a thief, but a traitor as well. What a cad I must be—to steal from my fellow thieves while betraying the country I fought for just a few years back." Kevin's voice shook with righteous anger. "How dare you—*how dare you* judge me like the Lord on Doomsday—you and your rag-tag pack of petty smugglers, who are too thick to figure out you've been escorting a spy back and forth across the water. If you weren't a woman I'd call you out for that."

Gilly's head came up and she stammered, "I—I really couldn't blame you if you did d-do it, what with you being so pressed for—for funds. Maybe—maybe you saw it as your only way out." Her voice gaining strength, she looked him in the eye and promised, "I wouldn't cry rope on you, Kevin, really I wouldn't. You can tell me."

All Kevin could do was shake his head sadly. "Your loyalty overwhelms me, wife. You'd betray friends and country for a man you have claimed time and again you despise. All that loyalty," he went on, "but not a single drop of *trust.*"

"Then you're innocent?" Gilly piped up in a hopeful voice.

"Ah, she rallies," Kevin drawled to the room at large. "*Yes,* you female Doubting Thomas, I am innocent. I only asked you about the smugglers to gain information about the spy the Admiralty thinks to be operating in this area. I'm under secret orders to ferret him out, if you must know."

All traces of remorse vanished from Gilly's eyes in an instant. "You mean to stand there and tell me you are on the hunt for a spy among Harry and his men and never told *me?* You used me, Kevin. Talk about a scarcity of trust. Where is *your* trust of *me!*"

Miss Roseberry, thinking she had been banished quite long enough, chose that moment to march back into the room (the loud voices she had been hearing, even through the heavy door, convincing her she wouldn't be thus subjecting herself to any further embarrassingly private goings-on) and clap her hands to gain the angry pair's attention.

"It is time and more my lady had a lie-down on her bed—*—alone,*" she said with great determination.

"Yes—yes it is. It's indeed more than time," concurred

Gilly, still looking at her husband with eyes that told him he was lucky she hadn't yet skewered him with her letter opener. Moving over to stand inside the protection of Miss Roseberry's stiff embrace, she said, "One more thing, O trusting one. I've promised Harry you'd meet him at nine tonight behind the stables for a talk. My fears that you were guilty were easily come by, but I refused to really believe deep down in my heart that you could be a party to such two-faced treachery. So thinking, I gave Harry my word you would help him discover his thieves in return for his help in trapping the spy. Now that I am completely assured you are innocent, as your role of deceiver was meant only to hoax and beguile your innocent wife into divulging information that might lead you to the spy, I wonder: would you have gone so far as to declare undying love for me to gain the information you desired? I am telling you about this meeting so that, perhaps, this matter as well can be settled once and for all. I am convinced this farce of yours—your so-public displays of affection—must be quite wearing on you even though you have doubtless had years of experience with this sort of ingratiating cajolery."

There, she congratulated herself, she had really said that quite well.

Her husband bowed deeply from the waist in acknowledgement, knowing now was not the time to try to convince Gilly she had misjudged both his motives and his emotions, and still more angry than he would like (for precisely what reason he was not sure), he thanked her stiffly and turned to leave without issuing a single word in his own defense.

"One more thing," Gilly called after him, now rather drunk with a sense of power that helped her to hide her heartbreak, "I'm going with you tonight."

"The devil you are!" Kevin countered as he began to retrace his steps, his eyes two chips of pale blue ice.

It seemed the battle was to be joined again unless a cooler head was allowed to prevail. "What a great piece of nonsense, my lady," Miss Roseberry intervened hurriedly before any blood was spilled. "Any time now that draught I gave you should begin to do its work. The recipe is a family secret handed down these many years and I will not divulge its contents. I will, however, tell you that it is at least three parts laudanum. By nine of the clock tonight you, my fine young miss, will have been already asleep at least two hours."

"Bunny, how could you!" Gilly exclaimed horror-struck. "I can't let this London dandy meet Harry and the rest alone. For one thing, he'd be a good hour late because he had trouble with his cravat. Besides that, anyone with a ha'porth of brains can see he's not the sort of man to be trusted with chasing down thieves and spies. Why, Harry would rather lug the womanish Willstone with him than drag a man-milliner like *him* along on a man's job. He'd only be in the way," she ended with a disdainful sniff that showed how well and truly she believed her husband's outward displays of laziness and soft living—all his hard work this last month and more on the estate not standing as proof he could hold his own in a fight.

"Oh, how sharper than a serpent's tooth is the edge of one's own wife's tongue as she puts forth her opinion of her husband's manhood," bemoaned Kevin, his voice fairly dripping sarcasm as he wisely decided to reassume his foppish mask. He had come too close to losing his temper completely, a thing he rarely did, as Kevin Rawlings in a temper was a sight to make brave men blanch in fear. "Wife, you disturb my peace."

Miss Roseberry fought to restrain her irate charge. "Good!" Gilly screeched. "Then my life has not been in vain!"

As Kevin tried once more to quit the room (before he gave into the impulse to turn Gilly over his knee and give her a half-dozen hard whacks that would make her other spanking pale in comparison), Gilly called after him, "At least take Jared and Bo with you. And Willie. And—and Lyle and Fitch."

An irrepressible chuckle escaped Kevin's lips. "Lyle and Fitch?Whatever for? I may be just another effeminate, ineffectual, posturing London dandy, but at least I can be relied upon as possessing some little bit of sense. Those two couldn't be counted on to even *find* their way to the stables before Boxing Day."

"I'm going with you!" Gilly vehemently declared one more time to his departing back, her fears for Kevin's safety outstripping her anger at the man for using her to learn about Harry—as well as for not letting her in on the secret about the spy lurking, as it were, right under their noses.

Yet when the hour for the meeting drew near, and Kevin and his two friends walked down the path leading to the stables, Gilly was not with them. Miss Roseberry's estimation of her draught's power was not overly ambitious—Gilly, in opposition to all her struggles to the contrary, was deeply asleep and not bound to waken much before the rising of the sun.

"Stop that!" Kevin hissed angrily. "You're thrashing about like a dog in a fit, making enough racket to raise the dead."

"Sorry," came Bo's strangled reply. "Cramp—in m'leg."

"Oh, good grief," sighed the Earl, shifting a bit in his cramped position behind a boulder to rub at his friend's tightly knotted calf. "There you are, sport, right as a trivet. Now let's see if you can stay quiet for more than five minutes, shall we? I swear, Bo—first you're thirsty, then you're cold and now—"

"Hush!" admonished the third member of their small party.

"What's forward, Jared?" whispered Kevin, wheeling on his toes to look over the top of the boulder, his eyes narrowed as he sought to pierce the darkness along the shoreline.

There was the sound of softly running feet coming up behind him, and then Harry was crouched beside him. "They be a'comin' soon now, yer lordship, iffen you were right."

"Are your men all in position?"

"Aye, that they are. But I still say we take 'em now—"

"And I still beg to disagree with you, my dear fellow. You landed your goods last night, and as I was with you and able to observe the amount of time it took you to stow that great mountain of cargo, it is obvious to me that these thieves you swear are making off with what's yours cannot move the cargo very far in one night without risking detection."

"That's right, mate," Jared added under his breath. "And don't forget the spy—he's one fish we're not about to let slip through our fingers."

The spy had come aboard Harry's tub from the cutter they met far out in the Straits, right along with the kegs of brandy, casks of cinnamon, and bolts of silk. Kevin, dressed in rough black garments, his face disguised with brass blacking, had watched as the man made preparations to spend the rest of the night in the caves with a bolt of paper-wrapped silk as his pillow. Everyone felt the spy, who was unquestionably the man who showed the thieves where to pick up the smugglers' cargo, would then travel to London at night, finding protection and camouflage amid the rough crowd of thieving overlanders.

Now that dark had come once more, Kevin and the rest had taken cover in the rocks and long grass outside and above the caves to await the thieves. While Harry was all primed for a fight right there alongside the sea, Kevin ruled that they would be better served to observe the thieves and follow them—undoubtedly ending up by locating the secret hiding place the thieves used to store the cargo and prepare it for overland shipment. After that it would be a simple matter of returning to the spot one more time the following night and apprehending the gang, the spy, and, Kevin devoutly hoped, the "gentleman" genius behind the whole dirty business.

Another half-hour passed in tense silence before the sound of jingling harness came to their ears. Within moments two dozen and one men (Kevin counted them for the sake of accuracy) passed by the crouching observers, just a few feet on the other side of the boulder, and descended the hill to the mouth of the cave. The man in the lead, a small, slim shape in the darkness, took up a position near the entrance and, with hand signals and a few soft French curses, admonished the gang to put their backs into it.

The cargo was first transferred to the top of the hill and then loaded onto donkeys. Following a discreet distance behind, Kevin and his band kept the small caravan in sight until, to everyone's amazement, the donkeys were led onto Hall property and brought to a halt at the rear of the two-acre Troy Town maze.

One by one the donkeys were relieved of their burdens, and the cargo was carried inside the maze. When all the kegs, crates, and bundles had been moved, the two dozen men and their pack animals moved off—followed by two of Harry's men.

The twenty-fifth man did not reappear. "Where's our little French friend?" questioned Jared, puzzled.

"No place to hide," Bo commented. "None."

Jared was on his feet, brushing twigs from his clothing. "Could he have left by another pathway, do you think?"

"Could have. No reason though. Closer to The Hall. Dashed silly move, if you ask me," reasoned Bo, the man most familiar with the construction of the maze.

Kevin convinced everyone there was nothing else for them to do that night and suggested they reconvene in the morning, at which time they could make a thorough search of the maze.

As the three men walked back to The Hall, Jared asked, "Are you thinking what I'm thinking?"

Kevin turned to face Lord Storm. "That would depend on what you're thinking. You have two options open to you I believe, especially if our friend Harry's suspicious eye-shiftings in my direction are to be considered. One, the thieves have discovered an entrance into Sylvester's underground warren or, two, that I am indeed behind this whole nefarious scheme."

"No! Not you, not our Kevin. Say it ain't so."

Jared clapped a reassuring arm about Bo's agitated shoulders. "Never fear, Bo, Kevin was only funning." Turning to the Earl, he admonished, "Now cut line you rascal before poor Bo here takes a fit. We all know the tunnels are the answer—even Harry. You did a bang-up job of convincing those men at that first meeting behind the stables that we had only their best interests at heart. Harry doesn't doubt you in particular; it's just the lifelong habit of doubting the entirety of the gentry—not that I blame him overmuch."

By now they had reached The Hall and were in the large saloon being handed glasses by their host. "Thank you for your trust, Jared—you too, Bo," Kevin told them, saluting both men with his glass before taking a restorative sip of port. "As I see it, all that remains come daybreak is for us to locate the entrance to the tunnels, capture the spy, who is at the moment hiding out inside, and then wait for the thieves to arrive tonight."

Kevin then outlined his plan for capturing the thieves. "We will block all but the maze entrance to the tunnels. Once the thieves re-emerge from underground, it will be a simple enough matter to herd them together and deliver them to the revenue officer in Hastings. Just think, Harry and his men may well find themselves to be local heroes."

They laughed at this vision of smugglers being praised by the authorities but then sobered as Jared asked just how Kevin proposed to keep the women in ignorance of what was going forward. Lord knew keeping them in the dark just these past few days had been difficult enough.

"The devil fly away with all females—I forgot about them," groaned Kevin, his handsome face twisted into a grimace at the thought of the chaos Gilly and Amanda could cause if they were to get wind of their plans.

"Send 'em to the shops? Any ruins nearby to visit? *Churches!* Ladies love to see churches," Bo suggested hopefully. "Got to throw a rub in their way."

"It's worth a try, Jared," Kevin said hopefully. "God knows we have to invent some farradiddle with which to fob them off. I wonder," he leered evilly, "do you think ropes and gags might do the trick—or locking them in the cellars?"

Standing behind the drapes in the window embrasure, two dressing-gown-clad women rolled their eyes at each other and grinned.

Chapter Twelve

IT HAD BEEN mere child's play to send the ladies off the next morning in the coach to view The Long Man of Wilmington at Alfriston, a scarce fifteen-mile journey, with the competent Harrow tooling the reins.

The three conspirators stood in the gravel drive waving to their wives as they leaned out the side windows of the Delaney traveling coach and waved their hankies gaily back at them. Then, just as soon as the coach was out of sight around the bend, the men fell to slapping each other on the back, congratulating themselves on the successful routing of the one hitch in their Machiavellian scheme—their nosey-parker wives.

Then it was off to the maze; wary Willstone, sleepy Lyle and Fitch, and feisty Willie tagging along behind carrying rakes, wooden poles, and an inlaid box containing Sylvester's prized dueling pistols.

Their search concentrated on the heart of the maze, the large open area that sported a miniature temple at its very center. Although Bo's small army of helpers had made great inroads on restoring the maze to its former glory, there had not been enough time to do more than scythe the long grasses in the clearing to a navigable height. Also, nothing had yet been done to refurbish the wooden pillars of the temple, which had once been artfully painted to resemble marble but now stood flaking and peeling and almost completely derelict.

"The grass—or should I say *weeds*—are surely trampled enough to show that the robbers came this way," Kevin remarked in an undertone, "but where the devil did they disappear to? None but the one path shows any signs of being traveled."

Jared, who had been poking about the turf with his toe

looking for Heaven knew what, muttered, "It's like they disappeared into thin air."

"Indeed," nodded Bo passionately. "Like Merlin. *Poof!* They're gone."

At Bo's words, Lyle and Fitch—never the bravest of men—turned to bolt from the area. In their haste to be gone they both turned at the same time, cannoning into each other with great force. The skinny Lyle bounced off the rotund Fitch and staggered backwards to careen against one of the temple pillars, which served in turn to send him reeling into Fitch's arms, the two ending in a crumpled heap on the ground.

The laughter that sprung to everyone's lips was immediately stifled when the temple—the entire structure: base, pillars, and vaulted roof—began to slowly rise from the ground.

Immediately the temple was the cynosure of all eyes. Motioning for silence, Kevin got down on all fours to inspect the three-foot-high opening that had been revealed and saw at once that the temple had been built atop a circular iron platform with a center iron pillar that operated on some intricate springlike mechanism. "Well, I'll be damned for a dolt, how could it have been otherwise!" he exclaimed in excited but hushed tones.

Signaling to Willie to hand over his dueling pistols—one to Jared and one to himself—the two men slowly lowered themselves by way of a ladder propped against one side of the exposed hole and dropped into the flambeaux-lit tunnel.

"There has to be a vent somewhere near or these wouldn't be burning," whispered Jared sagely.

Their pistols cocked and their bodies crouched in preparedness for anything, they pivoted about, noticing that the tunnels were a good twelve feet high and, just to add a bit of spice to the game, branched off in four different directions from the central area in which they now stood.

"Toss a coin?" Kevin grinned.

While Bo and the servants waited above ground, armed to the teeth with rakes, the two men made a systematic search of the first three tunnels.

One led to a large square room the robbers had used to store their pilfered cargo.

A second wound round and about for some distance, with several rooms cut out on either side, ending at a blank wall that Kevin supposed to be somewhere underneath the stables.

"How so?" questioned Jared.

Holding a fine lace handkerchief to his delicate nostrils, Kevin suggested his friend take a deep breath.

"Quite so," grimaced Jared, wrinkling his own aristocratic nose.

Further investigation disclosed a stone ring at the left side of the tunnel, which when pulled caused the seemingly solid wall to draw back a few inches until the old and uncared-for mechanism stuck fast. Peering through the crack, Kevin could see the main tack room of the stables, where just then one of the newly hired underfootmen was engaging in a round of slap and tickle with one of the housemaids.

"Whoops! Wrong door!" Rawlings drawled, withdrawing his face from the opening.

The third tunnel seemed to rise upward a bit along its length, ending at last at a heavy iron door, which, once the ring beside it was pulled, slid open easily on freshly oiled hinges to reveal the interior of The Hall's wine cellars.

"This has got to be the way our midnight intruder entered so easily," Kevin told Jared, "and it will be the very first to be stoutly bolted from the inside!"

That left one tunnel unexplored. "Isn't that always the way of it?" quipped Kevin irrepressively. Knowing that the spy was surely behind one of the half-dozen doors that lined that last damp corridor, the men trod warily, pistols at the ready.

By the process of elimination, they one by one ruled out all but the last door on the left. Silently they positioned themselves against the wall on either side of the door, and then, at a signal from Jared, Kevin wheeled and kicked open the door with one well-aimed foot.

The door flew inward to bang loudly on the earthen wall as, pistol at the ready, Kevin leapt into the breach.

"Sacrebleu! Mon Dieu!" shrieked the slight blonde man on the small cot who had been so rudely wakened.

Noting the three empty wine bottles—from The Hall's cellars no less—and the haggard, rumpled condition of their prisoner, Kevin and Jared apologized insincerely for the disturbance before bustling the now-groaning Frenchman down the corridor and up the rickety ladder to the surface.

"Lock this piece of offal in the oast house and come back here prepared to do a little carpentry work. We have some exits to seal before tonight," ordered Kevin, as Willie, chuckling over his own joke, prepared to "frog-march the Froggie" to the empty hop kiln.

That done, Bo—vexed to have been left out of the fray—said rather huffily, "Could have gone with the ladies. Nothing to do here."

"Oh, really?" quipped Kevin, winking at Jared. "I had hoped I could rely on you to figure out, now that Lyle has so providentially got the temple *up* for us, exactly how we might get it *down* again!"

"It's coming on to dark, but it's still too soon for our robbers to show their faces. What happens if the ladies return before we can set our plan in motion?" asked Jared with a worried frown, as the three men strolled towards the maze.

Kevin grinned and reassured his friends. "Harrow will take care of that little problem for us. I understand one of the off-leaders will pull up lame about, let's see—" he pulled out his pocket watch and checked the time—"ten minutes ago. Harrow assured me he wouldn't be drawing up in front of The Hall much before nine, and Rice is to then greet our wives with the happy fact that we three have gone to help one of the tenants deliver a calf."

"Good man, Harrow. Good idea too," nodded Bo, huffing and puffing to keep up with the long strides of his taller friends. "Don't like birthings above half though. Messy business."

The men met Harry and his fellow smugglers outside one of the entrances to the maze, and before too much longer Kevin had given his instructions and positioned everyone inside the maze in what he believed the best possible deployment of his forces.

When night came shortly afterwards the dark was almost total, there being only minimal light from the waxing moon that hung in a silver crescent high in the sky amongst some few stars.

Almost as if conjured up by some magician, the robbers suddenly appeared in the center of the maze. One of their number walked straight for the temple and began probing about the pillars, looking for the trigger to the mechanism that would raise the structure.

When he had tried his luck with three pillars without any success, another robber stomped to his side cursing, "Blast you for a fool, O'Keefe, we haven't all night!"

"Blister me if it ain't Glynis!" whispered Bo, aghast.

Sure enough it *was* Glynis, and as she pushed O'Keefe away, her position as leader of the group was firmly established by the way he and the rest of the men allowed her to take the initiative.

Now it was Glynis who went from pillar to pillar in an increasingly frantic pursuit of the trigger. "The damned thing is jammed," she swore at last, having pushed at the base of each pillar at least twice. "O'Keefe, you brainless dolt. What did you do to this thing last night? I should have known better than to trust you to do even one thing right, bacon-brained twit that you are."

A few of the robbers had joined Glynis beside the temple, all of them trying their luck at getting the thing to open. "Good job, Bo," Kevin murmured to the man crouched beside him behind a stone bench. "It certainly was simpler to lock the whole thing up right and tight that way than to take the time to block all the exits. Now pass the word—we move in on my signal."

With the robbers all intent on finding a way to reach their booty—at least those not arguing amongst themselves as to whether they would derive the most pleasure from beating Rory senseless or from merely slitting him gut to gizzard with a sharp knife—it was doubtful they would notice Kevin's group until they were completely surrounded.

"Stubble it, you unwashed curs," rasped Glynis as she flung her cap on the ground in disgust, allowing her golden curls to cascade down her back uncaringly. "You're screeching fair loud enough to raise the dead!"

Her words couldn't have been more prophetic. Just as she finished speaking, a hideously groaned *"Oh-h-h-h!"* reached their ears from somewhere in the shrubbery, followed hard by another, even more agonizingly moaned

"Ah-h-h-h!" that emanated from the opposite side of the clearing.

"Oh-h-h-h," the first sound was repeated with gathering force. *"Who . . . dares . . . disturb . . . my . . . peace?"* the disembodied voice asked despairingly.

"Ah-h-h-h!" the second voice answered. *"Who dares? Who dares?"*

"Not me!" One of Harry's men (the poor soul stationed closest to the second voice) shouted as he jumped to his feet and took himself off, crashing through the hedges like the Hounds of Hell were after him.

Two humanlike shapes seemed to float into the clearing from different pathways, the forms covered from head to toe in filmy white draperies that seemed to clothe bodies devoid of any real substance.

"I'll throttle the pair of them," gritted Kevin, running a distracted hand through his carefully arranged blonde locks. "I will, Jared, I swear to God, I will!"

But Jared, possibly because he had been married longer and was more accustomed to the mad starts adventurous women like his wife and Gilly were prone to go off on, and possibly because he too had a rather perverse sense of humor, was so busy choking on silent laughter, he could only shake his head and push Kevin back down as he tried to rise.

As the robbers huddled together like frightened sheep, Gilly and Amanda—for there was no doubt in Kevin and Jared's minds as to the identity of the *spectres* just now prancing about the perimeter of the clearing like demented gazelles, moaning and groaning and issuing threats of vengeance—reached into the folds of their garments and extracted small bags filled with a powder they then began to fling about the dumbfounded robbers heads as if they were damsels scattering rose petals on May Day.

"Grab them! Grab them you spineless ninnies!" Glynis was shrieking now. "They aren't ghosts, they're only—*Ha-choo!*"

Glynis's sneeze was only the first, as the powder being sprinkled so lavishly reached other nostrils, and soon the entire clearing was echoing and re-echoing to the resounding sneezes and sputtering coughs of twenty-four tearful, staggering robbers.

"Now!" Kevin shouted to alert Harry's men before he himself raced into the clearing—followed by Jared, Bo, Harry, and no one else. The rest of the smugglers—being as susceptible to Gilly and Amanda's histrionics as the robbers—had taken to their heels soon after their friend, leaving the four men more than a little short-handed.

Not that it mattered, as Bo was overheard to say later when he recounted the evening to his interested wife; for it had been mere child's play to round up the hapless robbers and hold them at gun-point until Harry's cohorts found their courage and returned to lend a hand.

Gilly shed her white cloak, revealing her face to her astonished audience, and boldly strode up to Glynis, looking the fuming woman up and down while grinning from ear to ear. "My, my, Glynis," she clucked ruminatingly, "We did say you looked your best in black, didn't we? Odd thing about that, though," she pressed on devilishly, "I don't believe those breeches are quite your style—as you're just a tad too overpadded in your ass-ets."

Then Amanda pushed back the hood of her white satin cloak and boldly joined her sister-in-crime. "Now, now, Gilly dear," she admonished with a giggle. "you mustn't offend Miss O'Keefe's tender—er—*sensibilities*. You know what a shy young miss she is."

"Damn if ye ain't a pair o'cards," declared Harry with a bit of awe. "Rare handfuls, the both of 'em. Pity ya, actually, yer lordships. Wouldn't want my Mary runnin' rigs like these two, beggin' yer pardon and all."

By now the robbers had been neatly tied together like a string of pack animals and were ready to be led off to Hastings.

"Gentlemen, there are three nails, very small nails actually, holding the temple locked in place," Kevin told the smugglers who were awaiting his orders. *"If* after depositing your prisoners with the proper authorities—remember, you came upon them by chance, along the coast, but several of them got away with, unfortunately, the cargo—you were to find your way clear to return here and *remove* those same little nails, and *if* the cargo now residing in the tunnel has suddenly disappeared by morning, I can see no reason to worry my head further on the entire subject."

At this statement there arose a rousing cheer for that "bang-up gentleman," the Earl. Harry promised, winking earnestly, "I ken keep my chaffer shut—mum's the word, right?"

The robbers were then herded, still coughing and sniffling, off to the lockup in Hastings.

That left Rory and Glynis still to be dealt with as, considering the gravity of their crime of treason, sterner punishment was called for.

"I never dreamed Rory was the traitor," Gilly commented, eyeing the two prisoners now standing dejectedly beside the temple.

"See why. Not enough in cockloft," soothed Bo. "Fella's revolting, actually. Sweaty palms, y'know. Never trusted 'im."

"That's one way of reasoning, I guess. And, combined with your past judgments, it gives you a perfect score on character assessment, Bo," pointed out Kevin before his humor seemed to disappear entirely as he advanced purposefully on his wife. "But as for *you*, woman, how did you manage to hoodwink us all and show up here tonight?"

Gilly ignored his tone and replied sweetly, "Did you know, husband, that Harrow mounted Amanda on her first pony? My goodness yes, he's known her since babyhood. Fair worships her actually—do most anything for her."

Jared turned to his wife, who was just then striking a pose that could have been titled "Sweet Innocence," and declared, "You never went to Alfriston, did you sweetings? Tell me, just how far did you get?"

"About a half-mile from The Hall," Amanda confessed candidly. "We picnicked on that hill over there and watched all the carrying on you went through today. That's when we got our idea—or actually Gilly did—I give her all the credit for her simply *famous* plan."

"Not all," interrupted Gilly honestly. "We were at a loss as to whether to use Malaba black pepper or Tchilecherry but, after discussing it with Miss Whitebread and Hattie Kemp, decided on the Malaba. So you see, we had some help."

While Bo and Jared only seemed capable of seeing the

humor of the thing, it was left to Kevin to point out that the two women could have come to harm with such a harem-scarem scheme.

"Harm?" scoffed Gilly, still drunk with her success. "Nonsense, Kevin. It was the greatest good fun, wasn't it, Amanda?"

"Oh my, yes," confirmed her co-conspirator. "After all, why should we stand by and watch while you all beat each other to a jelly in some dangerous melee or some such thing if we could help you?"

"True to form," Jared muttered facetiously. "Your solicitude for my welfare fair bids to unman me."

While all this bantering back and forth was in progress, Rory was otherwise occupied giving full vent to his feelings of self-pity. An out-of-work actor when Glynis found him, it had been mere child's play for that scheming woman to enlist him into her little company—playing gentleman to an audience that took in a whole section of Sussex.

It had been a fine time too—playing at tutor, going to bed at night on dry sheets and with a full belly, lording it over the villagers, hobnobbing with the gentry he aped so wondrously well—why did Glynis have to get so greedy and ruin it all! If only she had been content to take her cut from the smugglers and her pay from that Froggie Duval. But no, *she* had to try to have it all. Now look at them (not that he much cared what happened to that cold witch Glynis, who had for months shared the same roof with him but that's all), about to be marched off to London to be tried as traitors.

"Oh, the agony of it all," Rory groaned audibly. "It's hardly fair—all I did was act, why should that be such a crime? I am, after all, an actor, a Thespian. Would they have tied Kean to a ghastly fake Greek temple as a reward for merely playing a role?"

Glynis, who was tied to that same pillar, hissed in his ear, "Oh, stow yer clack," revealing more clearly than ever her less-than-genteel background. "These ropes are loose . . . there that does it. Now—quickly—slip your hands free and we'll make a run for it!"

Rory was nothing if not a quick study. "Like Bonnie Prince Charlie—we'll be away before they know we're gone," he improvised quickly, if not especially accurately.

"Huh? Er—sure," returned Glynis vaguely. "Now move a bit in front of me and wait until I give you the word—then we'll run for it."

Stupid clod, thought Glynis, rubbing her sore wrists while standing half behind Rory, as if I give a tinker's curse for *his* hide. Then, taking a deep breath, she placed her hands fully on Rory's back and gave him a mighty shove.

Rory cannoned into the small, celebrating throng, who were still trading quips back and forth in congratulation for a fine night's work. In the resulting confusion, Glynis, nearly invisible in her dark clothing, made hot-foot for one of the openings in the maze.

She might have made a clean break of it too if it hadn't been for the rusty length of metal lying half-hidden in the grass, an impediment to her progress that, when it came into contact with her dainty, booted foot, put a speedy period to her escape attempt.

"S'faith, Kevin," complained Bo as his friend picked up Glynis bodily and easily held her tucked under his arm as she kicked and cursed. "Make her stop. Shameful language. Shameful!"

Glynis's near-escape seemed at last to bring some semblance of sobriety to Gilly and the rest, and they all retired to their own rooms shortly afterwards, Glynis and Rory safely tucked up in a locked storeroom behind the stables until they could be removed to London on the morrow.

While the men shared a last victory drink, the ladies climbed the stairs, only to be met on the half-landing by a rare sight indeed—a thoroughly discomposed Bernice Roseberry.

"Now, now, Bunny," Gilly soothed the agitated dresser, clapping one reassuring arm about the bony shoulders. "There's no need to fall into a twitter."

"You stay out unchaperoned half the night doing Lord knows what, dressed only in a nightgown—not that it doesn't cover you decently—and with white flour all over your face like some sort of ghoul. Then, when you finally return, you're barefoot and the hem of your gown is drenched in dew—you'll probably catch your death—and you say I'm *not to worry*. Oh no, missy," poor Miss Roseberry objected heatedly. "I have every reason to worry. It appears to me that I am become increasingly nervous as each new day spent in this house dawns. Never have I had such problems—perhaps it is because I cannot recall ever before feeling any affection for my charges. However, I warn you, much more of these mad goings-on and I shall dissolve into a quivering wreck—a mere shadow of my former self."

Miss Roseberry's young mistress then further disconcerted the woman by drawing her into an embrace and planting a kiss on one flinty cheek. "I am prodigiously sorry, Bunny, truly I am," Gilly said with no little remorse. "Is it so *very* bad running herd on such a shameless scapegrace as I? I fear I have little practice thinking about how my actions might affect others. You see, there's always been such a scarcity of people who cared enough to worry."

While Gilly stood consoling the now softly weeping dresser, Amanda stole silently off to her chamber and her own worried servant, but not before she wiped a tear or two from her own eyes caused by the touching scene she had just witnessed.

Before Rory was put into the wagon that would transport Glynis and him to Hastings, he obliged Kevin by speaking loud and long on the subject of his leader—"Glynis O'Keefe." He told how Glynis, then known as Mae Wood, had grown up within sight of The Hall and how her father had been one of the men to help the late Earl dig the tunnels. The girl had always envied the people at The Hall and, once grown, had devised a way to gain for herself some of the riches she believed hidden there by the old recluse.

A bit of hair dye and some stylish clothes, combined with a new name and a hastily acquired brother were all the camouflage she needed. She set them up in the village and went about making her fortune—through smuggling, the transportation of French spies, and, she hoped, the midnight looting of The Hall.

Poor Rory. He was only a helpless pawn in the hands of an evil mistress—or so he said. Kevin was buying none of it, but he was glad to at last have the mystery of the tunnels set to rest. At least he could breathe easy that it was only Glynis, and not the French, who had discovered their existence.

Indeed, so relieved was he, Kevin found it in his heart to promise he could be counted on to write his friend Peter at the Admiralty, asking that man to put in a good word for the unfortunate Thespian.

Chapter Thirteen

THE DELANEYS and the Chevingtons were all packed and ready to depart. As Jared had told Kevin, "You'll settle down with Gilly much better if the place isn't stiff with your friends."

Glynis and Rory had been dispatched to London the day before under the guard of some soldiers from Hastings; the smugglers had regained their cargo, leaving behind three fine casks of French brandy for their great friend the Earl of Lockport; and the robbers were languishing in the Hastings lockup.

Amanda missed her children, and although her hands still itched to knock Gilly's and Kevin's heads together and make them admit they loved each other, she knew they could not be made to fall into each other's arms at her command.

Bo and Anne had made their farewells to the gardens they had performed their special brand of miracle upon in only a few short weeks, and were extremely touched when Lyle and Fitch, flushed and stammering wildly, presented them with a parting present—a small, sickly potted palm.

Everything was in readiness for the departure of the entourage when Nature intervened in the form of an unexpected but heavy summer thunderstorm, and there was nothing for it but to put off leaving until the weather cleared.

The restlessness of being cooped up indoors when there were places to go was being manifested in Jared's agitated pacing of the large saloon and the sound of Bo's rat-tat-tatting fingers endlessly drumming on an end table.

Amanda stood it as long as she could—which was no great length of time—before inspiration struck.

"I have a marvelous idea!" she told the room at large as

she returned from a quick trip to the library waving a piece of parchment in her hand. "Let's have some fun. Come on all you Friday-faced groaners—*what say you to a treasure hunt!*"

From her position reclining daintily on a small sofa, her hands folded lovingly about the slight mound of her enlarging abdomen, Anne eagerly voiced her agreement to such a plan. Bo was a dear, she told herself bracingly, but his incessant tapping could be said to grate a bit on one's nerves. Silently she wished upon her lucky star that he would be nowhere near when she was having the baby—she didn't think she could stand to have the poor dear nervous soul within sight (or sound) at such a delicate time.

The host and hostess of the soon-to-be disbanded house party, who were seated across a desk from each other discussing the advisability of sealing Sylvester's tunnelways forevermore (Kevin pro, Gilly con), were reluctantly brought to attention by their guests, who, seemingly bored to flinders just moments before, now were clamoring for an all-out assault on that perplexing unsolved puzzle.

Kevin, sensing this was a good way to entertain his friends (although he seriously doubted the late Earl ever meant his cryptic poem to be solved), quickly acquiesced to the scheme, but Gilly was another matter entirely.

She pooh-poohed the idea at first, hinting that it was all a sham, some twisted trick of Sylvester's equally twisted mind. When she was contradicted, she became openly opposed to the search, stating firmly that she had no need for the so-called fortune everyone was sure was hidden somewhere in The Hall (as Kevin had just once again then stated that the fortune, once located, was hers). Finally, declaring rather mulishly that she would not participate in any "damn fool treasure hunt," she departed from the room in a huff.

"Well, goodness sakes, whatever brought *that* on?" Amanda exclaimed, her eyes still on the door Gilly had slammed shut on her way out. "She almost seems *afraid.*"

"Panda box," said Bo flatly.

"That's Pandora's Box, Bo," corrected Jared. "But you may have something there. Perhaps Gilly believes solving the puzzle will only bring her more trouble."

"She knew my late uncle better than anyone else,"

Kevin supplied thoughtfully. "On reflection, she might be right, you know."

"Sleeping dogs."

"How's that, Bo?" Amanda asked.

"Don't bite. Can't, you know. Asleep and all that."

Anne slipped her arm around her husband's ample waist. "You mean we should leave sleeping dogs alone, don't you dearest?"

"Certainly. Said that. Don't bite then. Sleeping. Stands to reason. Don't bark either, come to think of it." Bo searched his friends faces, trying to understand the reason for their sudden laughter. "Fail to see the humor. Just simple logic. Dashed queer, you all carrying on. Not funny. Not funny a'tal."

Kevin wiped at his eyes with the corner of his handkerchief. "Sorry, old friend. We were thinking of something else I suppose. No one meant any harm. And you are right—sleeping dogs don't bite. Nor," he added, only a bit more seriously, "do they solve puzzles in their dreams. That being so, shall we, daredevil adventurers that we are, risk it—nipping dogs, dark predictions, as well as other numerous and sundry evils—and give it a go anyway? After all, ladies and gentlemen, we *are* English you know."

Jared took another look outside at the steady downpour that showed no signs of easing, shrugged, and drawled, "We've captured a spy, routed some thieves, exposed two traitors, and given aid and comfort to a gang of smugglers. All this entertainment and more our congenial host has provided for us. The least, the very least, we can do in return is solve his cursed puzzle for him. It's only fitting, dearest, don't you agree?"

His wife, who after all was the instigator of the idea in the first place, reminded her husband of that fact and, in the second place, that she was not one to take her leave when there was yet something unfinished. As her husband knew—"don't you, darling"—she dearly loved to tie up "loose ends."

And so, while Bo muttered dire warnings about dozing dogs and locked boxes and things best left alone, and while Gilly was off somewhere sulking like a child who, when the rest of the children refused to play by her rules, took up her toys and went home, the small group in the large saloon took turns at being Bow Street Runners out to solve an interesting case.

As she was the instigator of the project, Amanda outlined her plan of attack. They would first dissect the rhyme line by line, then word by word, or even letter by letter if necessary, until they had succeeded in gleaning its meaning.

" '*For now, on humble pie you dine—*' " Amanda quoted from the paper in her hands. "Who wants to be first?"

"Pies are baked in the kitchens," offered Anne vaguely.

"Kept in pantries," supplemented her husband. "Blueberry last night. Quite good, came down for more at midnight—pity it's gone now. Knew it would rain, could have saved some. All gone now, though. Pity."

Kevin pulled agitatedly at his shirt cuff and broke in on Bo's gastronomic reminiscences. "A person eats pie in the dining room—'you *dine,*' I believe it said."

Standing so that he could look over his wife's shoulder, Jared remarked, "There's eight syllables in that line." He paused for a moment to read further. "Eight in the second as well." He raised his head to look at Kevin. "They all have eight syllables. Do you think it means anything."

A glass of burgundy at his lips, Kevin paused and smiled evilly, "It means you can count to eight. There are four lines in the rhyme—that makes for a total of twelve, unless you combine the two as either forty-eight or eighty-four. Or you could subtract four from eight to get four, or multiply four by eight to get thirty-two, or you could—good God, who cares what you get. *I'm* getting a headache!"

They left Jared's number theory for the time being, and Amanda read the second line—" '*I give you, girl, an anodyne.*' "

"The girl is Gilly," Anne said unnecessarily, and they all agreed. "The rest of that line is simple too. You remember that anodyne means 'something that removes pain.' "

"That's my sweet wife," preened Bo. "Pretty *and* smart. Quite beyond my touch, actually. A lucky man, that's me."

Rice took that moment (while Anne and Bo were holding hands, gazing adoringly into each others eyes, and the others were busily trying to seem to be looking anywhere but at the billing and cooing twosome) to bring in the tea tray.

Amanda sat in for the absent Gilly and began to pour

the tea, before Kevin could recall that his wife was shirking her duties and thus create a disturbance by going off to drag her back to the large saloon, and Jared took up the reading of the rhyme.

"*'Your Fortune waits with endless time,'*" he intoned slowly, lingering over each word. "There's the 'time' that sent you racketing through The Hall peering into Sylvester's clock collection."

"Yes," Kevin concurred wearily, "and a bloody waste of time it was too, pardon me ladies for my crudity. The only good to be gained from that little episode was the money derived from their sale. That and the resultant peace and quiet that had for a space seemed impossible to achieve amid all that ticking and chiming."

"*'Two clues: your name, and this wry rhyme,'*" Jared concluded solemnly. "If this rhyme is a clue then I fail to see it. But what's this about a name—that seems as likely a place to begin as any."

"It must refer to Gilly's odd string of names," broke in Amanda. "Didn't you once tell us she had quite an assortment of names—like a person reading the roll at a girl's seminary I believe you said, Kevin."

He nodded and recited sing-song, "Eugenia Giselle Horatia Dawn Fortune. Ludicrous, ain't it?"

Anne disagreed. "I think they are lovely names. Let's see. Eugenia, like anodyne, is Greek, meaning 'well-born' or 'noble.' Giselle, on the other hand, is German, and that, while a pretty sounding name, has quite a depressing meaning—'hostage' or a 'pledge' of some sort."

By now Anne was the center of attention, with everyone on the ends of their seats hanging on her every word. "Go on, Anne," directed Kevin tersely when she paused, "you have our full attention."

Anne looked at her friends, saw their agitation, and hurried on. "There isn't much more. Horatia, from the Latin, refers to 'keeper of the hours,' and Dawn is English and simply means 'the dawn of day.' As for Fortune—that truly horrid surname your uncle was so cruel as to heap on poor dear Gilly's innocent shoulders, that is from the Latin *fortuna*, meaning 'fate' or 'destiny.' Oh, my!" Anne exclaimed as the full import of everything she had just said was brought home to her. "*Oh, my!* Do you believe it truly *means* something—everything put together?"

Kevin couldn't sit still any longer. Rising jerkily to his feet, he paced back and forth across the worn carpet, the cane he had plucked from its resting place against a chair now softly tapping against his left palm. "A wellborn hostage to fate—that's got to be it. Gilly *was* born out of wedlock, but when her twin brother died, Sylvester's grief turned into anger against Gilly—the girl-child who had dared to survive. Mrs. Whitebread told me Gilly's mother was an invalid from the time of the births until she died—obviously not a good subject for breeding purposes ever again."

"So Sylvester declared the secret marriage ceremony to be a sham and let everyone think his poor wife a mistress and his child a bastard," Amanda broke in, quickly grasping the situation as it had been nearly two decades before. "Sylvester probably wished to marry again in hopes of producing an heir—now that both his first- and second-born sons were dead. If he couldn't discount his marriage to Gilly's mother as a fraud, he had no hopes for siring another legal heir until the poor woman died."

Now Jared took up the story. "But he had reckoned without the reaction of the local gentry. Believing he had foisted his lightskirt on them for nearly a year, they all cut him from that day on. And since Sylvester was by then already a bit of an odd duck, never leaving the estate for more than a day at a time, he had no chance to find another gullible woman to wed. He stayed on at The Hall, refusing to repair the entailed residence he could not pass on to his sons, and slowly, as his hobbies became obsessions, he withdrew from the world entirely."

Kevin finished the story: "He kept the estate running reasonably well until his health began to deteriorate about seven years ago. For the last three years of his life, it was, ironically enough, Gilly who acted in his stead as best she could with little or no money at her disposal. God!"—he slammed his cane angrily against a table leg—"What a great lot of evil that man has to answer for!"

After everyone had taken turns venting their spleens on the subject of Sylvester's ignominious misdeeds, it was Anne who ventured to ask how the name Dawn fit into the puzzle.

And there lay the rub. It didn't fit. It didn't fit at all.

* * *

When luncheon was announced with Gilly still refusing to make an appearance, Kevin stormed out of the dining room, his appetite nonexistent in the face of what he had discovered.

Suddenly the enormous Hall seemed too confining. He had Willstone bring him his greatcoat and—dismissing the valet's cackling about ruining his Hessians in the puddles, not to mention getting soaked and probably taking a chill—Kevin went outdoors for a walk.

His steps led him eventually to the maze where, once he had reached its centermost part, he sat on a cold, wet stone bench and dropped his head into his hands.

Poor Gilly, he thought sorrowfully. His poor, deprived Gillyflower. How sadly they had both used her—first Sylvester, and now himself. He had forced her into marriage, made her a woman over her protests, and, he now realized—and this was the very worst sin of all—he had usurped her rightful place as heir to the late Earl's private fortune, which her father could and should have bequeathed directly to her.

She had been deprived of a normal childhood, but if only he hadn't blackmailed her into marriage, she could at least look forward to being one of the richest, most beautiful, most sought after young women in the *ton*. Her title, face, and fortune would have served as *carte blanche* for anything her heart desired. She would have been free to travel, to meet people—and now Kevin's handsome face was contorted with pain—to fall in love with and marry any man she chose.

Kevin's depression deepened. Gilly had been right, he conceded too late—they should have forgotten the puzzle ever existed. Sylvester's private fortune would still be theirs in less than a year, and they had been on their way to finding a good life together—even if it was a rocky road they were traveling.

Gilly had been beginning to care for him—Kevin needed desperately to believe that—but once she was told she was legitimate, sooner or later she herself would think of all the things he was already in the process of kicking himself over, and any chance for their future together would be completely and utterly destroyed.

Raising his eyes and his clenched fist to the skies, Kevin cursed aloud, "You've won, you crafty old bastard! I may live in the house you loathed to leave me, and I may reap the rewards of the estate you worshiped and the fortune you amassed, but you took from me my self-respect and made me wish to be nothing more than purse-pinched Kevin Rawlings once again. Oh yes, Sylvester, at last I understand why you let me have it: you knew that by the time I got it I'd hate every groat of it.

"And you did it so shrewdly, so cunningly, knowing I would be sickened to think I had taken advantage of a helpless girl like your daughter. But your revenge was even better than you hoped for—more devastating than even your most insanely devious dreams—for you gave me something I had never hoped to have and then snatched it away again once I had come to depend on it for life itself. You gave me Gilly—you gave me *love* —and then you took her away.

"I hate you Sylvester Rawlings!" Kevin shouted to the cloudy skies, "I hope you roast in Hell for what you've done!"

The rain had dwindled to a fine drizzle, but still Kevin's face was streaming droplets of water—mayhap there were a few tears competing with the raindrops—impairing his vision as he made blindly for one of the pathways out of the maze. He had gone no more than a few feet when the toe of one of his Hessians collided with something, and he found himself laid out belly-down among the weeds.

Cursing at the ruin of both his Hessians and his greatcoat (it seemed as if Willstone had wished this particular mishap on him), Kevin hoisted himself to his knees and turned to discover what had tripped him.

It was the same metal object that had foiled Glynis's escape attempt—he saw that, now that he could examine the object in the daylight—but what sort of object was it?

He pulled it upright, ripping it free of the vinelike weeds that held it to the ground, and at last realized that what he was holding was a style that had become another casualty of Sylvester's neglect. "There must once have been a sundial in this clearing," he mused out loud before suddenly shouting, "A *sundial!* Of course—*endless time!*"

Heedless of the damp and mud permeating the knees of his buckskin breeches and uncaring of the dirt that soiled his hands and shirt cuffs, Kevin scrambled about the clearing on his knees, searching for more evidence of the sundial's existence. After he located a dozen iron tablets, bearing large Roman numerals from one to twelve placed flush with the ground in a wide circle, it was easy to find the groove at the center of the circle into which the style had once been fitted.

This had to be it—this had to be the *"endless time."* Much as he wished he had never embarked on this treasure hunt, he now was in a fever to see it concluded. If Amanda had been right in her first supposition that Gilly's birth record and her mother's marriage lines made up the fortune, and if all their surmising earlier in the large saloon had been correct, he *owed* it to Gilly to give her what was rightfully hers—her legitimacy.

A thin, watery sun was just breaking through the clouds as Kevin raced to get the others, but he didn't notice it. He exploded into the large saloon through the French doors from the garden and, spying out Gilly, who had at last reappeared, he pounced on her demanding, *"When were you born?"*

Gilly was struck speechless. Her husband, whom a person would be hard pressed to fault for ever harboring even a speck of lint on his immaculate clothing, was somehow standing before her looking like a horse that had been ridden hard and put away wet. He had a smudge on his thin aristocratic nose and another across his chiseled chin. His glorious blonde hair was dark with rain and appeared for all the world like he had combed it with a rake. His clothing would have to be bundled up and put in the fire (there was no salvaging a stitch of it), and his beautiful patrician hands—the ones just now cutting off all the circulation in her arms from just below the shoulders—bore mute witness to the fact that he had been scrabbling in the dirt like an urchin.

Gilly's inventory of her husband had taken only seconds, but even that short span was too long for him. Again he asked his question, this time punctuating each word with a shake of the hands gripping her upper arms. "When were you born—what day, what month?"

"It—it was in April—April eighth. Why? What is going on? What's the matter with you, you look positively ill!" Gilly spluttered, truly upset at Kevin's bizarre behavior.

"Ah-ha!" Kevin crowed, releasing Gilly and turning towards the others—all equally dumbfounded by both his ap-

pearance and his question. "Don't you understand?" he yelled triumphantly. "April eighth. It had to be. Oh, I guess it could have been August fourth just as easily, but it was April eighth. Jared! Surely you understand. It was your idea."

Jared's frown cleared then and he grinned in understanding. "Four lines in the poem and April is the fourth month. Eight syllables to a line and Gilly was born on the eighth day. Very good, Kevin!"

"I have more than that, old friend, much more. What clock never has to be wound? What timepiece gives the time endlessly? And—and this is the best of all—what sort of timekeeper looks like a pie cut into segments? Think, friends. It is so simple I'm amazed we didn't see it before."

"Sundial!" shouted Bo in glee. "A bloody sundial!"

"Burn it if you aren't right, Bo," Jared complimented the happy man. He turned back to Kevin. "Out with it, man, I can see you're bursting to tell us more. Get on with it."

Instead of answering their questions, Kevin went to the door to the corridor and bellowed for Rice to send someone for a spade.

"*Buried* treasure?" Amanda smirked. "That's almost *too* much."

"Oh do be quiet, Amanda," Anne surprised everyone by scolding her friend. "I want to hear *all.*"

Kevin bowed in Anne's direction. "And so you shall, dear lady, seeing as how it was your brilliance that provided the key that first unlocked the puzzle.

"Gilly," he called over his shoulder to his unhappy-looking wife. "Do you know what time of day you were born?"

"Near dawn, I think," was all she could muster before sinking once more into an uneasy silence. She now knew what Hattie Kemp felt when she would shiver and say "a goose just walked over my grave." Maybe no one was waddling across Gilly's grave but someone was doing a mighty energetic jig all over her past, and she was convinced she was not going to be happy with the results of that nimble dancing.

"Dawn," Kevin repeated triumphantly. "I had guessed as much. And does anyone here have any idea about what time dawn occurs in the month of April?"

"About six—seven at the latest, I imagine," replied Jared, feeling like a puppet reacting each time Kevin pulled the strings.

"Close enough," Kevin agreed. "I would imagine that somewhere among Sylvester's copious notes concerning every bit of useless information to have occurred these last twenty years and more the exact time is recorded, but I have no time—pardon my poor joke—for such tedious research.

"Therefore, if you would all be so good as to follow me, I shall personally wield my trusty spade as I dig around the numbers six and seven on the sundial located at the center of the maze! Ladies first, please," he then cautioned, holding open the door and bowing again.

"By all means, let us adjourn to the maze," cooed Gilly nastily. "I am all curiosity to discover what it is that so excites Lord Lockport that he is suddenly all uncaring of his appearance. Indeed, this fortune must be of some import to him."

It took only a few minutes of digging before the spade hit upon something metal halfway between the two markers carrying the numbers six and seven.

Kevin dug more carefully now and soon could lift out a small oblong metal casket, which he carried over to place on one of the stone benches.

"I wish he wouldn't look so smug," Amanda hissed quietly into her husband's ear.

"He's not as carefree as he would have us think, Mandy, my love," Jared whispered back. "Look at his eyes—they appear almost feverish. He's under a great strain, our friend Kevin is, and I believe we both know why. Worse yet, look at Gilly—she's as white as a sheet, poor child."

The rusted lock on the casket broke after one blow from the spade, and Kevin hesitated only a moment before he threw back the lid to reveal the treasure.

There were three oilskin drawstring-topped bags inside, and Kevin dumped them one by one onto the bench.

"*Oh!* How perfectly lovely they all are!" Anne crooned as the diamonds, rubies, emeralds, and other precious stones that adorned the Lockport jewelry appeared before their awe-struck eyes.

For a moment—only a brief, heart-stopping moment—Kevin thought the casket was now empty. But then he saw a flat packet, similarly wrapped in waterproof bindings, reposing at the very bottom of the metal box.

Working carefully so as not to tear the brittle papers he found inside the bag, Kevin unfolded the two pieces of parchment, read them, then handed them to Jared.

"This is Gilly's mother's marriage lines, proving once and for all that Sylvester was married in a legitimate ceremony; and this second document is incontrovertible proof that our friend Gilly here was born Lady Sylvia Rawlings the eighth day of April in the year of Our Lord 1798."

"Sylvia?" squeaked Anne. "Not another name!"

"The Rawlings invariably name their females Sylvia, just as they curse their males by dubbing them Sylvester. I don't think my Rawlings ancestors cared much for children. Thank heaven my mother was a stubborn Irish colleen," Kevin supplied with a hint of his usual sarcasm.

"Well, I won't have it!" came Gilly's voice, clearly astounding everyone. "My name is Gilly. I *like* it. I won't be called Sylvia. It's a stupid name."

"I couldn't agree with you more, Gilly," Kevin told her silkily, crossing to where she stood some bit apart from the others. "What's so special about a name anyway? Shakespeare said it: 'What's in a name? That which we call a rose, by any other name would smell as sweet.' "

"Ha!" Gilly retorted, twin flags of color showing in her cheeks. "Try calling one a bastard for ten and eight years and then see if renaming it a rose will rid it of the stink!" Pointing jerkily to the papers in Jared's hand she jeered, "Do you think those scraps of paper have suddenly made everything all right? What about my poor mother? Where's her vindication? What rose does she smell?"

Gilly shook her head violently as if to ward off her own thoughts, then whirled on Kevin in a fury. "This changes nothing. Keep your papers. Keep your fancy jewels. Keep your fortune now that you've solved the puzzle. Keep The Hall and the estate, God knows you've earned them. I don't want any of it. And most of all—*I don't want you!*"

With tears streaming down her cheeks, betraying just how very much things *had* changed, Gilly took to her heels, her skirts held high above her ankles and one fist pressed to her mouth as she disappeared down one of the pathways, leaving Kevin looking like a scarecrow that has just lost half its stuffing.

Amanda approached him sympathetically, folding him into an embrace to which he did not respond. "She'll calm down, Kevin. Give her time. It was a shock, that's all."

"And when the shock is over and she realizes that the reasons for our marriage no longer exist—what then, Mandy? Will she demand her share of the money and her freedom, leaving this place and all its unhappy memories, never to return? I wouldn't blame her, you know."

"She won't do that," Amanda contradicted him earnestly, while the sound of Anne's soft weeping in the background gave the lie to her optimism. "She loves you, I know she does."

Kevin managed a small lopsided grin. "Sure of it are you? Well, Mandy, at least that makes one of us."

With most of the day gone, the Rawlings' guests decided to spend another night at The Hall, and as Gilly was locked up in her chambers with Miss Roseberry guarding the door, they spent their time one by one seeking out their host and giving him the benefit of their advice.

By now Kevin was sorely in need of mentors. Before Gilly had barricaded herself in her chambers, Kevin had confronted her, courageously recounting all his self-proclaimed sins against her and offering her a divorce if she wished one.

Her reaction was to be expected: she accused him of being in a rush to return to London and his many mistresses now that the terms of the Will had been fulfilled and the marriage between them had become superfluous.

He didn't try to argue with her. He resolved to be noble—to do the decent thing. She would thank him in the end. Kevin learned something as he watched Gilly turn from him in disgust—doing the decent thing hurt. It hurt a lot.

He hid in the library after a decidedly uncomfortable dinner with his friends, who were so excruciatingly aware of his unhappiness, and was well into his third bottle when Bo and Jared sought him out.

"Still feeling downpin?" Jared asked, eyeing the empty bottles.

Kevin lifted his head and looked at his friends through glazed eyes. "I've been thinking. Perhaps I should get away. Wellington needs good men still. I could enlist in a cavalry regiment under an assumed name."

"Not cavalry, Kev. Hussars, that's more the thing," Bo corrected him, happy to be of any service at all.

"Do you think, Bo?" Kevin returned.

"No. He don't think," cut in Jared, rolling his eyes at the well-meaning redhead.

"Gilly. How is she? Missed her at dinner," Bo improvised quickly, vainly trying to cover his *faux pas* with yet another one.

Kevin raised one expressive eyebrow and gave a hollow chuckle. "A marked friction has developed between myself and Lady Lockport. I cannot say how she is faring, as it is difficult to converse through four inches of solid oak door."

"Send up some flowers. Women like flowers," Bo suggested hopefully, gaining him a groan from the man he was trying to cheer into better spirits.

"I'd sit at her feet on a leash if it would make her happy, but somehow I believe it's my absence, not my presence, that she most desires."

Amanda, who had come on her own mercy mission, heard this last statement and admonished, "Nonsense. The last thing Gilly wants is to have you disappear from her life." Putting one finger to her lips she added, "Of course, on the other hand, I also cannot see Gilly content to have a husband who resembles an overgrown lapdog. Knowing Gilly, she would soon be disenchanted with such slavish displays of devotion and dash off on a smuggling run or some such thing to escape the boredom."

That drew a faint chuckle from Kevin, and correctly reading his wife's silent signals, Jared took Bo's arm and neatly steered him from the room.

"All right," Amanda said bracingly, "now that we are alone, I want to know something. *Are you out of your mind, Kevin?* What on earth are you doing—giving Gilly up without so much as lifting a finger to keep her?"

Kevin straightened a bit in his chair, the better to face his attacker. "Amanda," he reasoned, "Gilly has led a life filled with nothing but poverty, drudgery, and shame. My advent into it gave her a name she already owned—not that I knew it, I do allow myself that one balm to my spirit—and took away what little freedom she had.

"Now, even if she takes only half Sylvester's private fortune, she'd be rich enough to buy an Abbey. She's legitimate. She's young. She's pretty. She has the whole world at her fingertips. At least she would if she weren't married to me. How can I ask her to give all that up when she deserves it all and so much more, just because of her father's demented Will?"

"How?" Amanda railed at him. "You ask me *how?* You silly, silly man. You ask her because you love her, because she loves you, and because you'd both be only half a person without each other.

"I know love, Kevin. We're very lucky, Jared and I—we found each other. Silly pride and stupid fears almost kept us apart, but our love was stronger than those things, Kevin," Amanda said finally. "I don't know if I believe you really love Gilly. No man who loves a woman like you say you love Gilly would give her up without fighting for her. You disappoint me, Kevin. Until now I never would have taken you for a coward—or a fool."

Rising from his chair, Kevin went to Amanda and placed a kiss on her cheek. "Now I know why I at one time believed myself to be in love with you. I never had a woman for a friend before. You're my friend, Mandy, my good, dear friend. Thank you. I'll go to Gilly tomorrow, on my knees if I have to, and try to win her." He smiled. "And if that doesn't work, I'll put the heartless chit over my knee and spank her!"

"Goose. How you do run on," Amanda told him huskily, her golden eyes bright with unshed tears. She reached up and kissed his cheek. "Good luck, *my* dear, good friend. You've found your true love at last—may you always be as happy as Jared and I—you deserve it!"

The grass was still wet with early morning dew when Gilly spread her skirts to sit beside her mother's grave. Dressed in a becoming morning gown of mint green, embroidered Spitalfields silk, she looked the picture of youth and beauty—unless one looked too closely and spied the age-old weariness in her eyes.

"Good morning, Mama, Tommy. I have some very happy news for you today," she began and then went on to tell of the discovery of the casket and its contents the day before.

A person could have filled volumes with the things she left unsaid: a lifetime of remembered hurts, years marked by never-to-be-forgotten slights and snubs, but Gilly didn't speak of any of this. Instead she concentrated on the bright things—the disclosure that her mother had indeed been Lady Lockport and Tommy a Viscount. Gilly would have her family moved to the Rawlings mausoleum on the estate, she told them, there to have them sleep their endless sleep surrounded by all the Rawlings that had come before them as well as those who would join them in years to come.

She told them about the fine Rawlings jewels that she, little Gilly, would wear as she presided at gala balls and dinner parties once The Hall was restored to its former glory—as it could be now that all the money was at last available.

After a time though, her voice lost most of its cheery lilt and her head drooped more and more towards her chest. At last she could hold back no longer and she laid her head against her mother's headstone and began to cry.

"Oh, Mama, I'm so unhappy," she sobbed brokenly. "At first, when I heard the news about us, I could only be angry. All I could think about was how *unfair* it was for Sylvester to have treated us the way he did."

She sniffed and wiped at her nose with the back of her hand, clumsily, like a small child. "Then I realized that Sylvester must have been insane—real Bedlam-bait like Harry would say—and wasn't really responsible for what he did. I guess it nearly killed him when his first son died and when Tommy died too, leaving him nothing but a puny girl who couldn't inherit—he just slipped round the bend entirely. I'll never forget how he wronged you, Mama, but I can learn to live with my memories.

"No, there's something else that is wrong, and I just don't know what to do. Oh, Mama," her voice broke a bit, "never in my whole life have I missed you more. If only you could talk to me, maybe you'd have an answer for me."

For a long time there was nothing but the sound of the breeze rustling the leaves of some nearby trees and some birdsong off in the distance. Then Gilly, gathering her courage, spoke again.

"It's Kevin, Mama. Our marriage was not his idea, you know that. Come to think of it," she said with a bit more force, "it wasn't *my* idea either. Anyway, there have been times, even whole days, when I think that our marriage was the only good turn Sylvester ever did me.

"But there are other times," she sighed, "a discouragingly *vast* number of times, when we seem to get on like cats in a sack—fighting and clawing at each other, and for such silly reasons, over such silly things.

"Kevin has always objected to what he calls my 'inconsiderate mad starts,' but I don't set out to upset him. It's just that I am so unused to having to account for my whereabouts or actions. I must be more thoughtful, I know; why I even put poor Bunny through hoops fretting over me, and I certainly have no reason to cause *her* pain."

Gilly plucked a long blade of grass and began to twirl it between her fingers. "Ever since you died I've been on my own except for Hattie and the rest, and, to be honest, that's the way I liked it. If I didn't let anyone too close then they couldn't hurt me when they—you know, died or went away.

"Now it seems like I'm up to my rump, er—I mean, now it seems as if I'm surrounded by people who say they like me and want me to like them in return. Anne, Bo, Amanda, Jared, Bunny, even Rice—they all say they care about me. It's nice, but it certainly is a responsibility. I have to account for my comings and goings or they worry I've been hurt or kidnapped or worse. And much as I like them all, I'm afraid to let them begin to mean too much to me because then I'll have to worry about *them* and if *they* are all right, or if they'll stop liking me and leave me alone again."

Gilly sat silently again for a while, building up her courage to tell her mother the worst of her news. There was a slight sound from somewhere behind her, like a twig snapping underfoot, but she was too lost in a brown study to hear it.

She stirred restlessly, reached for the daisies she had filched from a nearby grave to give to her mother, and began making a daisy chain to occupy her fidgeting fingers.

"I think I was finally beginning to trust Amanda and the rest when Kevin showed me I had been right not to trust anyone too much. You see, Mama, Kevin never said he cared for me—I mean *really* cared for me—but there were times when I was sure he did. I came so close, so very close, to letting myself love him.

"I really believed I had finally found someone I could care for, someone who wouldn't leave me or turn their back on me because of what I am—like the villagers did when I started to grow up and they remembered I was a bastard.

"But yesterday changed all that. Oh, I know I was more than a little upset when I first found out what Sylvester had done—I just knew his so-called fortune was better off left alone—and I know I was a little unfair ranting at Kevin the way I did."

She stopped for a moment and then continued, "Actually, Mama, I was a lot worse than unfair—I was a bloody shrew, screaming at him like it was all his fault.

"But before I could apologize he came to me and—calm as you please I'll have you know—offered me a divorce if I wanted one. *A divorce!* Oh, Mama, can you see now how I had been right not to trust him? Now that he has what he wanted he can't wait to be shed of me?"

Gilly crushed her daisy chain in her hands and cried, "Why couldn't he have left me alone, Mama? Why did he come here and show me what it's like to care about someone and hope they care about you?"

Her flame-topped head buried in her hands, she sobbed brokenly, "I was all right before he came, I didn't need him to pretend he cared about me—to make me want to care about someone else, to make me remember how much it hurts when the one you care about goes away.

"I could have lived all my life without ever knowing Kevin Rawlings existed. I was happy in my ignorance. But now, now that I have had a taste of what might have been, I am at a loss to see how I will ever be able to live the rest of my life without him.

"Oh, Mama, I love him, I must love him—why else do I feel like I'm dying inside? I don't want the fortune or the jewels. I just want Kevin. Why can't he love me too? Please, Mama, why can't he love me?" Gilly asked desperately, knowing she would hear no answer.

The nattily dressed man standing quietly behind the weeping girl was for the moment too overcome with emotion to trust his voice. But her sobs were breaking his heart—she for whom he would gladly lay down his life to spare her the slightest pain.

Taking a deep steadying breath, he leaned down behind

Gilly and clasped her shoulders in his hands. Raising her to her feet, he turned her unresistingly towards him and lifted her chin with the bent knuckle of one finger. Willing himself to refrain from giving in to the impulse to crush her to him and kiss her until she became faint from lack of breath, he looked searchingly at her upturned tear-wet face, arched one eloquent eyebrow, and smiled his most ingratiating smile.

"Idiot," he drawled caressingly. "My dearest, sweetest, most adorable idiot . . . whoever said I didn't love you?"

Epilogue

STORM HAVEN was a perfect reflection of its owners—Amanda and Jared Delaney—warm, inviting, and pulsing with life. The grounds, on this warm late June day, were a picture-book setting for the domestic group now gathered on the velvety green east lawns.

Two sturdy dark-haired toddlers were happily frolicking with several deliriously delighted fat tan puppies of questionable pedigree, while their indulgent Nanny looked on from overtop her knitting.

A table sat nearby, beneath the shelter of a large oak tree. Gathered around this table playing a game of Brag were Amanda Delaney, mother of the twins; Anne Chevington, her serene beauty even more apparent since the birth of her son four months previously; and the redoubtable Aunt Agatha, a tiny, wiry lady who had been happily cheating and (even more happily) coming up the winner of nearly every hand dealt.

Bo Chevington was stretched out on his side on a carriage blanket amusing a chubby red-haired baby, who was delighted by the toy rabbit that, once his daddy had squeezed its fuzzy tail, sat still for a few moments and then suddenly hopped into the air.

Jared Delaney, on his way to join them, stood some distance away from the group, pausing to smile over the warm feelings the scene stirred in him. Then he walked over to his wife and dropped a kiss on her nape in greeting.

"I have a letter here from Kevin," he told her, laughing as she squealed and grabbed it out of his hand.

"This simply *must* be the one we've been waiting for," she said. "Gather round and I'll read it aloud:

Our dear friends—

I hope this missive finds you all well and safely past the danger of Bo bending your collective ears unceasingly about his son the Nonpareil—surely he cannot maintain such eloquence even in such a worthy cause.

"Naughty jackanapes," Aunt Agatha commented aloud while silently breathing a fervent *Amen* to Kevin's concern for her battered ears (and nerves—honestly, anyone would be justified in thinking Bo performed some miracle producing little Edward—even if he was a most engaging child).

My regards to Aggie, of course. I would give a great deal to see her face now that I have confounded all her grim prophecies and settled down here at The Hall.

"Faugh! Is it any wonder?" Aunt Agatha was goaded into saying. "How could I place any confidence in a fool I first encountered in my drawing room in London practicing spitting tobacco juice into my best Sèvres vase and trying out curse words in an attempt to ape some low-bred mail-coach driver?"

"We were young then, Aggie. Boys do grow up, you know." Jared defended the misadventures of his youth.

"You came about nicely once you met Amanda—well, perhaps not that soon. At first you behaved most reprehensibly. Why, I remember Honoria writing me from London about your exploits, and let me tell you young man—"

Jared held up his hands in protest. "Spare my blushes, please, Aggie, I beg you—not in front of the children."

Amanda interrupted this friendly squabbling with a shriek of pleasure. While her husband and his aunt had been bantering back and forth, she had read ahead silently and at last discovered what she was looking for.

"Oh, that trickster," she exclaimed, "how like him to gammon me by writing as if this was just any old letter. Listen to this!

By the by, friends, you may offer us your congratulations. I have been so diverted else I would have written sooner, but by the time this letter reaches you (considering the state of the King's highways) it shall have been some three weeks since Gilly, my most splendid, brave Gillyflower, presented her adoring husband with the most beautiful, perfect baby girl a man could hope for.

We have named her Alicia, after Gilly's mother. The little creature has been fortunate enough to favor Gilly, although my diplomatic wife vows Alicia has my ears.

"It can only be considered a blessing if she escapes inheriting anything more than a pair of Rawlings's ears—at least she can hide 'em under her hair," put in Aunt Agatha facetiously.

"Aunt Agatha," protested Amanda, "that is a singularly infelicitous remark. Just don't ever let Gilly hear you talk like that—she fair dotes on Kevin, you know."

"Pshaw!" scoffed the old lady, flicking a stray flower petal from her lacy shawl. "And you told me she was an intelligent little thing. Sounds a bit queer in the attic to me."

"Oh, Lady Chezwick," Anne giggled nervously. "You're such a wicked tease."

The elderly lady leaned over and patted Anne's hand. "Don't fly up into the boughs, my dear. I only tease people I'm fond of, you know. If I truly disliked Kevin Rawlings I would treat him with extreme civility and never utter an unkind word about him."

"In that case, Aunt," suggested her chuckling nephew, "you must *adore* our Kevin, judging from the way you are always roasting him."

"May I get on with this?" demanded Amanda, waving the letter in front of her. She started in once more:

As I told you before, Aunt Sylvia has responded wondrously well to Gilly ever since it was brought home to her that she was her niece. Indeed, Gilly too had to get used to the idea that she had suddenly acquired an aunt after thinking herself entirely without family—on the right side of the blanket, that is. Already Aunt Sylvia is haunting the nursery, as she and Elsie were our first official visitors since the birth, and Gilly has had the happy notion the old girl will be very good with Alicia now that my dear wife has been spending so much time with her, drawing her slowly back from her dreamworld. Gilly says to send you all her love and promises to write soon, herself, telling 'all' *about the baby. That should prove to be a weighty tome, I fear. But never fret, Jared, I promise to go bail for the postage—happily, my sponging days seem behind me now. Until we hear from you, hopefully with the news you and Amanda and Bo and Anne (who I am sure are still visiting at Storm Haven) will agree to stand godparents to Alicia, I remain, yr. obedient, etc., Kevin.*

"Already three weeks old, huh?" Jared mused. "That's our Kevin all over—late again."

"Well," added Aunt Agatha with no little satisfaction. "So that's that. I hate to admit it, but I'm proud of that boy. He seems to have really matured in this last year. Yes," she nodded happily, "Kevin Rawlings has at last become a sober, responsible citizen."

Aunt Agatha might not have been so complacent if she could have been privy to the conversation just then taking place elsewhere between Kevin and Gilly as they watched over their slumbering child.

"Look at her, Gilly, darling," Kevin was saying. "Just look at her. Isn't she just the most splendid child ever born?"

Gilly couldn't quite suppress a giggle as she caught sight of her husband's fatuously preening expression. "Of course she is, dearest," she agreed wisely. "Didn't I say she had your ears?"

In a burst of exhilaration, Kevin lifted Gilly into his arms and waltzed her out of the nursery and into their shared bedchamber. Whirling her about dizzily, he exclaimed, "We shall fill The Hall with our children!"

Lifting her head from where it had been buried against his broad shoulder, Gilly responded breathlessly, "You deliciously silly man. Do you have any idea of the number of bedrooms there are in this great pile?"

Kevin, his blue eyes twinkling as his mouth lowered to claim hers, sighed theatrically and murmured, "It is an awesome task we are setting ourselves, I agree—but nonetheless a challenging one. I can only suggest we make a beginning."

And they did.

THE END . . . OR IS IT?

Author's Note

One of the primary attractions of a Regency novel is its historic setting; therefore, an accurate portrayal of the events, real characters (and there were some real *characters!*), language, modes, and manners of that glorious time in history become a major concern for the Regency author.

Yet I found myself compelled to include mention of the vast underground excavations carried out by the Fifth Duke of Portland in this book, although according to DeBrett's the Duke was only twelve the year my story occurs—just barely past the sand-castle stage. My reason for this is that such tunnels—large enough to drive a coach and four through—smack too much of a figment of the imagination to be believable.

I wished to be able to lend Sylvester's tunnels, by means of referring to other such construction, some basis in fact so that you, dear reader, wouldn't think you were being asked to swallow some farradiddle I had made up purely to fit the confines of my plot. If this bending of the truth offends anyone's sensibilities, I hereby apologize.

AVON REGENCY ROMANCES

LADY OF INDEPENDENCE *Helen Argers*	*64667-6/$2.75*
HER LADYSHIP'S COMPANION *Joanna Watkins Bourne*	*81596-6/$2.75*
THE IVORY FAN *Valerie Bradstreet*	*79244-3/$2.25*
HEART'S DESIRE *Deborah Chester*	*84798-1/$2.50*
THE WICKED MARQUIS *Marnie Ellingson*	*65821-6/$2.50*
BETHING'S FOLLY *Barbara Metzger*	*61143-0/$2.50*
THE EARL AND THE HEIRESS *Barbara Metzger*	*65516-0/$2.50*
THE BELLIGERENT MISS BOYNTON *Kasey Michaels*	*77073-3/$2.50*
THE LURID LADY LOCKPORT *Kasey Michaels*	*86231-X/$2.50*
THE RAMBUNCTIOUS LADY ROYSTON *Kasey Miachels*	*81448-X/$2.50*
THE TENACIOUS MISS TAMMERLANE *Kasey Michaels*	*79889-1/$2.25*

Buy these books at your local bookstore or use this coupon for ordering:

Avon Books, Dept BP, Box 767, Rte 2, Dresden, TN 38225
Please send me the book(s) I have checked above. I am enclosing $________ (please add $1.00 to cover postage and handling for each book ordered to a maximum of three dollars). *Send check or money order*—no cash or C.O.D.'s please. Prices and numbers are subject to change without notice. Please allow six to eight weeks for delivery.

Name ____________________

Address ____________________

City ____________ **State/Zip** ____________

Regency 2-84

Dear Reader:

If you enjoyed this book, and would like information about future books by this author and other Avon authors, we would be delighted to put you on the mailing list for our ROMANCE NEWSLETTER.

Simply *print* your name and address and send to Avon Books, Room 1210, 1790 Broadway, N.Y., N.Y. 10019.

We hope to bring you many hours of pleasurable reading!

Sara Reynolds, Editor
Romance Newsletter

Book orders and checks should *only* be sent to Avon Books, Dept. BP Box 767, Rte 2, Dresden, TN 38225. Include 50¢ per copy for postage and handling; allow 6-8 weeks for delivery.

Reader 10-83

IT'S A NEW AVON ROMANCE LOVE IT!

HEART OF THUNDER
85118-0/$3.95
Johanna Lindsey

Set in the untamed West of the 1870's, HEART OF THUNDER is the story of a headstrong beauty and of the arrogant outlaw who vows to possess her father's land—and her heart.

WILD BELLS TO THE WILD SKY
84343-9/$6.95
Laurie McBain **Trade Paperback**

This is the spellbinding story of a ravishing young beauty and a sun-bronzed sea captain who are drawn into perilous adventure and intrigue in the court of Queen Elizabeth I.

FOR HONOR'S LADY
85480-5/$3.95
Rosanne Kohake

As the sounds of the Revolutionary War echo throughout the colonies, the beautiful, feisty daughter of a British loyalist and a bold American patriot must overcome danger and treachery before they are gloriously united in love.

DECEIVE NOT MY HEART
86033-3/$3.95
Shirlee Busbee

In New Orleans at the onset of the 19th century, a beautiful young heiress is tricked into marrying a dashing Mississippi planter's look-alike cousin—a rakish fortune hunter. But deceipt cannot separate the two who are destined to be together, and their love triumphs over all obstacles.

Buy these books at your local bookstore or use this coupon for ordering:

Avon Books, Dept BP, Box 767, Rte 2, Dresden, TN 38225
Please send me the book(s) I have checked above. I am enclosing $________
(please add $1.00 to cover postage and handling for each book ordered to a maximum of three dollars). ***Send check or money order*****—no cash or C.O.D.'s please. Prices and numbers are subject to change without notice. Please allow six to eight weeks for delivery.**

Name ________________________________

Address ________________________________

City ________________ **State/Zip** ________________

Love It! 2-84